BACKBEAT

A NOVEL OF PHYSICS

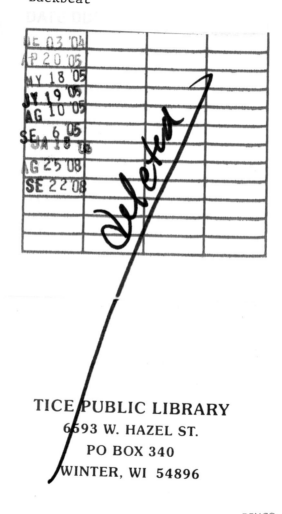

BACKBEAT

A NOVEL OF PHYSICS

~

J. Frederick Arment

Blue Hot Books
Key West, USA

Printed in the United States of America

First Edition

Library of Congress Cataloging-in-Publication Data
Arment, J. Frederick, 1953-
    Backbeat : a novel of physics / J. Frederick Arment. — 1st ed.
        p. cm.
    ISBN 1-889749-18-4 (ppk. : alk. paper)
    1. Orphans—Fiction. 2. Physics—Fiction. I. Title

PS3601.R57B33 2004
813'.6—dc22

                                            2004003915

Publisher's Note: This is a work of fiction. Names, characters, places and incidents either are the product of the author's imagination or are used fictitiously. Any resemblance to actual events, locales or persons, living or dead, is entirely coincidental.

Books are available at quantity discounts when used as teaching aids or for promotional activities. Please contact the publisher for details.

Blue Hot Books
Correspondence: 5818 Wilmington Pike #320, Dayton, Ohio 45459-7004 U.S.A.
www.bluehotbooks.com

—For my children, Collin and Emily

ONE

I don't believe in death, not the kind that sends souls to heaven or turns ashes to ashes, dust to dust. It's children scaring children, the Whirl once told me. Death is a myth so strong it defies the laws of physics. Not only will it take your life, but death gives you hope. That's the danger, he said, that's the choice, life or hope.

—Wake up, kid.

I open my eyes and blink. Green shards of glass splinter the morning light. Thin rays of dust shoot across the warehouse like dirty lasers. I wasn't sleeping, just dreaming and drumming, quarreling with the past to postpone the cold. The night wind has iced the steel girders a crystalline blue, like the country house in *Zhivago*.

—Do you hear me, Romey? a voice says and feet shuffle closer.

Asleep in my arms on the concrete floor is Violet with her bleached hair coiled flat around dirty ears. If I didn't know better, I'd think her innocent, but Violet's blue-shadowed eyes twitch from the sound of the voice and her red lips crease in a mumbled curse. What horrors inhabit the dreams of whores?

—Wake up, Romey, you've got business.

With the sole of his wingtip, Oscar Fine nudges my shoulder. In the scattered sunrise, the lawyer's fiber optic hair shines green, but I know it's the silver of coins. It seems a lifetime ago since I've seen his troll face and wrinkled, white skin, now so out of place among these browns and dirty pinks of the sleeping Hovelites.

That's what we call ourselves, dwellers of the Hovel, but only to mock ourselves before others would. Runaways and castoffs, a dozen of us sleep like rodents on the third floor of this abandoned building with its paint peeling and Escher stairs that stop and start.

—Come on, Romey, Oscar says and kicks my gym shoe and makes my knee bump against Violet, who pushes away until stopped by a crystalline pillar. I grab her pant leg and hold her while the rest of the Hovelites scatter like mice.

—What the hell's the matter with you, Oscar? I say. What are you doing here?

Violet reaches under the blanket and lifts the black and white kitten that purred between us through the night. Now its spine is arched like Violet's, and it's all I can do not to jump up and smack Oscar for scaring them, but I slide three fingers through my greasy hair until they catch in knots at my shoulder. In a broken mirror leaning cockeyed against the wall, I glimpse what I've become: hollow eyes and swollen lips, green pants smeared with grease, a dirty sweatshirt cut off at the shoulders. Swirling on my upper arm is the beautiful red and blue tattoo that still stings from the needles. Crab Nebula in the flesh.

—Car's waiting, Oscar says and I can see revulsion in his eyes, but Violet says she likes my look, a young Brando, only on smack. Come on, kid, Oscar growls and hoists his shoulders. I don't understand, he says, why New York is always so damn cold.

As Violet pulls her leg free from my hold, the kitten scratches her arm, which makes the Hovelites recoil in pain. I sit cross-legged and rub my face with rough hands. Usually, I would stumble down the rusted stairs to the second floor and pee a rainbow to the trash cans in the alley, but the Hovelites are churning. Two nights ago some loud drunks from the Bowery moved to the fourth floor and everyone's been freaked ever since. That was the night the kitten showed up. Crawled out of the sounds of crashing beer bottles and obscenities, so Violet named it Tuf.

—I'm not coming home, I say to the lawyer who hulks over me. I told Frank when he was here I wasn't coming back. Now go away before my friends realize you're not a cop.

On the outside, Gabby and Brownie and the rest of the Hovelites are still as the icy pillars, but on the inside they're spinning like tops. Squinted eyes and pinched lips, they're cursing me for not getting them away from this exposed warehouse and moving to somewhere lost in Harlem. What they don't know is the cash I took from the Whirl nearly a year ago has finally run dry. I get paid this Friday, first time legitimate in my whole life—Won't the Whirl be proud?—but drummers, they warned me, make little but noise.

—Frank's sick, Oscar says.

—Get a doctor.

—Real sick, Romey. The doctors say he's not going to make it.

—That's bullshit, Oscar.

—No bull, he says and rearranges his pinstripe coat so it falls smoothly over beefy shoulders. Someone poisoned him, Oscar says and with a shrug of his shoulders and the calm of jurisprudence, he tells me my guardian, Frank Whirlpool, has ingested enough strychnine to put him in a death-grip.

—They don't know who did it, he says, but Frank hasn't got much time, Romey. He would want you with him. He has a right, all he's done for you.

—Who the hell is this? Violet says as she cocoons the kitten with the blanket and holds it away from the intruder.

—It's all right, I say to her. He's just a lawyer.

—What's a shit drummer like you got a lawyer for? she says. And who poisoned who? He said somebody got poisoned.

—It's okay, Violet. Go back to sleep. I'll handle it.

—Then handle it, she says and rocks the kitten as if it were a baby. We don't need nobody here with a damn lawyer.

I stumble to my feet and push Oscar to the stairway, but he plants his feet and pushes back hard, and I don't blame him. Known him all my life. When the Whirl needs help, Oscar Fine is there, like part of the family, what family there was.

—Frank needs you, Romey. That's all I should have to say.

—And I come running, right, Oscar? I sure as hell don't trust you, all I've seen you do for Frank, and he came here a month ago with some bullshit about how he was going to die. I'm not buying it from either one of you.

—Jesus, kid, Oscar says, think about what you're doing. Frank is dying. You could lose everything, and for what? Oscar scans the crouching Hovelites and shakes his head. For Christ's sake, he says, give me a break.

As much as I try to hold it together, my lips start to quiver and my shoulders shake. It might be true, that's the thing. It's not so hard to imagine someone trying to kill the Whirl. Maybe the bastard is poisoned and lying somewhere retching and dying. Serve him right. A bit of justice would be good, only he wasn't supposed to die, just suffer a little. Maybe ask forgiveness.

I leave Oscar at the dark stairway and stoop low beside Violet. I give Tuf a two-finger pet and he stretches his body as if he's in mid-leap. I try to put my arm around Violet, but she pushes me away and I see Oscar shake his head. It's embarrassing and my heart skips like a stone across water, but I know Violet loves me, or I love her. First time I saw her, it shocked me what happened, the oscillations back and forth, up and down, slapping us apart and drawing us together. It was the strong force, nuclear, the bond of a proton to a neutron. As I fixed on those sad brown eyes and glazed copper skin, I thought she must be everything I was not, so outwardly wounded with a green angel tattoo on her leg and glistening silver ring in her belly. Slight taste of salt the first time we kissed, and fearless, that's what really got me. Walking alone on the streets of New York City, a waif selling sex like newspapers on the corner. Not the kind of love that matters to her, so why should it matter to me?

—Just let it go, baby, I say and kiss her on the cheek.

Violet's eyes are slits. She nods up and down, not at me, but at Oscar as if she's decided he's not due any more respect than the other men on the street that she points out with their double grins of arrogance and desire. She talks about it sometimes, how a few will stop and follow through, while others get spooked and glide on to the big hotels and better stock. It's ugly any way you look at it. The trick, she tells me, is not to look.

—Dammit, Romeo, Oscar says, we don't have much time.

So that's it. Impatience always brings it out, or frustration, not Danny, or Ricky, or Junior, but something out of a freak show. Romeo Quark Argasti, it gets caught on the tongue, but I can't really blame my given name on the Whirl, and my parents are dead and gone.

—I'm not kidding, Oscar says. Frank is going to die, and you gotta be there.

—I told you. I'm not coming back.

—You are coming back, he says, if I have to carry you back.

He steps forward so I stand with my fists clenched and we stare into each other's eyes until we both feel ridiculous and look away. On a cold morning when death hangs just a thought above us, the whole world seems a little ridiculous.

I lower my fists as a stray thought tunnels into my head. Binding energy. Hardly something to think about when a lawyer comes threatening, or your lover spurns you for the warmth of a stray kitten. It's from having a physics geek as a guardian, rather than a plumber or banker. It's why Frank Whirlpool will always be near me, alive or dead. Binding energy is the amount of energy needed to break apart an atom, but it's not the definition that counts. It's the interference, the manipulation, the abuse. It's why I shake but don't ache with the thought of the Whirl dying, and why I have this nebulous tattoo covering the scar he made when he busted me with an empty whiskey bottle. It's why I sleep on this cold concrete floor and dream these incessant thoughts of a thousand definitions and principles of physics no more real than binding energy, causing me to split from the Whirl with all the sadness of a nuclear blast.

—I'll call the cops, Oscar says. They'll take all these kids to jail. I'll do it, Romeo. How would you like that, all these kids in the slammer?

—Asshole! Violet thrusts her middle finger into the air and the Hovelites hop in vectors back and forth. If I don't do something fast, they'll figure Oscar's tough stance is a ruse and beneath that thousand-dollar Armani is blood and bone.

From a pile in the corner, I grab my jacket with the broken, silver buckle. Two drumsticks fall from the pocket and clatter on the concrete floor. I stuff them diagonally down the front of my pants and slam my arms into the filthy leather.

—Get the asshole gone, Violet spits, and you go with him, Romey, whatever the hell he called you, Romeo, Romey. We don't need nobody with a damn lawyer, do we, Tuf?

The kitten tries to escape, but Violet scoops it in the blanket. She slides closer to Brownie Newsome, who is hunched next to Lacky Giovano, Sarah Connell, Gabby Straughn, and others whose names I don't remember, but who over the last few months have taught me more about family than the Whirl ever could.

—I'll be back, I say and kiss Violet's hand. I promise, baby, in a couple of days I'll be here. Tell the band at Bonner's I'm still going to play. I might miss a night or two, that's all. You tell them, baby. I've got to take care of something. Don't forget. Promise me?

She nods, but I don't believe her. She'll forget. Maybe they'll all forget. I follow the squat lawyer under a steel gray beam and through a hole in the wall and down two flights of shaky steps to the street. A black limousine waits with engine running. We climb into the back and I pull the drumsticks from my pants and stash them on the seat beside my leg. Oscar motions for the chauffeur to go, and the car winds around piles of trash and abandoned cars until we find a major avenue toward the New Jersey Turnpike.

—Place gives me the creeps, Oscar says.

—You don't know anything about it.

—I know Frank is dying, and I know how much money is at stake.

—Lots, you don't have to tell me.

—You could say that, he says and shakes his head as if he's patented the move. I guess you could damn well say that.

The car swoops with headlights flashing up a steel ramp to the turnpike. People stare from other cars, but they can't see through our tinted windows. Absorption, the taking up of energy by something moving through a medium, waves of arrogance built from waves of ambition.

—Let me get this right, Romey, Oscar says. You've decided to live in a pit rather than in one of the grandest estates on the Atlantic coast?

—It's not a pit. It's a hovel.

—Jesus God, what's happened to your mind? First, this drumming nonsense, and now you're hanging out with criminals. Never seen a kid so inconsiderate. All the opportunity in the world and you shit on it. Adopted kid, for Christ's sake.

The driver holds the speedometer at ninety-five. The Whirlpool estate is in the Remington District of southwest Jersey where the world changes from graffiti-coated block to green lawns and velvet ivy. Vermont granite walls make the mansion look more like a museum, or mausoleum, but it's the only home I've ever known. Until last year, that is. Like an electron at higher and higher energies, I skipped from orbit to orbit, on and on until there was no more room to move. That's when the Whirl pushed me to the threshold. Gave me the extra jolt to jump, and I suppose I can thank him for that. The final argument was over physics, which may seem insane, but it's the only language the Whirl and I share.

TWO

The guard nods our limousine through the gate and we roll up the long, cobbled lane toward the mansion. It must be the way of homecoming, the senses reaching for what they've been deprived of, a jackknife splash into the warm swimming pool, the metal-to-metal clash of train and rail on the wooden floor of my room. The apple trees in the north grove are just beginning to bud, but I swear I can smell the fruit rotting.

—It's a shame, Oscar says and points west of the lane to a split rail fence that's teetering back and forth like a DNA chain. Place has gone to hell, he says. I don't know why Frank ever built this place. The Foundation takes all of his time.

—Fighting with Silvie takes all of his time, I say and Oscar shrugs.

—I suppose the place gives his brother a political base, he says, but that's all going to change. Philip was here when Frank was poisoned. The nurse found him on the bathroom floor. You've been away for what, a year or two?

—Eleven months, I say.

—Seems longer. Philip announced his candidacy for Senate last month. Senator Philip Whirlpool, how's that sound? Not that he has much of a chance with the voters, but he has a brother with money. The place is crawling with consultants and bankers, now doctors and police. I don't know where it's all going, Romey, I really don't.

Oscar takes a folded handkerchief from his pocket and wipes his forehead. The air conditioning in the limo turns our chilled breath to white clouds.

—We put a lid on the journalists, Oscar says. Philip is trying to control the media, but the whole shebang is about to explode. Whether you like it or not, Romey, you're smack in the middle.

The limousine bends around two New Jersey State Police cars and under the canopied entry. Two maids in black and white dash out and stand like rockets beside the door. You'd think I'd be grateful for a childhood lived in such splendor, but it was far from natural, like being raised on a movie set. The staff was on the payroll, the tutors were drop-linked from satellite. I was Frank Whirlpool's pet project, an experiment, a prodigy to be given the best of everything and everything that was best.

To me, the Whirlpool mansion was endless hallways and cavernous rooms of knocking pipes and creaking floors. I remember when I was nine or ten, like an alchemist searching for childhood, I transformed those sounds into a menagerie of invisible friends. For several months, I was in kid heaven as I laughed and conspired with those echoing companions until the nanny turned me in to the Whirl.

That's when I took to music. Anything but silence or adults speaking to adults, and music was an acceptable pursuit. The Whirl was obsessed with antique instruments. From Vivaldi's viola to Benny Goodman's clarinet, they hung on every wall and stood in all the corners. Winds, strings, percussion, it didn't matter to me, I tried them all and I had the gift. The Whirl ordered violin and cello lessons, but in the end I chose the slam-dunk of harmonic discord. In a corner of a guest bedroom on the third floor of the mansion,

I discovered Gene Krupa's very own double bass drum set with a conga on the side and a high-hat cymbal that reverberated through the halls like a children's revolution.

—It's hard to believe, I say to Oscar as the car slows to a stop, that the police haven't figured out who did it.

—They're on it, he says. A detective is interviewing the help. About ten o'clock yesterday morning, Frank was found on the bathroom floor. It's bad, this strychnine. Philip said Frank was all bunched in a fetal position.

—It was Philip.

—You don't know that, Romey. The nurse was the first to find Frank.

—He couldn't wait for Frank to die, Oscar. That's the way it's always been.

—Don't start, he says, and whatever you do, don't talk to the press. Philip is Frank's only brother. He's family. You've got to be careful. You don't understand all that's happening, believe me, you don't.

The car halts parallel with the main door and its bronze knocker made from physicist Werner Heisenberg's right shoe. Not a replica, but his actual shoe, a size ten with strings hanging loose from the knot. "Uncertainty lies within," I can still hear the Whirl whisper to visitors and chuckle as if the joke was on them.

—Ahhh, Romeo, you're here, Philip says as he lopes out to meet us. Just in time, he says. We've missed you. It hasn't been the same without you.

Philip sniffs his beak nose to cover the lie. Dressed in a double-breasted gray suit with a red tie and Cordovan shoes, the younger Whirlpool is a snippet of Frank. He has the Whirl's deep-set green eyes, but Philip's face is thin like the relatives from Baton Rouge. The chandelier's artificial light makes his balding head nearly disappear, so his eyes pop like a lizard's.

—Let's go up, he says and motions us to follow.

He curves his long spine forward and around a yellow taped-off area with a state trooper at attention. He leads us through the sitting room with its array of instruments that hang like trophies of a great hunter. Tubas and trumpets, marimbas and gongs, violins and guitars, rare and dusty instruments replace the works of art you would expect to find in a great mansion. But this is no stately home of old money. It's a technology perk. The marble exterior is still white, and ivy barely grabs hold. Instead of a ballroom or a smoking lounge for the aristocracy to huddle, there's an underground lab and a fully functional observatory that mars the clean lines of the tiled roof.

—Frank isn't really a Methodist, Philip says as he leans toward me, but Reverend Walker agreed to attend. Such things don't matter in the end, now do they?

I shrug the same as Oscar shrugs. We climb the wide stairway to the second floor and walk the stretch of hall to the master bedroom in the west wing of the house. When I was younger, this room with its huge windows always seemed a cauldron of light, but now the curtains are drawn. A partially exposed pane lets a thin line of yellow shoot across the rug.

—Go on, Oscar says and pushes me around a policeman and a doctor and into the mobile hospital that the Whirl's bedroom has become.

I stand stillborn at the foot of the bed. The drumsticks dig in my stomach, but I can't take them out in front of all these people or they would think me a kid with a toy. If the Whirl saw me playing in the metal band at Bonner's, he would scoff, too, but now he's motionless, covered with blankets to his chin. His fleshy eyes are closed and his face is pale except for the folds of red wrinkles as if, inside, he's on fire.

—We ask in the name of Jesus, prays a triangular man with a Bible sandwiched between thick, white hands, that You be with

Frank in his time of pain.

This isn't right. There's got to be some kind of prank here. Where's the lesson, Whirly, the sardonic laugh? Pop those bloodshot eyes and say, Ah, ha! Surrounded by these doctors and would-be mourners, you've gone way too far.

—Help him cope with mortality, the reverend says. Keep Frank's thoughts always on You, Holy Father, and he will be blessed by the grace of God.

We circle the bed like spotters around a trampoline. Family and friends, every one of us undoubtedly suspect for murder: Philip, Oscar, Reverend Walker from the Riverport Methodist Church, the Whirl's three tight-lipped nieces in their long dresses and ruby lips, and the chipmunk-cheeked Leslie Patrick, the latest of the Whirl's private nurses. Even the ungrateful adopted son.

—Is he still breathing? asks a small woman with a thick Norwegian accent. The Whirl's lover for thirty years, his business partner for twenty, Silvie Nels fixes her eyes on the dying man as a master would a slave.

—Not as strong as before, nurse Leslie answers and wraps her plump index finger and thumb around the Whirl's limp wrist.

Silvie nods once. Her perfume drifts across the room with its scent of lemon and roses. Her silver hair is pasted back as if a cold wind had frozen it fast in a cold, grandmotherly look. Twenty years ago, Silvie and the Whirl started the Foundation for Frequency Research. Now she's president and he's chairman, or the other way around. Who keeps score? Like Philip, she's a good one for how the Whirl explained evil. It's more what you do with the field, he said, and less what the field does with you.

—Only Your goodness and grace, Reverend Walker moans, allow us peace with the knowledge that all of us must leave this earth.

Is the moment of dying for the billions around the world always this false-hearted? Are the ministrations of mourners this impure?

Not only are eternal life or damnation at stake, but a fortune so large it could make the weak recant and the strong believe.

—We leave this earth, oh Father, says the reverend, to join You in heaven to be judged.

The light from the windowpane snakes across the room to a small table covered with tissues and brown pills. As the sun goes behind the trees, there's a simple change in the frequency, yellow to orange.

I remember on my fourteenth birthday, the Whirl gave me a triangular prism. When you think of an object as a certain color, he said, it's only an illusion. White light from the sun has all the frequencies in the spectrum, he explained as he held the prism to the light and showed me the violet and red and the rainbow in between. When photons, or waves of light, hit an object, he said, some frequencies are absorbed, others are reflected. The colors are those frequencies reflected and detected by the eye. So visible color is not a primary characteristic of the object, Romey, rather the ability of the observer to see.

I listened that day, as I did to all of the Whirl's bits on life cloaked in the language of physics. I was in awe of my guardian. His picture was on the cover of *Time*. Other scientists came to do him honor. In the Whirl's bloodshot eyes was a world in which objects dissolve and the vacuum goes on forever. Yet for all his lessons in physics, what he failed to teach me was that we could lose our ability to see color. These mourners with their pitch skin and transparent pupils absorb the entire spectrum. Black as onyx; gray as clouds; white as paste.

It makes sense in the *logos*, the Whirl told me with his eyes as bright as the prism. I've been too long in understanding, he said, but it's just what your mother knew, Romey. She was better than us, you'll see.

The bedroom light has darkened. The air is swirling matter. Thin streaks of sunlight from the window retreat and leave a few silver photons to flash and disappear. It's as if these spotters have sucked all the energy from the Whirl and now they're working on me. Fear is heavy in the room, avarice and ambition, and as surely as these people believe in evil, they believe in death.

—Your heavenly gifts are rich, swoons Reverend Walker. We pray that Frank has made the commitment to reject the power of earthly gifts for one much greater.

The Whirl is moving. The room smells like plastic decomposing. His chest raises the blankets. The others in the room are frozen in bow-headed mourning, and I know what the preacher is thinking. Philip dragged me to the Methodist church enough times to know. Does Frank regret the way he lived? Will he repent at the end? Does he believe in death more than in life?

Not the Whirl, absolutely no way. I should call his name, try to revive him before these mourners write his obituary in their words. He has a right, all he's done for me.

—Be with all of us, the reverend says, so You might give us strength and understanding that all things are part of divine providence.

Mechanical gasping. Now even the air has become the Whirl's enemy. The molecules keep away from his lungs just as intelligently as he begs their comfort. Electrons flee from clouds of hydrogen and oxygen. The Whirl is a faltering pump. His chest seizes. He takes a short breath, then exhales long. Too long. Seems as if he's never going to stop, then he does.

No more gasping. No more rising of the blankets. The great Frank Whirlpool is silent as a ghost. A long exhalation? A last burst of air emptying the pipes? It's strangely consoling, a cool breeze after a horrible storm.

—Father, we thank You for the blessings we receive. I know Frank thanks you for the blessings that have come to him in life.

My own breath stalls. My head tips down and I shake it side to side. Does he forget that breathing is the most important act of physics? A great drawing in, a dry breath returned, soundless, a whistle over chapped lips, is that all there is?

The preacher's head is still bowed, as are the others around me. They don't realize what has happened. They go on as if he remains the brunt of their jokes, while I stand here feeling as though I've lost an arm or leg. I should throw myself on him, warm him, bring him back from death, but I'm frozen stiff. If I'm not careful, I'll pass out and they'll rush to me as if I were more important than the dead.

—Romey, Oscar whispers in my ear, it's time to go.

I stare at the lawyer, then at the Whirl, then back at Oscar, who is the only other person in the room without downcast eyes.

—He did it, Oscar whispers. He set it in motion, Romey. Now you need to know.

THREE

When I look back on this Romey of a different time, I remember every beat of his heart, my heart, and every thought in his mind. My mind. It has been several years since I lived with Violet and Brownie and the other runaways in that New York warehouse, and retrieving the past is nothing more than rewinding a favorite song or feeling, once more, the warmth of a lover.

Time is really a trick, you see. The frame of the moment is cubed, as in a Picasso painting where the same perspective shows past, present and future. Time can feel unbearably slow or regrettably fast. As Einstein taught us, one twin can stay on earth to grow old and die, while the other twin travels at the speed of light and goes on forever. At 300,000 meters per second, in fact, there is nothing but energy. Time and space disappear.

According to contemporary scientific knowledge, when two atoms collide, energy is released. New particles are created as photons, leptons, quarks and other names that mean nothing to ninety-nine percent of humanity. Past, present and future, the Whirl ingrained in me, are trajectories that come together as an exchange of tiny particles. This is the complexity of physics, or simplicity. It tells us that time is a function of motion, and motion depends on energy, which is equivalent to matter.

Nothing to it, really. So why should we fear something that stretches so easily and contracts with the mood of math?

We shouldn't. We can choose, you and me. One timeframe is as valid as any other. I prefer remembering the past in the present tense. Not so much because the present is any more real, but because the past and future are more detached in my mind, just as you must be from the words in this book. How could you understand the life of another, when your own past, present and future are colliding and separating in the roiling froth of physics?

Fortunately, we have a way to solve this mathematical problem. In our case, just as Picasso tied together and froze the frames of a cubist moment, something happens in my future that connects my past with the present. In a few short weeks from when this Romey of another time looked upon his guardian in death, the trajectories of time will collide. I will find in a London archive a stack of letters written over nineteen years before by my mother, Maria Elana Argasti, the beautiful and talented daughter of Tuscany in all its glory and shame.

I know little about her, and less about her lover, American physicist Justin Albert Bishop. After I was born and my birth parents had died, their former business manager, Frank Whirlpool, adopted me out of civic duty. There was little contact with the Bishop or Argasti families. That's why the letters Maria wrote her twin brother Alberto have become so important to me. With the same sense of confession that close siblings whisper into each other's ear, Maria revealed in these letters to her twin how she felt about music, and my father, and a life without tradition to guide her.

The letters gave few details. When the two siblings finished school, Maria and brother Alberto had left their home in Mariano and went separate ways. While Alberto followed his father's urging and pledged to become a priest at the Holy Father Seminary in Florence, Maria fled from their time-frozen village and dedicated herself to music. With a talent and passion for the cello, she won a full scholarship to the Royal

Academy of Music in London, and it was there in the spring of 1985
that she met Justin, a doctoral student in physics at Royal Holloway
College. To the horror of Maria's family, the two unmarried students
moved into a small flat in Bloomsbury at the center of London.
The result was me, a singular event in time. Yet as I have come to find,
it was more than the birth of a bastard. According to Justin's waveform
theory, it was the constructive interference of waves, a superposition of
energetic frequencies, the combination of two forms of courage that had
potential to conquer life's fear. Or it could have, if not for my parents'
untimely deaths.

September 17, 1985

It was just as you said, dear brother, only far worse. Papà stayed
with us for three long days and I begged the clock to keep striking
until it was time for him to leave. His garlic and tobacco are still
thick on the chairs and I know Justin thinks they will never come
clean.

When I finally took Papà to the train, I told him I loved him
and that he would always be welcome. How could I say such lies,
Alberto? How can you look at him without thinking of how he treats
me, how he sees me as sin? Why should I care what an old man
thinks? I have Justin and music, and you for listening.

I wish I could forget all about Mariano and the endless grapevines
on the hills and the bronze steeple that jabs the sky. Papà could only
talk of the priesthood and you, but I do not hold this against you. I
am glad you are getting what you want. Do the priests at Holy Father
know they are gaining more than they bargained for? You as a dutiful
pledge, dressed in black and so silent with devotion to God! What
about those nights when we whispered and risked our souls?

Devotion should not be so lifeless, Alberto. I have found a
different kind of devotion and, for me, it is life. I am a disciple of
Justin Bishop. It is not only his beauty, though he stops my breath

with his blond curls and spotted blue eyes, but also his ideas that make this dull world vibrate like crystal. That is devotion! This is religion, brother.

Papà could never hope to understand what is between Justin and me. On the way back from the station, Justin and I took a long walk in Bloomsbury Square. I tried to tell him the truth about Papà and the black nights in Mariano. The park at Bloomsbury is one of the few places in these cold streets of London that remind me of the wooded slopes and green fields of home. How we laughed as innocents and sang by the creek behind the barn. *Glory to our Savior! The Kingdom of the Lord is come!*

I can't wait until you meet him, my twin. Justin will change the world. His ideas are like those in the books you read at night when I pestered you with gossip. Justin's thoughts are for those who know the heart speaks a deeper language. I only wish you could come to know him as I do. He makes my knees weak and my heart so happy.

You should tell them! I taunted him as we walked in the park. You should shout it, Justin! I took his arm and pulled him along the path. People on green benches read crumpled papers and fed the begging birds. Justin shushed me and kissed my forehead so sweetly that I felt a rumble deep in my chest. Stop running, he scolded me. You make me dizzy, he said. Only Justin does not know that I am already so turned around by him, that front seems back and the past fades from my head.

You come back, Papà had the nerve to say before he boarded the train. You can imagine the way he talked to me, Alberto. He took me aside and said it many times. *Vieni a Mariano, Maria, Vieni a Mariano. Subito!* He was fuming, so angry that his eyes bulged. It was as though he believed the power he holds under the skies of Tuscany could follow him to the streets of London.

He is worried about his daughter, Justin tried to convince me. Any father would be worried, he said, but I laughed. Justin thinks

Papà is a tiny man, but his arms still look to me as though they could burst through his shirt. Papà thinks I am so mystified by Justin that I can no longer reason, but I am deeply in love and that is something a stubborn man from Mariano, especially Sergio Argasti, will never understand.

In the park, I pointed to the people on the benches. They will listen, I said to Justin. Everyone should know about this physics, the waves that make us vibrate with energy. This is the most brilliant physicist in the world! I yelled, but a woman on the bench shushed me. She pulled her red cloak around her so tightly that the book she was reading fell to the ground. I ran to pick it up, but she growled at me. You're scaring the bloody pigeons! she said and it shocked me because these Londoners are usually so silent. It is as if they have already lived and know what will come.

I did not mean to bother you, I assured the woman, but she sniffed and I noticed her wrinkled face, how it looked like Mamma's. Not only the white wrinkles of skin and crow's feet around the eyes, but the way she clutches her purse and gathers the folds of her dress into a space that seems to hold such secrets.

I stooped and kissed her red cheek, Alberto. It was a rush of feeling for Mamma, I am sorry to admit, and Papà. Justin pulled me away and we drifted by more benches with strangers and their threadbare gloves. Such a pigeon you are, I told him. Afraid these people will not understand, but they will. You have found something beautiful, Justin, that makes sense of the world, even the bad.

The sun went behind the trees and from my coat pocket I took the purple hat you bought me, Alberto. I pulled it tight against the cold. My stomach did not feel so good. We had not eaten since lunch. I should not have let Papà come. We had no money to feed him. He should have stayed in Mariano with Mamma, but he always goes where he is not wanted.

I rested my head on Justin's shoulder. He put his arm tight around me. The trees along the avenue are just beginning to lose their leaves and the pavement was slick from rain, but the black and white cabs roared along the street as if there were no danger. Our apartment was cold inside. Justin shut the window and you can imagine after so many days with Papà, how Justin was looking forward to being alone. He kissed my lips, but I felt a thought buzzing in my head. How I tried to be rid of it, Alberto, that Justin's hands are not so unlike Papà's.

I pushed him away. I made an excuse. I said if we made love, he would not be able to hear my new composition, and that I should play for him. I ran to the bedroom to get my cello. I sat on the bed and pulled the bow slowly across the strings. Papà's tobacco was clogging the air. I wrapped my legs and arms around the cello and the notes trailed across the floor and seeped out the window and down to the people who sit on the cold benches.

I am so happy with this new music, dear brother. You would like it, too. This string quartet sounds like wind in some places and storms in others. Now Justin sleeps with his eyelids closed over beautiful eyes and I sit near the lamp and write this letter, which you must never show anyone, or even confess. No one can understand the shame I feel for Papà, or my anger for Mamma. Memories are never forgotten, but forgiven, and I know in my heart that Justin's hands are not like Papà's, but rather like God's. And for this, I give Justin my love.

FOUR

I'm dizzy with death, almost giddy. The air is helium. My heart pumps dry as I watch for the Whirl to do something more than suck a warm breath and blow it out cold. A last exhalation, a mortal sigh, like the passing of a dog or cat, this can't be enough for human death, especially murder. A great wind should blow open the window; an angel should appear in a blinding flash of light. The Whirl will surely rise and tell us he was right all along, and that death holds no sway, but the room has lost color, no red or blue, just a ghostly translucent gray.

—Oh, my God, nurse Leslie says and puts her ear to the Whirl's mouth.

The reverend closes his Bible, leverages against the bed and rises to one knee. The doctor rushes to the bed. A policeman steps from the hall and clears his radio.

—May God be with you, Frank Whirlpool, the reverend says as the doctor searches for signs of life and finds none.

The floor shakes. My legs quake. The Whirl's face is as white as the sheet, but his brother's eyes are coal black. Silvie Nels and the four haunting nieces flutter against the wall. The reverend mumbles incantations that make no sense to me, but everyone is swaying to and fro as if locked in a dirge. These people can make life so dead, and death so alive.

I feel Oscar's hand on my arm. He tries to pull me from the room, but I take the drumsticks from my pants and hold them with white knuckled fingers. He lied to me. The Whirl lied to me all this time. I press against the wall and beat the sticks beside my legs, left hand once, right twice, bam, ba, bam. A short riff, grating on the ear, but it feels raw and alive. Bam, ba, bam, bam, the plaster flakes like snow.

Oscar grabs me with both hands. I hit the wall again, bam, bam, as I see Silvie Nels suck a warm breath and blow it icy toward my face. Philip's thin lips turn down with contempt. The silver tongues of the four nieces from Baton Rouge jingle like tiny bells.

—Let's go, Romey, Oscar says. Now!

I hit against the wall once more, then stuff the sticks into my pants. With me in tow, Oscar plows past the policeman in the hall. Adrenaline sweeps through my limbs. I pass Oscar and run down the long hallway, so he huffs and puffs to catch up. The square walls are huge and surround me like a box. We flee down marble steps to the first floor hallway where the sun breaks through thin panes of glass that blanch the furniture. We stop on the eastern end of the house at a door to the Whirl's study.

—Damn, kid, the lawyer says and stops to catch his breath, what the hell was that? He grabs my hand and pulls me in. He locks the door and turns on a lamp that sits on top of the Whirl's dusty desk. I'm sorry about Frank, he says, I truly am, but you've got to be more careful. The police won't understand that kind of behavior. They won't.

I stand in the middle of the room and look out the glass doors at the rolling lawn that's thick from spring rains. Undulating waves hang low in the sun's light, but I still can't see the green that I know is there. Oscar throws his coat over the couch, points to an armchair in front of the desk and nods for me to sit. The long case on the west wall is lined with textbooks on physics that the Whirl drilled into me, day after day. Dented and broken musical instruments are piled high in corners. Like notes on a sheet of music, seven saxophones hang vertical on the horizontal paneling.

—The person that murdered him, Oscar says, will be caught. They'll burn in hell, you can be sure of that, Romey. It was deliberate. That's what the police said. Nasty stuff. Strychnine is in all kinds of off-the-shelf poisons. Anyone could have done it, but they'll find the killer. The detective assured me.

Oscar shuffles two stacks of paper on the desk into one pile, then he goes to the north wall. He lifts a Vermeer reproduction from the paneling and exposes a black steel door with a combination lock. He places the picture on the floor against the wall, and I watch as he spins the dial to the left, then right, then left until the thick door jumps open.

—It was damn good timing, Oscar says. Frank would have liked you being there, Romey. He was a huge man. He loved you. He made provisions for you.

Oscar rummages his right hand in the safe and pulls out a stack of cash like the one I stole the night I ran away. I had thought I deserved it, earned it, but the Whirl turned me in. I spent two nights in jail, then he dropped the charges.

With his left hand, Oscar removes from the safe a black velvet tray with an array of gemstones. I have seen them many times before, diamonds, rubies and others more exotic. These were the stones that Silvie and he had used for their dog-and-pony show, the original frequency tests that made the cover of *Scientific American*. The gems were used to demonstrate a new technique for measuring composite frequencies. Their outputs showed how frequency changes can be predicted by altering inputs. Part science, part medicine show, it made sales of the Foundation for Frequency Research's commercial drug line go exponential. People will do anything, the Whirl told me, to avoid dying, except to live. What do any of his words mean now?

Oscar shifts his hands deftly and moves the gemstones from one rack to another. He picks up a monstrous jagged ruby that loosened from handling. The ruby is by far the largest stone in the collection and the light from the window roils inside it like a flame. Oscar resettles the stone in its velvet indentation and puts the tray and the pile of money back inside. Then he takes out a stack of documents, rummages through it, tucks one under his arm and closes the safe.

—It's not a simple will, he says. Then what can we expect? Frank Whirlpool wasn't a simple man.

—Not simple, I say and wipe my twitching eyelids with my fingers, then harder with the backs of my fists. The Vermeer is dull and lifeless, and the grass outside the window is still gray. Oscar unfolds the document and spreads it on the table.

—The will has language, he says, about the way Frank wanted the estate to be administered, but for the most part it sets out in pretty simple terms the beneficiary and the stipulations attached.

Oscar sits in the Whirl's chair and stares at me. Another face morphs over the lawyer's with thick glasses and gold chain curled around pocked cheeks and ears. Compared to the gaunt vertical of the Whirl's, Oscar's face is thick and horizontal.

—You may be surprised, Oscar says as the other image fades, but Frank has done something extraordinary. He did right by you, Romey. More than right. It's as if he knew something was about to happen. He called a few weeks ago, had me draw up a new will. The thing is, the new will gives the entire Whirlpool estate, the house, the money, everything to a single beneficiary.

I rub my eyes harder, as if hurting them might somehow bring back the color.

—He left the estate to you, Romey, Oscar says, all to you.

The rubbing is only making my eyes hurt more. The room is still gray as stone. Losing your color must be similar to losing your ability to touch or taste. The floor and ceiling are chalky, the desk has the sheen of wet ink, and the will that Oscar smooths on the desk is almost silver.

—Worth about two billion, he says with his eyes as wide as windows. And it's yours. Does that surprise you?

—No, I say, but he blinks as if I've given the wrong answer so I say, yes.

He looks at me cockeyed. I stop rubbing my eyes. What the hell was the Whirl thinking? That I could be pulled back so easily into this empty house with its echoing halls and payroll family?

—Which is it, Romeo? Are you surprised, or not?

—I'm surprised he bothered to make a will.

—Why is that?

—He liked to see people fight.

—Nobody said there won't be a fight, Oscar says. Just because it says something in this will doesn't mean there won't be a fight. One hell-of-a fight, I'd say. And now, with murder hanging over us, we'll be lucky if it's ever settled.

I sit back in my chair. My stomach is in knots. I need a drink, or a smoke.

—As far as the details go, Oscar says, the stipulations might appear to be a little eccentric. I told Frank he was asking for trouble in the courts.

He spins the will so it's facing me. His fingers chart the words as he reads, but I can't follow. I think of Violet and wonder if she's okay. I try to imagine what the Hovelites are doing now, talking, eating, scraping together enough money to buy food or reefer.

—There's a catch, Oscar says. In order to inherit the estate, Frank wants you to do something. Find something, really. He's sending you on a mission, Romey, a quest. It makes sense, I suppose, with this drumming career and all. Music runs in your family. Where's that place you play? Bonner's, is that a club?

—It's a bar.

—Well, we all have to start somewhere. You inherited talent from your mother's side, no doubt. A violinist.

—Cellist.

Oscar takes a photograph out of his vest pocket and places it in front of me on the table. I've seen it before, the one with my mother standing on the second step in front of a huge building in London. Mounds of black hair fall on her shoulders and thick eyebrows break horizontally with only a slight gap above her nose. She's wearing a long coat and her arms are wrapped in front of her. Her lips are slightly open, as if she's talking to the camera, telling the photographer to hurry because it's cold.

Years ago when the Whirl first showed me this picture, I thought I looked a little like her, but only the dark eyes with pupils that overpower the white. I could never understand what the photo was supposed to mean to me. There was resemblance, but it was more an irritation, like trying to remember a place you've never been.

—I don't know much about my mother, I say and push the photo back to him.

—Apparently, she wrote some very beautiful music.

—Why are we talking about my mother, Oscar? Frank is up there dead, and you start a damn conversation about my mother.

—I'm sorry. I really am, but you don't have much time to get this through your head. He wanted you to do something that's going to cause all hell to break loose in this house. He wants you to find a piece of music your mother wrote before she died. It was lost. He wants you to find it.

—Why would I do that?

—That's the stipulation, Oscar says and frowns. To get the money, you must find these sheets of music.

—What the hell does that mean?

—It's the way Frank wanted it written, Oscar says and shrugs. The law says you can put anything in a will, you know. According to Frank, there's a musical score—it says here a *string quartet*—your mother wrote before she died. She was killed in a plane accident.

—I know how she died, Oscar. She was my mother.

—It's kind of sentimental, really, he says and pushes the will toward me and points to the language that spells out the stipulation. "My legal charge," he reads upside down, "Romeo Quark Argasti, is to receive the benefice set aside in this will, if he recovers within one year of my death an unpublished string quartet in A minor, entitled *Logos Sonores*, which was composed by his mother, Maria Elana Argasti."

I try to read it, but the words jumble.

—She died with my father, I say, two months after I was born. They both died in a plane crash. She played the cello. He was a physicist. That's all I know.

—Frank was introduced to them a couple of years before they died, Oscar says. He was their business manager. According to him, your mother was a gifted musician. Your father was working on a physics thesis that eventually merited a minor nomination for a Nobel Prize. You come from one hell-of-a gene pool, kid. Apparently, Frank was taken by Maria's music. Maybe he wants you to know something more about your mother. Anyway, that's the way he wanted it written.

—Who cares what Frank wanted? He's gone. He left me with bullshit.

—Have a little respect, Romey. After all, it's your mother's music. It should be important to you.

—He could have found it himself.

The drumsticks in my pants dig into the skin. I stand up and pace below the saxophones that hang on the paneling. I have an urge to grab the fake Vermeer and smash it on the wooden floor, but it's fake, just like everything the Whirl said about death and dying.

—Look, we can't know what was going through his mind, Oscar says, but he knew something was about to happen and did little, as far as I know, to stop it. As much as I hate to say this, I think Frank wanted to die.

—He told me he wouldn't die.

—We all say that, but we know better. I told Frank this will was going to cause problems, but he told me to mind my own business. That's how he was, Romey, you know that better than most.

—I don't want to talk about the will.

—Unfortunately, you must. The will has been filed in the county courthouse. It's legal. Whether it's crazy or fair, you inherit nothing if you can't come up with this piece of music.

—Then who will?

—That's up to the court. Others have very good claims and the desire, certainly. Philip needs money for his Senate campaign. Silvie will want the money to go to the Foundation. Reverend Walker is champing at the bit to have Philip fund a new church sanctuary. Even Frank's real family. . .

He stops and stares at me as hard as I stare back.

—It's just you could end up with nothing, he says. Frank wouldn't have wanted that.

—He manipulated people, I say. He's manipulating now, even when he's dead.

—In some ways, the dead have more rights than the living. That's what fear can do, I suppose.

—I'm not doing it, I say and sit down hard in the chair. I take out my drumsticks and click them on the desk, da dee, da dee dum.

—Jesus, Romey. Oscar's mouth puckers until I stop the beating. He gathers the will and folds it into a tall rectangle, then ties the ribbon. There's one way to put this behind you, he says and opens the top drawer. I'm not recommending it, mind you. He pulls another document from the drawer and puts it in front of me. I took it upon myself, he says, to prepare this legal instrument in advance. Just in case. Once they speak to their lawyers, Philip and the others will have a disclaimer prepared, anyway. If you sign it, you renounce your claim to the estate. It says you refuse the stipulation in the will. You can go back to your life, but I would advise you to think about that very carefully. Once you sign, it's done. You lose everything.

—You're working for Philip.

—I resent that, he says. Frank was my friend. He wanted the money to go to you, and that's what I'm trying to make happen, but it's your choice. That's the law. This document is just an option.

—I'm getting out of here.

I slip the sticks into my coat pocket. I've got to get back to the warehouse. Violet will be wondering. She won't last long. She doesn't have the power to be loyal, to trust someone.

—Maybe you haven't the stomach for this, Oscar says and taps his finger on the document. I don't blame you. If I were your age and I saw the sharks circling, I would want out, too. Whoever murdered Frank didn't do it for sport. Not with this amount of money involved. They could just as easily kill again. If you sign this letter, I'll witness it. Then it can be all over and you can go back to your pit.

—Hovel.

He goes to the door and twists the knob. Then with a shake of his head, he steps into the hall. I hear the door close and the floorboards creak as he walks toward the western end of the house. Oscar's heels are almost noiseless, leather against wood.

In time, the room settles into an eerie silence. I stare at the fake Vermeer that shines in a beam of sunlight that tracks from the window across the floor and up the wall. Even with shiny gems hidden in the safe, it's a dreary room. I glance at the document. Black lines of type run border to border. I can't get the Whirl's bloodless face out of my head. Will that be the way I remember him? I touch the tattoo on my right arm. For nothing he hit me with the bottle, just because I wouldn't listen, because I wouldn't understand.

Minutes slip away. I hear sirens and commotion in front of the house. I hear the second hand of a clock on the far wall of the den urging me to act, but I won't. That's what Violet tells me, that I wait too long for things to happen. I need to stake out my life, she says, or people will stake it for me. They'll use me, in her words, destroy me, like every night they try to destroy her.

The door suddenly opens. My legs are numb from sitting too long in one place. I've rubbed my eyes until the spots no longer fade. I should see a doctor about this. I could be going blind, but how do I explain to a doctor that a dead man has stolen my color?

Click, click, click, like drumsticks on the metal frame of a snare drum, I hear footsteps behind me. I mustn't show Oscar I'm wracked with doubt. The document is unsigned on the desk. The steps come closer. Click, click, click. Not the same. Different shoes than Oscar's. Leather, not wood.

I spin in my chair. Stars explode in my head. As I fall, I see thin cracks in the wooden floor planks grow huge, then only black.

FIVE

Later, when I found the letters my mother wrote her twin brother Alberto, I noticed they were bound together with the brown hemp string you'd find on any ordinary package. The knot was a butterfly bow with one end pulled through until only one wing remained intact. The outermost envelopes were brown, and except for the edges the inner ones were still ivory. The stack included thirty letters written between 1985 and 1987. Curiously each letter was sealed and never opened, and even now there are times when I wish that is how they remained.

September 27, 1985

Until this day, brother, I had not seen this side of Justin, a temper that makes him forget what he believes. He reminds me of the old men at the café in Mariano, quarreling for no other reason than to hear their own voices.

He had gone to University to get our week's mail. I was washing dishes at the sink and playing in my mind Verdi's *La Traviata*, one brilliant note upon note, when Justin burst into the room as if someone was chasing. Yet it was only a letter.

The bastard! He cursed and threw the letter into the air. I spun at the sink. A plate slipped from my hands and shattered across the black and gray tile. *Cos'ha,* I screamed. Look what you made me do!

Then like Papà caught *ubriaco* by Mamma, Justin's face turned red as blood. The broken plate scattered around my slippers and stretched in beads of water beneath the sink. I stooped to pick up the tiny shards, being careful not to cut my fingers, but the red dots soon appeared.

It was frightening, Alberto. You remember Abalona Reveri from school, how she cut her fingers with a kitchen knife. The doctor told her she would have scars and she would never have the same feeling in her hand. If I did the same, it occurred to me, all my dreams of music would be lost. I would end up in Mariano and Papà would have been right all along. Commit to God, he always said to me. Musicians are like too many shoots on the vine. Well, brother, he may be right about wine, but not about me. Verdi and Mozart were right, and Papà has always been wrong.

I wrapped a napkin around my finger. With a small sponge from the sink, I wiped the dishwater from the tile and squeezed it into a rusty bucket we keep on a bottom shelf. I went to the bathroom sink and poured alcohol over my wound and it was all I could do to hold my scream. Even now, the red dots show and my finger feels numb, but I need to write, if only to make you understand that the person I have chosen as my lover has weakness, but much strength.

When I came back to the kitchen, Justin was slumped in a chair at the table. I was still angry, but I kissed his cheek and told him he should not be discouraged. This Dean Harrad does not understand anything, I told him. If he knew you like I know you, Justin, he would change his mind because these ideas need to be heard.

I reached for a pan beneath the sink and for the can of coffee I keep beside the flour and sugar. An Argasti tradition, you remember, Alberto, as the clock strikes the hour, *caffè* at six in the morning, *del vino* at noon, and *una birra* at seven in the evening. It is one of the small things that make me yearn for Mariano and the voices of

Mamma and Papà, but it is you I miss the most, dear brother.

You must write and tell me how you are preparing for the Church. Are you still seeing Verità? What will you do when the Church asks you to be celibate! I remember how at night you would escape through the window of your room and not be back until morning. I will not tell your secrets, but I will always remember waiting for you, looking out my window toward the black hills as the light slowly changed to gold.

I know what you will say when you read this. You will tell me to forget what is gone, and I am trying to do that. Life is still good with Justin. I love him and he cares for me. When I cut my fingers, he was very concerned. I told him to pay my wound no mind. It was not noticeable, no more so than that letter.

It was you, Justin, who told me so, I said as I took the coffee cups from the shelf, careful not to drop them and add to our troubles. Ideas are all around us, you said, like spores that travel in the air. If you did not think of them, others soon will, so it does not matter if Dean Harrad will not listen. I will listen and others will listen, too.

He did not answer or look at me. I asked him to tell me again of his thoughts, just as he did when we were first together. It was why we are together, I believe, his ideas and my music. When he told me about the energy that is all around us, I could actually sense it, the vibrations, these waves that go into us and through us. Sometimes I can see them, Alberto, as if sunlight filters through a vapor of diamonds. Just as the thick air wavers on a hot day, or as our breath becomes a cloud on a cold day, these waves that Justin speaks of are so real, sometimes, I think I can reach up and pluck them from the air. I so wish I could show you, brother, how beautiful it is to see the world as waves. You would say they come from God.

I realize, now, the letter Justin received that day in the fall of 1985 was from Dr. Leon Harrad, the Dean of Science at Royal Holloway

College. *Justin had submitted a proposal for a highly speculative doctoral thesis, which he had begun to call the waveform hypothesis.*

His proposal was rejected with no reason offered, which meant things had to change. Justin would no longer receive grant money from the college and Maria's scholarship at the Royal Academy of Music was too small to pay the rent. One option was for Justin to stay in London and finish his degree with a more acceptable thesis, but he realized he would risk an academic life in obscurity and relative poverty.

Another option would be for him to return to the United States, use his father's connections and take a gamble that his theory would eventually triumph. His old professors at Berkeley, he knew, would accept his return. American universities were in a constant state of competitive recruitment, especially in the field of physics. His sister, Hope Bishop, had written to him that there were plenty of grants available from supporters of Fermilab National Laboratory near Chicago. The director of the lab, she said, still fondly remembered their father, James Bradley Bishop, once the lead engineer on the original particle accelerator design. All bets among the elder scientists at Fermilab were for the prodigal son to exceed his father's legacy.

There was only one real problem with that plan. It did not include Maria. Though she knew it would take several years for her to finish her degree at the Royal Academy, she tried to encourage Justin to go without her. His research, she told him, was as important as her music and her music was too important to lose.

Yet she confided to Alberto in her letters a fear that Justin's ability to commit in the long term was too fragile. He depended on constant encouragement, she said, and she wondered if her lover had the passion to sustain a difficult dream, or even to sustain their love.

When she revealed this fear to Justin, he was furious. Passion was not the point of science! His ideas were not some dream of one individual, he told her. The waveform hypothesis was built on the hallowed ground of legends. Scientists for centuries had gained fame by methodically adding one small part to the great, unfinished puzzle that was knowledge. It was observation, correlation and experimentation that made progress, not the passion of dreamers.

The trouble with his argument, Maria realized, was that his waveform hypothesis was as unwieldy as passion. The waveform concept was difficult to frame within the scientific method, even Justin admitted. Not only was the quantum level too small to observe, but the mathematics of vibration involved differential equations too complex to solve with the most powerful computers. Few scientists of the twentieth century, with exceptions such as physicist-philosopher Wolfgang Pauli of the Pauli exclusion principle, were secure enough in their profession to make public their conjecture that energy was the true essence of the universe. Like Pauli, Justin believed matter might, indeed, be easier to conceive of than energy, but it was only a derivative. Energy is a priori to matter. Energy is that which is conserved, as the law of the conservation of energy expresses. Only the form in which energy appears actually changes, such as the transition from water to steam and on to the work being done in a turbine.

For thousands of years, Justin's proposal outlined, scientists had been grappling with this puzzle. They had searched their laboratories and wracked their brains for the essential building block of the universe. This puzzle was at the root of the most important questions of physics. What is the smallest form of matter? How did the universe appear at the beginning of time? If you cut through the complexity of form, what is the basic tool of creation?

At the height of Greek civilization, Justin recounted in his paper, Empedocles identified four basic elements: earth, wind, fire and water. Democritus went further to name the basic building block the atom, the undivided. Yet what is important is not the smallest particle that makes up matter, Justin proposed. It is how we think of the world in our minds. Is the universe really fixed in matter? Or is the matter we see everyday as fluid as energy?

These basic questions, unfortunately, are wrapped in a cosmic mystery. Between Albert Einstein's theory of relativity and Niels Bohr's work on quantum mechanics is an apparent conflict in the way we perceive how things work. Energy is equivalent to matter, Einstein proved, and matter is equivalent to energy. At the smallest levels, as many scientists began to realize, the distinction between matter and energy breaks down. Even in the emptiness of space there is a constant fluctuation of energy and matter. During these fluctuations, particle pairs of electrons and their antimatter positrons erupt, or condense, out of the void for split seconds of time. Stretching and retracting within the laws of energy conservation, the universe around us is an infinity of spontaneous creation and destruction. Space is virtually teeming with activity that we can barely imagine and still not conceive.

Still, scientists continue their obsessive search for the smallest particle. Physics texts are filled with clever ways for us to preserve our material world. According to the standard model of particle interactions, tiny entities called quarks and leptons make up the matter of the universe. Examples are the proton and electron. According to the elemental chart of chemistry, only one proton and one electron are needed to make the smallest element, hydrogen. At a higher level, two hydrogen molecules bond with an oxygen molecule to create water. Then, according to the equations of mechanics and thermodynamics, when a thermal force is applied to water it turns into steam, which can be harnessed by an engine for use as power.

To actually complete this clean explanation of the building processes of the universe, Justin wrote, would still require a further breakdown of matter below even the quantum level of quarks and leptons. It still requires us to find our way beyond matter to the realm of energy. It leads us to a universe such as the one scientists believe may have existed just after the Big Bang, before matter was created, when the four forces of the universe—the electromagnetic, the strong, the weak and gravity—were combined in a unity of spontaneous creation.

This world of spontaneity strikes fear into the hearts of many philosophers, theologians and scientists. They fear this drive to energy. Some believe we probe too deeply. What if we find the universe is simply vibrations and waves? Would it unsettle our solid existence or offend our spiritual roots? To those who feel threatened by these fears, it is as though our lives will somehow be demeaned if we break from our enduring faith in matter.

To his credit, Justin did not suffer from this variety of fear. He believed his waveform hypothesis would eventually revolutionize the way we think of the universe. Yet as Maria saw it, Justin had other fears just as profound, and the more he tried to ignore his passion, his spontaneity, the more these fears threatened his ideas, and their love.

Letter continued...

Justin has always been full of hope, Alberto, but now he seems defeated. According to his ideas, there are those who take energy and those who give it, and Justin usually fills me so full of energy I think I must explode. All I want to do is sit with him on the metal stairs outside our window and play the cello to the traffic on Currington as it races by as if motion will go on forever.

You cannot let this stop you, I said to Justin, but he slammed his hand on the table and pushed out his chair. He told me he has been into some trouble in America. When he was at Berkeley, he was arrested for using his computer to go where he did not belong. All that is behind him, he said, it was nothing. Yet he seems to still feel the shame.

He went to the stove and, as if it was poison he was about to drink, he poured hot water into the cup and slowly stirred the steaming coffee. I put my arms around his waist. The past is nothing, I said. You did something that kids do and you must forget about it. Talk to me, Justin, I whispered, about what is now. When we first were together, you told me what was in your head every moment.

Why not now?

I need to justify my ideas, even to you?

I tried to stop the tears, but I did not succeed. I am not his enemy, Alberto. I am his lover, and I want to know everything he thinks. What Justin believes makes the world less frightening for me. His ideas are medicine. They heal, like prayer they clear away sickness.

Why bring religion into everything, Maria?

I breathed deep to let the hurt pass, then I told him I am no longer Catholic, and he knows that. He should not try to hurt me by accusing me of religion, when Papà accuses me of the opposite. I believe in God, but not in the *rosario*.

Why do you keep it by the bed? he asked me, but he saw how his anger was making me cry, so he took my hand and held me, and I held his.

People like this, I said and picked up the letter from the Dean and shook it, will always be blind. They look for matter, like you say, Justin, when it is energy they need to find. They should know music. They should feel its energy. Music is just as your physics, you see. These waves, are they not the energy that carry the notes?

He did not laugh at me this time. I wish I could convince you, Alberto, of his power as well as his weakness. He can use either one to make me stronger or to wound me. It is what you feel when you stand at the ocean and feel the energy push and pull in the motion of waves. The waveform, Justin says, is fundamental to life. I believe him, Alberto. It is also fundamental to the Church, and the baby Jesus, and especially to music, these vibrations I feel in the notes. The waveform is the form of the universe. It is what began at the beginning. It is the way of the field that takes in everything, the earth and the stars. A priest, Alberto, should understand this simple idea. What God thought at the very beginning was the first waveform, and that thought is what created all things.

When I play the cello, I am closest to understanding Justin's physics. The truth is in the frequency and wavelength, the pitch and roll. When I sweep the bow across the strings, it reminds me of his ideas. Energy is dissonance and resonance. At the deepest level everything is a wave, including music and physics and all the religions of our ancestors.

This thought is wonderful, my brother. Matter and time and space are the movements of God. At this very moment, there is an intense field that connects brother to sister. Even from our distance, beyond our local nature, our waves interfere. Constructive or destructive, we choose the way we live.

Later, I went to the bedroom and took my cello from where it leaned against the wall. I realized my finger was still wrapped in a napkin, but I began playing with four fingers instead of five. While I played, Justin was silent and I could tell he was thinking about a universe beyond what most learn in school, but of which he is slowly teaching me.

It is spiritual, I said to him as he listened to my song, but he opened his mouth to argue, so I pulled my bow across the cello so it made an irritating sound.

You should not close your mind to this, I chided him. It is what my twin brother understood when we were still young, that there is a profound beginning. What you believe, Alberto, is not unlike what Justin believes, that the breath of God, the very first breath, began all things. It is what the Bible calls the Word, and physicists call the Big Bang, and the ancient Greeks called the *logos,* the fertilizing wisdom of God. It is just notes of music, I told him, the simple melody that is everything we know.

Religion is an emotion, he said. Physics is much bigger.

Than love? I stopped the bow in mid-stroke. Nothing is bigger than love, Justin, no matter what you think. If your ideas are worth anything to those who need them, it must be a physics of love!

SIX

—How well do you know him? the detective asks Oscar Fine.

—Very well, in fact. I've been the family's lawyer for about fifteen years. It's terrible to see Romeo like this. I left him alone in that room. I feel as thought the whole situation is my fault.

The back of my skull is pounding. The lawyer and detective have been in my hospital room for several minutes. I try not to move. I think of anything that comes into my head but breathing, moving. It's difficult to keep from jumping up and yelling my innocence, but I overheard the nurse and doctor talking about a crime, and they were talking as if I were the accused.

—You say, Mr. Fine, you were outside the house when the robbery occurred?

The detective's voice is hoarse, maybe tired, impatient. My eyes are closed tight, but I know his eyes are focused on me.

—After Frank died, Oscar says, I took the boy to Frank's office on the first floor. We reviewed the will. I left Romeo alone so he could think about it. The coroner arrived to take Frank, so it took me awhile to get back to the office. That's all I know.

In a high-energy particle accelerator, such as Fermilab in Chicago or CERN in Geneva, a minuscule proton is often the center of attention. At a quantum scale, I remember the Whirl teaching me, 938 million electron volts, so far below the visible world it defies human ability to comprehend, the proton becomes for a split second the protagonist in one of the most optimistic and horrific experiments known to humankind. This tiny, positively-charged proton is launched then accelerated, tracked and bent one way then another through a small tube that runs in a circle for miles just a few feet below the ground. Meanwhile, an antiproton, its antiparticle with a negative charge, is released in the opposite direction and spun at similar speeds until the moment of impact when the two particles collide in a mirrored doom. Bam! The Whirl smashed his hands together and scared the life out of me.

—And you don't think the kid broke into the safe and stole the gems? the detective says. He has a history of theft.

—No, I don't.

—And you don't think he murdered the old man?

—Doesn't make sense, Oscar says. I've known him since he was a little kid. He and Frank had a falling out, but I don't think Romeo is capable of murder.

The impact of a proton and antiproton is spectacular, the Whirl went on that day, both visually and spiritually. When a form of matter and its antimatter opposite collide, both particles cease to exist. Pure energy results, which transforms into a host of Frankenstein-like particles, such as quarks, photons and neutrinos. Luckily, he said, there is very little antimatter left in the universe, or we would still be witnessing the destruction of matter at super high rates, which is what the early universe was like soon after the Big Bang. And that would not be conducive to humanity. Fortunately for us, the Whirl said, matter won out. It seems nature, if not science, is far less intent on demolishing matter into smaller and smaller bits.

—I talked to the deceased man's brother, the detective says. No love lost between him and the boy.

—I hope we can count on your discretion, Oscar says. We've got enough problems without the press digging up family dirt.

—Philip told me the kid was living somewhere near the Bowery with some meth-heads, so why is it so out of the question for him to go the whole way?

—I guess you'll find out soon enough, Oscar says with a sigh. They had some rough times, he and Frank, but I think they truly cared for each other. Sometimes when Frank was drinking, he kicked the kid around a little. You'll find that out when you interview the help, but nothing to warrant murder. Romeo never fought, Frank told me. Never threatened him. No reason to believe the boy would murder his benefactor. And the theft of items from the safe would have just shown stupidity, and Romeo is far from stupid. There were some bonds and cash, a few diamonds and stones of some substantial value, but not enough to tempt someone who understood the extent of Frank Whirlpool's wealth. The real money was not in that safe, and Romeo knows it. He has a decent chance to get it all.

—A chance?

—The boy has to do some things before he inherits the money. He reacted badly when I told him, said he didn't want the money if he had to do what Frank had asked.

—That's motive, the detective says. Maybe he knew what was in the will. Maybe he couldn't wait, so he plopped a couple of tabs of strychnine into the old man's drink.

—He didn't know what was in the will, Oscar says. And he was nowhere near New Jersey. No idea Frank had been poisoned. There are a lot of other people who had motive. Frank had plenty of enemies.

—You say there was about two hundred thousand in cash and bonds? The stones would be a little hard to turn, but the kid might have thought he could pawn them. The doc says he tested positive for cocaine. It takes a lot of money for that kind of habit.

—Maybe I'm naive, but I just don't think he would risk it. He's a runaway, not a murderer.

—Might be true or not, the detective says. The kid's prints are all over the safe, but he lived in the house, so that won't hold much water in court. We'll let the District Attorney decide once we know what the kid did between the time you left him in the office and when we found him in Harlem.

—Harlem, you say?

—On 104th Street about two o'clock this morning. That's probably where he got the wound on the back of his head. We found a tire iron with some hair and blood on it. We're having it tested at the lab. Maybe a buy went wrong, who knows? Doctor says he's got a bad concussion, but we're going to have to ease up on the sedatives. We've got to question him soon. With Philip Whirlpool running for the Senate seat, the press is going to be all over this.

—What now? Oscar says.

—I'll come back in the morning. We've got an officer posted at the door. Dave Budding is on until eleven o'clock. The doctor promises me the kid will be ready to talk. Meantime, I've got a few questions for the business partner.

—Silvie Nels?

—Yeah, he says, then the nieces, and that cute little nurse he had, and the dozens of others who have been hanging around Frank Whirlpool with bags to catch the money. You're a lawyer. You've seen it. What people will do for money, especially this kind of fortune. Compared to some cases, poison shows some generosity.

Wobble-wheel gurneys and shuffling rubber shoes screech in the hall. I wait until I'm sure the detective and the lawyer are gone before I open my eyes. The heart monitor beeps with signs of life. Patients walk the hallway with IV's in tow. Nurses and doctors scuttle to their next patients.

—Glad you're awake, says a nurse with a white hat. She's bent over me smiling. How do you feel?

She gives me a drink that's absolute zero and it burns my throat. She rubs the tattoo on my right shoulder because she sees the scar. Lining the walls and window ledge are flowers with cards from people I don't know, banks and insurance companies, relatives of the Whirl I can't remember meeting.

—You've been sleeping a long time, Romeo, the nurse says. That's a nice name, Romeo from the play. I love Shakespeare. Do you have any pain, dear?

I shake my head. The pain is delayed but it hits like a fist.

—Your wound is healing nicely. You've got to be a little careful with the bandages, but once you get some rest I think you'll be fine.

In a particle accelerator, the Whirl explained to me, the control room is full of scientists and luminous screens linked to back rooms with huge processing computers that record images and correlate data. Like a pitcher for the Yankees, a gifted geek releases some protons of hydrogen. Magnets send them around and around the accelerator ring at speeds measured in millions of electron volts over the speed of light squared. Mostly the geek on the mound manages a few simple strikes and balls, but once in a great while a proton smashes in a spectacular home run that reveals, by computer imagery, a tiny patch of the universe before unknown.

—Blood pressure is back to normal, the nurse says. The wound is taking the stitches well. I think you'll be on your way very soon. Would that make you happy?

—Maybe you could look at my eyes, I say.

—What's wrong with your eyes?

—I can't see color.

She pushes my right eyebrow up and pulls down my cheek. Then she tries the left eye and shakes her head. She writes notes on my chart.

—Your pupils are dilated, she says. Your muscles are twitching.

You've had a lot of stress. I'll ask the doctor to take a look. In the meantime, I'll have someone bring you something to eat.

She disappears through the door. I raise my head and see the shoulder patch of the policeman sitting in the hallway with his back to the door. I feel the lump of dressing on the back of my head, and I scoot further up in the bed until the pain surges in my head like a gangsta rap or some Brazilian mamba. A nurse's aide brings me my meal, chicken and noodles, applesauce, a biscuit and some carrot cake. In the movies, when there's an officer posted at the hospital room door, it's time for the hand-held camera. The killer always returns, and poison is so easy to use.

I push the food cart aside and put my leg over the mattress. The mamba gets louder. I touch the floor with my toe. In an accelerator, thousands of particles are put in harm's way. Some disappear into energy, others collide into bits and pieces, and some survive whole. I wish I had listened more closely to the Whirl when he explained the variables that make the difference, but now he's dead, if not gone.

Palms flat on the mattress, I launch myself to a standing position. The room feels as though it's a vacuum, no sound or motion. My pulse flutters, but walking is similar to riding a bike and I remember how to shuffle and stoop. I check the drawers and closet. No clothes, no effects. Shit, I can't find my drumsticks. I open the curtains and look down three floors to the busy street. The massive window above the heater is sealed with thick, black caulk. In the reflection of the window, my eyes are sunken into dark holes. The bandage looks like a beret that's slid back too far. I raise my arms and stretch, but an ocean of pain rises and breaks against rocks.

I slide barefoot to the door and listen. The policeman sucks a breath as if he's sleeping. It's now or never. I take the plunge and step through the doorway, then without looking at Officer Dave Budding, I sprint as fast as I can down the hall.

It's only seconds before I hear him scream. Dave Budding has tipped his chair and is cursing. I blur past the nursing station and open doors of rooms with other particles yearning for freedom from pain, or death, or worse. I reach the elevator and look back to see the confused officer running toward me with his hand on his holster.

The elevator doesn't cooperate. I mash the down button with my palm, then with my knuckle. The fist in my head is still punching. I see the stairs and blast through the door and fall down two and three steps at a time. One, two, three, four, five platforms, then the doors to the basement fly open upon the concrete and cars, black grunge and graffiti.

I race into the smelly air of a New York street and see people walking, shoving and shifting in Brownian motion, molecules bumping into molecules. Everyone looks familiar, a guy with Oscar's nose, Gabby's sleeveless vest, Philip Whirlpool's balding head, Silvie's pulled-back hair. The Whirl's four nieces, not so much their faces but their tinny voices, seem to squeal from the storm sewers that steam into the cold daylight.

I burst into a small clothing shop not far from the hospital. I've got to shed this ridiculous gown. It's as if a cold metal hand has gripped on my spine. From the sale rack, I grab the first thing that comes to my hand, a jacket. The store clerk is freaking. The kid says nothing, but he rushes for the desk and the phone.

—I'm sorry, I say to him. There's nothing I can do.

By now, Dave Budding must have called in and the guards and police must be combing the halls. The hospital alarm is pulsing like a supernova. I find a pair of pants near my size and stuff them on as if I'm stepping into a gunnysack.

—Do you have shoes? I ask.

As if his life depends on his answer, the clerk nods to the back of the store and I find a right and a left from different style loafers that nearly fit. I apologize to the poor kid, then explode like a madman to the street.

SEVEN

—You're out.

—I'm not out, I say and try to nudge Danny Cheever off the drum throne. You're the one who's out. I missed a few sessions, so what? It's my band.

—Who says so?

—The crowd says so. You've heard them, Danny, so clear out of the seat.

—What's with the head, anyway? He hits the snare drum hard and points the stick at my bandage. You fall on your head, boy? You go a little dense? The band needs a drummer, not a freakin' veggie case.

Chalice stumbles down from the singer's platform to where Danny Cheever pokes the drumstick at my head. If it takes a fight, I've never been more ready. Danny and Chalice, the whole damn place, I don't care. I just need to play, feel the sticks in my hand, if only for another night. I need to be rid of this buzzing of hospitals and police, but instead of squabbling with this no-talent drummer, I should be fighting with Oscar, or Philip, or the Whirl. It's tough enough to keep calm when you can't see right. Is Chalice red hot or fiery blue?

—What the hell are you doing here, Romey? he says and whips his thick, bleached mane back from falling into his face. The police came asking questions, man, he says. I can't afford that crap, not from a damn drummer. We've got a show going here, and whatever you're doing on the outside, don't bring trouble in here. You got it?

Chalice is Dave Tiemba, the front man since Benny Jacoby left for Florida. Chalice renamed the band Grimace and changed the whole play list, but we finally landed a paid gig at Bonner's. He's a raunch rocker and doesn't like my style. Too techno, he told me. Skipping the third beat drives him crazy, but the beat's more personal than genre. And there's jealousy. The crowd comes to see me.

—Who busted your head? he says.

—Poor boy fell down, Danny says and slams both sticks on the hi-hat.

—I came to play, Chalice.

—Tell him to get lost, Danny says.

—Damn drummers, the singer says with another shake of his dirty mane. Wish I could do without a damn drummer. Stick man I had with my last band, the bastard sold our equipment and disappeared. Swore I'd find a way to skip the drummer.

—Look, Chalice, I say, Violet must have told you. I just missed a few sessions. Death in my family. You can't expect me to be here when there's a death in the family. I'm in, man. No trouble. I need this.

—Can't do it, Romey.

—Just one more night. Tonight's the last. You can pay me and that's it. I need the money.

—Uh huh, he says. Well, that's the trouble. We're trying a new sound and you're still playing the old way. Danny's like fire, Romey. No big deal, you left us in the lurch. We gotta have someone who's on the same wavelength, man. You aren't. Never were. Not your fault, but there's nothing I can do.

—They'll follow me, I say. I'll take the crowd to some other band. I don't want to, Chalice, but that's how it is.

—You threatening me? Look, shithead, we're going to try this with Danny. Maybe it won't work. Maybe we'll want you back, I don't know, but you threaten me and I'll kick your stupid ass.

Danny leers. I want to punch them both, but I limp back to where the lights are not so bright, where I can stew in the dark. My head is pounding and every time I move too fast my eyesight blurs. Concussion. Malfunction of the synaptic firing in the brain. The electrons move in a current down the neurons only to find there's no way across the gap to the next nerve, so they wait.

People pat me on the back and ask me where I've been and why the hell I have a huge bandage on my head. The waitress, Jenny Fraley from St. Paul, brings me a vodka and beer because she thinks I'm still a part of the band. I swallow the liquor and chase it, and it makes my head spin like a spiked neutron. An hour goes by just watching the band despite the fact that Danny can't see the opportunities to interject the sympathetic beat. He's got his troubles firing, too. It hurts me to listen. It's difficult to focus, and it doesn't help that I feel this overpowering dread, this sad throbbing in my mind that the Whirl is dead and gone and I don't have a home, never did.

Vodka burns my throat. It must have been painful for him, burning mouth, scorched throat, retching and buckling as the strychnine spread through his body. Anyone could have done it, like Oscar said, but who would want money that bad, no matter what the Whirl did, no matter how many enemies he found at the bottom of a whiskey bottle? He made his brother feel worthless, screwed his business partner and ignored his relatives. Even Reverend Walker had come calling to the most notorious stone-faced sinner in the neighborhood in hopes of funding a kingdom of Heaven on Earth.

I'm about to cover my ears to keep from hearing Danny clunking the drums, when I see Violet. She slips through the back door with her work clothes on. Though it's freezing, she has on skin-tight hotpants and a strapless tube that I know are clashing reds, but I see them as light gray and black. I think how cold she must be, and how cold the Whirl must be. Does he drift across the Styx like an Egyptian pharaoh? Does he ride through space as spent energy? I wonder if he'll do eternity in a casket, or get fired in a crematorium and buried in a cardboard box.

Violet slides through the crowd to the bar. Though she's dressed for it, I don't think she's working. Over a month ago, she told me she quit, but that was when I had all kinds of money. Now I'm busted for good. So what if she hooks? To love is not to possess, or that's what the poets say. It's the violence, I've got to remember, not the sex, and Violet looks virginal, hair frizzled on bare shoulders, black lipstick from a teenager's makeup kit. That's her draw, she tells me. Just right for old men who want nothing more than to recapture the pulse of youth.

I make my way to her. She's talking to Chalice. He points to the door as he starts the next song. Violet scans the crowd, but I'm still too far in the dark for her to see. She turns away a greaser who puts his fat hand on her shoulder. She's too high priced for someone who frequents this kind of dive, kids without money or lost dreams.

I make it to the stage and swing around in back of Danny and spot his extra pair of drumsticks. I slide them out of the case and he sees me, but he's playing and can't stop. He mouths a threat I can't decipher. I nod and smile, then shove the sticks lengthwise into my pants and head for the door. I try to catch Violet, but she's walking fast as if she's trying to outpace the cold. Her heels peck on the concrete. She finishes one cigarette, then with the embers she lights another. People turn as she passes them, as if the frosty breeze from her movement is creating a magnetic field. She's almost to 27th Street before she stops to see who is following. She's all too familiar with the stalk, the indecision, the final checkout before the approach or falter.

—What the fuck you got in mind? she says and turns with her hand on hip. She takes a puff from her cigarette, then recognizes me. Romey! she screams. Damn, where you been? Then she finishes the gap between us and hangs onto me with her face buried in my shirt and the front tip of her stilettos on my mismatched loafers.

—How are you, baby, I say. I missed you.

Her body is cold, then warm as she presses harder against me. We're in front of a closed bakery and the security lights are shining in our faces. Her eyes are like a wild animal's illuminated by car lights. I haven't been gone long, but already she's let the past creep in.

—You okay? I say.

—What's this? She touches the bandage on my head. Someone hit you? Who hit you, Romey? I'll kill the bastard.

—It's okay. Don't worry about me. Let's go home, Violet.

She stares into my eyes as if she's trying to see if I'm the same person.

—Let me take your hand, baby, she says. I was just going home. Chalice said you left the bar and I was about to find you. I've been waiting. I'm not kidding, we'll kill the bastard, Romey, whoever did this to you.

We walk fast across the glistening black concrete that rolls in front of the retail district on Century Street. It's a cold night and moist. The wind is from the north and it feels like it's about to snow, but the Hovel is the warmest place on earth. Even on the bleakest nights, the air is constantly folding inward, rising against the cold as if everything's happening for a reason that's no reason at all.

—The drunks left.

—I thought they would, I say.

—Just up and left. Don't know why, but it's better. They were making trouble. Brownie got into a fight with one, but I don't think that's what made them go. It's just Brownie that's got a new cut.

Right along his jaw.

She shows me by slicing her right cheek with her index finger. Hand-in-hand, we climb the metal stairs to the third floor. We don't say much to the others who look up as we go by. Brownie's got some wine and a dirty bandage on the new cut. Sarah is cozying up to him for a drink. They've got cardboard wedged against the broken windows. Gabby has two friends over next to a candle where they hunch their shoulders and smoke hashish.

Even if the cops come to find me, the others won't tell. You can trust people who don't trust others. Violet grabs Tuf from where he's hiding in a corner. I grab our blanket and a large piece of cardboard. We make our way, the three of us, to the fourth floor and, just like home, unfold the box and crawl inside.

—You put something on this? Violet says. Something medicine-like? She pokes my bandage until I jerk. I'm not kidding, Romey, you tell me who did this.

—I don't know. I push two fingers on the kitten's head and stroke down its thin body. They hit me from behind, I say.

She puts Tuf aside and pushes me down onto the cardboard floor, then pulls the blanket up so it covers us. She unbuttons my shirt and the cold air curls the black hair on my chest. She blows warm air on my nipples and unzips my pants and takes out the drumsticks and, because she's seen me do it before, tucks them safe under the blanket. Then like a nurse ministering to a patient, she starts to make love, but there's more. Every few minutes, she takes a look into my eyes as if she's wondering if it's making me feel good and safe, and it does. We wake at four o'clock in the morning to smoke a cigarette and watch the neon sign blinking over the bakery.

—It was that damn lawyer, wasn't it? she says.

—You don't have to worry about Oscar.

—Did he do this?

—He was there, I say, but I don't think he had anything to do with it. It's a long story, Violet. There's a lot of shit going on. The Whirl was murdered.

—Murdered? That's your dad, right? He's dead?

—I'm adopted.

—But you liked him, didn't you, baby? Murdered? Who the hell would murder him?

—I don't know. They think it was me.

—Did you do it?

—Hell, no, I didn't do it!

—Hey, I was just asking, you know. He hit you, though, didn't he, baby? You told me you ran, I remember. You said he was messing with you too much, that's what you said.

It seems a billion years ago, the night he came to me drunk as a skunk, going on about how he wished he'd never taken me in. I thought he was going to hit me, so I hit him first. Cuffed him on the right cheek and left him on the floor. If I could change the world, you'd think I would do it differently, but I wouldn't. I couldn't have stayed one more day, when staying anywhere was out of the question. There's no such thing as perpetual motion or no motion at all. Energy changes, it moves on. Sometimes you try to stop it, but it doesn't work, like love in a box.

I'm crying. I can't help it. Violet puts her head on my chest. Tuf snuggles between us. I fight the tears back and tell her how the Whirl took his last breath and that I'm having trouble with my eyes. She tells me the clinic will be open in the morning, but those doctors know a lot about pregnancy and dying, but nothing about physics. Then against my better judgment, I tell her about the will.

—Jesus, Romey. Are you shitting me? That's got to be it. The bastards are trying to frame you. They're trying to screw you. You can't let them do that.

—What am I supposed to do? I say. They almost killed me, Violet.

—So you run? You got a chance for that kind of money, and you run? Jesus Christ, Romey. Go back and jack the bastards.

—It's rigged. The whole thing. They never did buy into it, the Whirl bringing me in, Philip, Silvie, the whole damn family.

—Doesn't matter who in the hell buys into it, she says. People would do anything for that kind of money. Anybody would.

—It's the Whirl's fault. He's just screwing with me.

—The bastard is dead, she says. I'm sorry, Romey, but that's the truth, and he hit you. So let him play if he can, more power to him. Two billion, what the hell is that? Here we are sleeping under a damn box. You're scared, that's what it is.

—I'm not scared.

—They slammed you, now you're scared. I see that in you, Romey. You're always running from something. I don't take to that shit. I don't take to cowards.

—I'm not running.

She puffs on the cigarette at a higher rate than oxygen and heat can mix. It sparks and pops, and scares the hell out of Tuf, who scats down the steps to find the others. Against the bakery sign on the left and the Dillard's Moving and Storage sign on the right, Violet's thin profile fluctuates at a tempo that makes her look as if she's part of the neon.

—You're going back, she says.

—I'm not going back. They'd arrest me.

—You're going back and telling those bastards you want the money. Fuck them. You didn't murder nobody. Look at this place, she says. You saw Brownie down there with a new cut. With a hundred bucks you could make his day. And Gabby, she's got bills. An abortion, what the hell, Victorio says he's paying for it, but there's all kinds of expenses, and Victorio, shit. Gabby could have the baby, for Jesus' sake, think of it, Romey.

Violet's eye shadow is smudged. She isn't crying. It's as if she can't cry. The tears just well up until they reach equilibrium with the air. I put my palm flat on her face and she kisses it.

—Oscar will give me some money.

—How much?

—Maybe a million.

—Shit, you think? No way, not if they don't have to. They'll ditch you, Romey. Blame the whole thing on you. They got it all planned. You need someone to watch your back. That's what you need, someone to watch your back.

—This is serious, Violet. Someone killed him.

—You don't trust me?

—I do.

—Then we get this thing taken care of. You just trust me. I'll watch your back. We'll do it together.

I know she's working me, but I'm too tired to argue. And scared. I see a little of the sky through the dirty windows of the warehouse and between the two buildings on the corners of East River Drive where they open to a view of the Brooklyn Bridge. To actually see stars in this city is out of the question, but it might help sometimes. When you think of what's out there, an infinity of particles and compounds and gases, billions of galaxies and zillions of stars, it makes everything on this earth seem a little smaller. No matter how much violence and money there is in New York City, it couldn't possibly make an impression on the vast, unimaginable void.

—We love each other, right? she says. Right, Romey?

—That's right.

She scoots over until she's in my arms. I hear the others on the third floor still laughing and playing poker. People like Violet and Brownie and Gabby could care less that the universe is made of carbon and hydrogen and the heavy elements of stars and planets and people. Only so many composite ideas can be absorbed by anyone, no matter how interested. People gloss over the facts, even the most brilliant people, then with mythology and religion they create a universe of their own. All you do is put two molecules together and make something comfortable. Yet whatever you make is really the same as all the rest, nature in its simplest form. One thing causes another, then that thing causes another, and so on.

But that doesn't really do it for me, or for anyone. There's more, much more. Something beyond what the Whirl could teach me. Something that makes people struggle to find it. If, as physics tells us, spontaneous creation of the universe is true—and it doesn't matter so much whether it was pure probability, or divinity in the guise of probability that first caused it—then what we see as pleasure and pain is more than just some dust moving dust.

It's creation, the universal synapse. In humans it's a jumping of the gap between neurons, a consciousness, a will. One electron communicates with another in different parts of the brain, the theory goes, the same as we communicate with each other arm-in-arm. It's the same as when one electron on Earth knows what another does on Mars, non-causal, non-local, immediate communication, all according to the theories of physics. The world is a living, breathing place, just as human beings are living and breathing. It's the natural state of the universe, a hotbed of spontaneous creation, and though all this physics may seem senseless in the face of death and murder, the truth of the stars remains. If you stare into the darkness and think of it deep down, a person could find God, or at least find the courage to go on.

EIGHT

October 13, 1985

Have you taken a vow of silence, Alberto? Now that you are studying in *Firenze* maybe you are too busy for anyone but God. Have you received divine wisdom? Is that it? I hope so, brother, for both our sakes. You must be ready to advise me on good and evil, because I need your insight now.

An odd event occurred last night. As if we had hoped him into existence, a stranger came to our flat to offer money and a future. He was vain and rude in manner, yet I saw in his eyes the pride of someone who believes he does right. He is famous, he told us, for turning science into fortune and he might turn Justin's physics into a fortune, too.

Should we be wary of this stranger and his money, Alberto, or should we think him a godsend? Justin and I had been talking in the kitchen. Not more than a moment before, I had said we should not stoop so low as hand-to-mouth and that something would come to stop our indignity.

A knock at the door made us jump. We stayed silent as the echoes ceased, then Justin opened the door slowly as if, instead of a person, he expected to see *salvezza*. The stranger with his deep voice and fine leather briefcase pushed the door wider and stepped inside. A mutual acquaintance, he said, thought it would be good if he and Justin met. Then he asked whether we knew Dean Harrad, so I waited for the explosion, but Justin simply let this man walk further into our lives.

Frank Whirlpool is an enormous man with long arms and wide shoulders that seem too large for our tiny flat. He has a thin face and deep furrows beneath black hair that curls long around his ears. He was dressed more elegantly than do most Americans. He had a fine blue suit and red tie with a Wellington knot pulled loose.

Though he was looking at me, he extended his hand to Justin, who introduced me as his girlfriend, a musician, an Italian. Then in a most extraordinary way, the stranger took my hand in front of God and everyone and he kissed it!

I love to hear a cello, he said, or as you would say, Maria, *violoncello*.

I pulled my hand away and put it behind me. Cello is fine, I said. It seems a long time since I was in Italy.

Call me Frank, he said, both of you. We should all go to the London Symphony, the three of us. Then he turned to Justin and told him Dean Harrad had said Justin's ideas might be of interest to investors.

When did the Dean begin to care about ideas? Justin said, and I could tell he did not like how this stranger had kissed my hand.

Frank Whirlpool only laughed and said a person in the Dean's position must remain skeptical. Politics is in everything, he said, even in physics.

I was sure, especially after the letter, that Justin would ask this man to leave, but Justin simply let Frank Whirlpool make himself at home.

The problem with physics, he said with a wave of his hand, is that it may take centuries for people to adapt to new facts. Even scientists have a hard time believing.

Justin took from the drawer the Dean's letter and stuffed it into Frank Whirlpool's hands. The stranger tossed the letter onto the table as if it was nothing. He said the Dean would do anything to have what Justin has. Even insult you, he said, just as you, no doubt, have insulted him.

How could I have insulted the Dean of Royal Holloway?

By going beyond him, the stranger answered Justin. There is always resentment from the uncreative toward the creative. Otherwise, we would all be creative.

Justin took the man's overcoat and handed it to me, but since I was not so sure about what he was saying, I simply held it in my arms.

He told us about his partner, a Norwegian who has many connections in America and Europe. Silvie Nels, he said to Justin, will handle the money, I will handle the market and you will handle the product. *Ménage a trois.*

Then he told Justin about another student's idea their Foundation is funding, a Harvard student who devised a compound so strong, he said, it bonds steel to steel without the need for welding. Two pieces into one, as if it comes from the same roll.

If an invention is already a product, Justin asked, why do you still need the inventor?

Frank Whirlpool just smiled and without asking permission or worrying about whether the window could be opened, he drew a lighter from his pocket and lit a huge cigar. The smoke lingered in a dirty cloud at the ceiling, and I bit my lip, not because of his rude habit, but because he was looking at me as if I was a product, too.

You should not smoke, I said. And Justin does not need a *ménage a trois.* He will get his grant without you or this Silvie Nels.

Justin jumped from his chair. Maria thinks only of music, he said and took Frank Whirlpool's coat from me and hung it so carefully in the closet I thought it might have golden threads.

The stranger continued to smile his Cheshire smile as if Justin was his wonderland and I was his Alice. He asked me if I would make some tea, so I looked to Justin who would not meet my eyes. I opened the window, and turned on the stove and filled a pan with water. While Frank Whirlpool told Justin more about his partner and this Foundation the two have started in New Jersey, the water began to roll and Justin began pacing. I put our good white cups onto the table and tried not to listen, but I could not help being surprised that Justin was so willing to tell this stranger about ideas that he has only revealed to me.

What could it be about this man, Alberto, that Justin would trust him so completely? Is the attraction of money so strong in men that they can deny the overtures of strangers to their lover? Justin says of gravity that the closer one object gets to a second, the more each of them pulls the other. How can I stop the force of nature, even though it be the pull of sin?

Though he was twenty years younger, the man who showed up at their apartment door that night was very recognizable to me. I remember when the Whirl walked into a room, he filled it with a restless energy so there was little room for others. Like all charismatic personalities, I would imagine, he knew how to project, to push his electrons outward so they interfered with others, wave upon wave, superimposing, building with some, destroying others.

After living with the Whirl all my life and seeing the faithful line up at his door, I know how overcome with his presence the two young students might have felt. Frank Whirlpool, undoubtedly, made Justin feel both powerful and weak. He made Justin forget his own mortality for the moment and think of hope. As matter drifting to the event horizon of a beautiful and immense black hole, Justin was drawn to the Whirl's bottomless dream of fortune and fame.

And he gave Frank Whirlpool what he wanted. Justin revealed that night the core of his waveform hypothesis. It was an idea that could be expressed no better than by the interplay of the three as they spoke for the first time in that small London apartment. Unfortunately, waves were colliding and reflecting in ways that none of them at that time could foretell.

There are many theories, Justin must have explained, that predict the way the universe works, particle theory and field theory. They all stop short of describing the essential unification of the cosmos. They get caught, Justin believed, in the endless search for the root of matter. Yet the fundamental structure of the universe is not matter. It is not an atom or electron or quark. It is energy, pure energy that creates the motion of a wave.

The Whirl was a physicist by degree, if not in practice, but that night he must have withheld judgment because Justin told him ideas that were beyond the realm of reason. Higgs Field Theory, Justin had written in his paper to Harrad, was just the beginning. Scottish physicist Peter Higgs had contended there were many different kinds of fields around us, literally permeating the universe. Matter, according to Higgs, is created at the intersection of these fields. Different fields create different forms of matter, such as the electrons of atoms and the hypothetical gravitons that create the pull of gravity.

Yet Justin's ideas were not just a rehashing of other ideas. According to his doctoral proposal, he believed science had evolved from Maxwell's equations on electromagnetism and Einstein's relativity theories. It was well proven that energy and matter are interchangeable. If matter could actually be accelerated to the speed of light, it would be pure energy, and pure energy has no mass. Many scientists believed as an inevitable conclusion of the work of such men as Christiaan Huygens, Erwin Schrödinger and Wolfgang Pauli, that in some ways energy can better be described as a wave, not a particle.

If energy is in the form of a wave at the highest speeds, Justin reasoned, what happens to the wave at lower speeds? It takes the solid form that we see as matter, but it does not cease to be a wave. Energy slows down, becomes a particulate, but it still rolls through time and space. Whether it seems a motionless or moving wave, potential or kinetic energy, it's a wave all the same.

To Justin, this conclusion should have a huge impact on the way we think about the universe, yet it had received little credence from the scientific community. It meant a fundamental change in the historical search for the building blocks of nature. It meant a change in the goal from a quest for matter to a quest for the root of energy. Vibrations, or oscillations, create a one-dimensional field, he conjectured. The vibrations roll in sequence through time to create a two-dimensional, sinusoidal wave. Different waves interfere with each other and resonate, which creates a third dimension, which is the field of the four forces and the field of matter. This combination is what we see as the components of matter, the quarks, electrons, atoms and molecules of our world.

Almost immediately, the Whirl realized what Justin's waveform hypothesis implied. If the universe is composed of waves, then identifying one-by-one the different types of matter was only the beginning. The essential unification of waves meant everything in the universe had a common ground, and that meant a formula. It was definable, predictable and transmutable, which for thousands of years was the end goal for the original and most notorious of capitalists, the alchemists, seekers of gold.

The Whirl was quick to realize the implications for himself and the Foundation, because he began to bind his future to Justin's hypothesis so tightly that he created a huge and perplexing wave that has rolled through time to me.

Letter continued...

So Justin grows silent with me, Alberto, but not with strangers. He was so willing to spill his ideas that he ran to the drawer for paper and pen. He drew for Frank Whirlpool the difference between his hypothesis and string theory, for which there is much excitement at Royal Holloway. He stays all night at the college with his friends talking about this revolution in physics where tiny strings not only make up matter but also the forces of nature.

You do not have to be a scientist to understand this physics, Alberto. String theory is only a way of looking at the tiny level of the universe, where everything is made of vibrating strings instead of particles. To understand Justin's ideas, just change the strings to waves and you'll have most of it. Waves intersect to create the structure of things. The universe is energy that travels by waves. This energy creates the fields of what we can see and touch, the sounds and sights, the invisible rays of the sun. They are simply Justin's waveforms.

Frank Whirlpool, I could tell, was impressed because he began to ask questions that went deeper and deeper into Justin's physics. Are all things just composite waveforms? If you take this to a logical conclusion, this stranger who seemed to have become Justin's best friend said, you might say that humans are simply waveforms. Then our fate, he said, is contained in a wave!

Justin shrugged his shoulders, but I knew this is what he believes. The interference of waves, either constructive or destructive, creates larger waveforms, including us.

I know what you are thinking, Alberto, that this separates us from God, but it does not. Because all waves begin at the tiny quantum world, they only have what is called probability. They do not have a destined fate that we can know without God. They have many potential paths, or histories. They have frequency, wavelength and amplitude, just as notes of music have ways to be measured. Waves depend on a cause, like the pluck of a cello's string, but they can also occur without a cause, or spontaneously. Probability, Justin says, ensures that certain things in nature occur without the need for a cause.

Is this not close to what we spoke of as children, brother? A world of music? A universe composed of the prayers of children? Anything is probable. Anything is possible. It is too large an idea to be hoarded by scientists. It is the physics of love, I believe. Your theology, my music, Justin's physics, they lead to a universe of waves that give and take our energy. And we have seen both in our lives, have we not Alberto, both the give and the take?

It was late when Frank Whirlpool finally left. He asked for his coat, and stood at the door and I could tell he was already beginning to doubt what Justin had said. These ideas are too difficult to keep in our small minds. Justin has told me over and over, but I still do not understand it all. I see only the parts. I have an infinite number of possibilities, but I can choose only one path, one turn at an intersection. When I decide something, once and forever, the probability wave, as Justin says, collapses. Only one possibility remains.

Frank Whirlpool said he would talk with his partner. He said we must be careful with such ideas. There is a trick with capital. There are billions of paths—he used Justin's words—but only one leads to fortune.

Justin was exhausted, but so excited he could not sleep. He believes this stranger might be the answer to our problems, but he fears it is too good to be true and that Frank Whirlpool might not return. I know better, Alberto, and it makes me have another fear. Behind those prideful eyes that stare at me with such longing and ambition is a troubled soul. How can we expect such a man to understand a physics of love?

NINE

Violet and I share a cigarette near a phone booth on Water Street. I search my wallet for Oscar's number. The bandage is loose and my head is throbbing, but less than last night when every siren and grinding gear erupted in my head.

A small grocery is a block away, so Violet goes to find some breakfast while I make the call to the law offices of Boyer, Fine, and Roberts. The receptionist answers and I tell her who I am. She hesitates a moment, then she asks me to hold. As if I could lose my one connection to a world that's slipping away, I've got the receiver in a death grip. No decision is right unless it feels right, and it's not that this decision feels wrong. It's just not much of a decision. No reason to stick around New York and be a victim of circumstances beyond my control, so I'm giving up my future for the quest of a man who, undoubtedly, is rotting in hell, if hell is real.

—Mr. Fine will pick up. Thank you for waiting, Mr. Argasti.

I see Violet with a bag and some leaflets that she stuffs into an overflowing trash can at the corner. This morning, she changed out of the hotpants and tube top into jeans with holes in the knees and a sweater cut off at the midriff. Her white-blond hair is spiked from inattention and it looks more natural, kinky and thick like the mane of an albino lion. Waiting for the traffic light, she leans against the signpost and swills from the carton of chocolate milk.

—Romey, Oscar says as he comes on the line, where the hell have you been?

—Nowhere.

—You have no idea how much trouble you've caused. The police are looking everywhere. I should have told them about that damn warehouse, but we can't afford to let it hit the papers. Are you all right, boy?

—I had nothing to do with the murder, Oscar, and I didn't break into the safe. Someone is trying to frame me.

—You could have told that to the police.

—You tell them.

—It's not that simple.

—Frank would have wanted you to help me, Oscar. Now I'm asking.

I move the receiver to my other hand and lean against the booth. Violet runs across the intersection and holds up a strawberry filled donut. The hollow payphone noise buzzes in my ear, and I know Oscar is silent because he's weighing his options. In law, there's a comfort level with probable cause. It's only spontaneity that causes the trouble, indefinable actions like forgiveness and trust, and that doesn't work so well with a legal system that depends on precedent.

—There's a diner on East River, I say. Annie's, near Hopkins Street. Can you meet me?

—I've got some appointments, but I'll break them. Three o'clock, is that good?

—No cops, Oscar.

—It's to everyone's advantage to keep this quiet.

I hook the receiver onto its cradle. Violet hands me the donut and an open milk container. I take a long drink. It's sweet and rich and such a change from the cigarettes and booze of last night that it nearly gags me. I push Violet's hair over her ears and notice the black roots.

—You should let it go natural, I say.

—That's not what my clients wanted. They wanted fantasy, you know, Marilyn Monroe types, sex on a spoon. Where you been, Romey?

We wait for the Don't Walk sign to change, then we coast across the street and finish our donuts and chocolate. The air hasn't warmed from the sun, but the jacket I stole from the shop by the hospital has a lining. If I had the chance, the only thing I would do better is find the same loafer style. And maybe steal a pair of pants one size smaller. And some socks, maybe, that would be good, warm socks.

—Oscar won't be here until three.

I swig the rest of the milk and take a mouthful of donut. Violet can't keep her hands still, so it looks as if she's on something, but we haven't had anything but a few tokes. A street cop comes by and nods us away from the store front, so we wander toward Hopkins to a second-hand store where a friend of Brownie's works the register.

—I can't stand it, Violet says. The thought of all that money is driving me crazy.

—It's bullshit.

—Jesus, Romey, two billion. What are we gonna do with it? You ever really thought about that? How about Florida, or an island or something? Just you and me on an island, all that sand and sun. Just thinking about it makes me get hot, kind of. It makes me want to get it done faster, Romey, like now.

—Get what done?

—The music! Jesus, I can't believe you sometimes. The library, maybe? Think the library would have it? We could look up your mother's name. Figure out where she died.

—I've been to the library. She died in the English Channel, but I already knew that.

—What's the English Channel?

—A sea between England and France.

—Shit, she says, maybe the music went down with the plane. How are we supposed to find it then?

—Maybe we can't. Maybe we were never supposed to.

—You can't talk like that. You hear me, Romey? The only thing impossible is to let that kind of money go. So, he's coming, right? Oscar's coming?

—To Annie's, yeah.

—He bringing some money? For expenses?

—I didn't ask.

—What the hell did we say about that? You've got to ask him for some expenses. Let me call him back. What's the number?

She runs to a payphone and picks up the receiver and hands it to me, but I grab it and put it back.

—So that's why the homecoming, I say. It's the money, isn't it?

—Hell, yes, it's the money, she says. What do you take me for? Now if you mean, do I want you, too? And that's what you're asking, then just ask it.

—I guess I am.

—You've got some balls, she says and starts walking again. Only you got no balls. She pulls her sweater over her stomach, but it pops back up. She walks faster and I have to run to keep up.

—Violet, stop.

—You let people walk all over you, she says and stops in the middle of the sidewalk. Listen, Romey, I like you and all. I may even love you, but don't press me on this shit. You take me or leave me. I can't force you to do this. You got to be a man and think about how we can get this done. I don't have any schooling, but it seems like you need someone, and I'm what you got. So, that's it. How's it going to be? You tell me.

She sits on the window ledge of a store that sells used CDs. She crosses her legs and bounces her foot up and down. I sit next to her and we eat another donut. The sugar is changing my chemistry fast and I'm awake as hell. We don't talk, but sit with arms touching. In a while, we walk one block to the second-hand store where Brownie's friend lets us take some black socks to keep the cold wind off my ankles. Under the marquee at the Ridgeway Cinemas, we sit and watch the front door of Annie's until Oscar arrives.

—I'm glad you could join us, Miss—?

—Violet, she says.

—Well, I'm glad you could join us, Miss Violet.

—You think? she says. And it's Violet, just Violet. Don't call me Miss Violet.

—She's okay, I say. You don't have to worry, Oscar, or not say something because she's here. If we do this, it's her and me.

—I'm glad, he says. I wasn't being disrespectful. I'm glad you have company.

—I'll bet you're glad, Violet says.

Oscar stirs cream into his coffee and we wait for the waitress to bring our order: two steaks for Violet and me, and a vegetable plate for Oscar. I see him staring at the bandage on my head.

—It hurts, I say. It was Philip, had to be.

—The detective thinks it was you. He thinks you broke into the safe, and that you got double-crossed in Harlem. He says you had motive, and that makes you a prime suspect for the murder.

—You know different.

—I believe you had nothing to do with it, but it looks bad. They're checking your whereabouts before Frank died. You knew his habits, Romey. You knew the combination to the safe, so when I left you alone, they think you stole everything. That's how they figure it. You decided to kill Frank, and when you found out what was in the will, you decided to take what you could get rather than wait.

—How did I get to Harlem? Did they figure that one out?

—Part of the mystery. It's compelling.

—I was set up.

—By whom?

—You know the way Philip and Frank were always going at it, Oscar. All this money and Frank so tight. Or Silvie, what about Silvie?

—I don't know anything about anybody, and neither do you. Lots of people had motive. Philip is desperate enough, there's no doubt. Silvie and Frank were in the middle of a power struggle at the Foundation. He spent the last few months of his life engineering a take-over of the Board. The Foundation was nearly bankrupt, so Frank packed the Board with his own people. I don't think she would kill Frank. She loved him. After all these years and bullshit, when it comes down to it, they were still in love.

—Philip loved him, too, I say and start to break up, but I hunch my shoulders and fight it. And so did the other people who hated him, I say. That's the way it was with him.

—You might be right, he says in a softer voice. The courts try more cases about love than about greed. Your guardian made a lot of enemies, Romey. His nieces were hanging around. His live-in nurse, Leslie, may have had plans. I don't know what Frank told her, if he led her on. Even that Walker fellow, with the Methodists, is a suspect. Philip has been talking with him about a Whirlpool trust to build the sanctuary, as long as they named it for Philip. Hell, everyone had a little to lose by him staying alive, including you, Romey, including you.

—I got out, I say. I was nowhere near the place when he was murdered. I don't want the money.

—The hell you don't! Violet says.

The waitress arrives with our order, but Oscar pushes his plate aside and drinks his coffee as if he's impatient to leave. I've lost my appetite, so I push my plate aside, too, but Violet is putting hers away as though she hasn't eaten in days.

—The stolen items are not really that important, Oscar says. Insurance will cover them. I think I can get the police to leave you alone about that. Maybe you should get away for a little while. Let things settle down, not only with the police, but with the family. The nieces from Baton Rouge have already contacted a lawyer. It didn't take long.

—I'll be damned, Violet says between bites. They'd like us to stay away.

—If you'll excuse us, he says, this is really a family matter.

—I told you, Oscar, she's with me, forever.

—Hey, watch what you're saying there, fella, Violet says. Jesus, Romey, forever.

Oscar can't quite turn his frown to a smile. I take a small bite of steak, but it's tough and I take it out of my mouth with a napkin.

—We're not running, Violet says. You tell him, Romey. How am I supposed to help you, if you start caving in? They killed the Whirl and they tried to kill you. Hit you in the head with something damn hard. That's attempted murder.

—There's no proof anyone associated with the estate tried to harm Romeo, Oscar says. It could have been a burglary, plain and simple.

—That's bullshit, I say, and you know it. We just need to know if it was Philip, or Silvie, or the little weasel nieces, or one of the thousands who lived on Frank's payroll. We need to find the murderer. He deserves that, at least.

—All I know, Oscar says, is that they could have killed you, but they didn't. It was a warning.

He opens his coat and pulls out some photos and a slip of paper. He spins one of the photos around. It's the same one of my mother on the steps at the Royal Academy of Music with the glossy lipstick and long coat.

—Wow, Violet says, that really your mother, Romey? You look like her, except around your mouth. Your father must have had a big mouth, Romey. That's what happens. I was watching TV about this genetics stuff. It's all coded in, everything.

—After the plane accident, Oscar says, your father's things were sent to his family's house in Chicago. Maria's family lived in Italy, but there were bad feelings over Maria and Justin living together without being married. They didn't know about you until the court told them, and they didn't want to know any more. The best lead I have is an aunt on your father's side who still lives in the family home in Chicago. Her name is Hope Bishop, Justin's older sister. I'm not sure how much she knows. She was living with a woman at the time, and that didn't sit well with the courts. They refused her adoption hearing. When Frank took you in, he came up with a letter signed by your mother making him, as the couple's friend and business manager, the sole guardian. There was no contest from Maria's family. Only from Hope, and that didn't play with the judge.

He hands me a slip of paper with the address. I put it and the photo in my pocket.

—We'll need some money for expenses, I say.

—That may take a few days.

—How much you got? Violet asks.

He shrugs and takes out his wallet and flips through the bills. He takes out a fifty and puts it onto the table to pay the check. Then he pulls the rest from his wallet and pushes the money toward me. I take it and hide it below the table. Five fifties and four twenties.

—I've got another appointment, he says. I'll work on getting you cleared of the burglary charge, but it will take some time. I know the district attorney. There's no strong evidence you had anything to do with the robbery, and they know Philip can't afford the publicity, so it won't be too difficult to get it dropped.

—We need a car, I say.

—I'll get you some money next week. In order to pull funds from the estate, a judge has to clear the amount for a specific use.

—We can't wait that long. The longer I hang around here, the better the chance I'll get busted before you can fix the charges. And we can't buy a car on two hundred, not one that runs.

—I have no more cash. I'm sorry.

—The limo, Violet says. We can take the limo. That'd be cool, Romey.

—The limousine is estate property, Oscar says.

—So how are you driving it?

—Absolutely not, he says. I need to get to my appointment.

—Call a cab, she says. Let's take the limo, Romey. They'd never stop a limo.

Oscar is sweating above his lip. Violet stares at him until he spins the keys across the table.

—I'll do my best to fix things, he says, but I can't stop the legal maneuvering of the family, or the threat of violence. You're on your own, Romey. You've got one year from the moment of Frank's death to deliver the goods. That's it. Someone has given you a warning. Next time, who knows?

TEN

A wave is a disturbance, the Whirl showed me. On one of our walks around the estate, he had tossed a rock in a pond. The waves move outward, he said, in concentric circles until the energy that caused them dissipates. Another example would be a radio transmitter, he said, that sends waves at the speed of light to an antenna, which if it's tuned to the same frequency picks up the sound.

—You steal it?

—No, Brownie, Violet says and pats the top of the limousine. It's Romey's. He's rich, or he's gonna be.

Some waves interfere with other waves, the Whirl said and tossed two rocks at the same time into the pond. We watched their expanding circles collide with each other to increase or decrease the size of the waves. Others types of waves, he said, don't interfere. When two radio waves cross, the sounds go on like nothing happened. It depends on the length of the wave and how fast it oscillates. It's because a radio wave has a super long wavelength and a frequency of one to 100 megahertz. Water, on the other hand, has a frequency of about one hertz, so nearly anything creates a disturbance. Humans have a frequency of about eight to ten hertz, so it's not hard to imagine how people interfere, sometimes to the negative, sometimes to the positive.

—You stole it! Brownie says. I wondered why them cops come 'round. Good deal, man. All this time, I thought you was a scam.

He runs the flat of his palm along the side of the car, careful to avoid the chrome as if he might mar the finish. Gabby is hanging onto Brownie by the shoulder chain of his leather coat, which means she's his lover, and that's news to Violet and me. They never seemed to get along especially well. Gabby is a flower child who likes drugs and talks in circles as if the world is too beautiful to fathom. Brownie is more a street urchin who needs the taste of distilled corn before he smooths his edges. Yet love's got more on its agenda than similarity, and Gabby is tending to Brownie's face, which is healing from his epic battle with the drunks. His cut is still bright pink, which means he'll have a scar even larger than mine.

—No more free drinks at Bonner's, Brownie says, that's the shit part. To hell with you two for leaving. Brownie hugs me and slaps me on the back, then apologizes when he remembers my head wound. Now, where we going to get a little Jack Daniels for free? he says and adjusts two braids that fall over his eyes. Violet, how can you leave with this guy? Such an asshole.

Gabby playfully slaps Brownie on the shoulder and reaches up and kisses my cheek. She whispers into my ear that she'll take care of Brownie while we're gone, and I know she's taking her place in the order. Violet was the undisputed queen of the Hovel, now there's a void to be filled.

—We'll be back, Violet says and throws a plastic sack full of clothes and things into the front seat. You guys might not be around, you know, things change.

—You take care, Brownie says. Whole lot of suckers to take advantage of you, especially with this car. It's a target, man. You look like some kinda royalty and they'll rip you off royal, that's what they'll do.

—He's got me, Violet says and hugs Brownie, what's to worry?

I hug Gabby and whisper to her to stay off the horse, then I hug Brownie who hugs Violet once more. Then we reverse the whole thing, and Gabby has tears in her eyes. I check inside the limo to make sure the sound divider is down, then pitch my pack into the gaping back cavern. I've got an extra pair of pants and two shirts, a book of short stories, a driver's license and passport, two pairs of underwear and one change of socks. I slide into the driver's side, and Violet moves all the way across to the passenger side and holds her plastic bag. I close the door and press the window button so the glass on my side disappears into its metal frame.

—We'll see you, I say to Brownie, win or lose.

—Losers, man. Don't be that way.

I start the engine and put the limousine in gear, then I remember something we left. I slam it back in park, push open the door and run up the stairs to the third floor. I see Tuf under Gabby's blanket, so I grab him and fly down the steps and back to the car. I pitch him over to Violet who smothers the kitten in her arms. Her smile is soft and sweet and she scoots with Tuf over next to me. We say goodbye to Gabby and Brownie one more time, then I put the car in gear and we take off down the cluttered street, slowly at first, then faster as if we're hovering above the pavement.

—Thanks for remembering, Violet says and rubs her face on the kitten. It hasn't sunk in, you know, that we're not coming back.

—Not for awhile. You okay with that?

She nods, but keeps staring ahead. The road glistens from an oil slick. I try to figure out the buttons on the dash, but there are too many and I soon give up. Violet starts eating chips and drinking cola from a sweating can. The cool air rushes through the louvers of the glossy oak panels. The smell of pepper blows in from the street, then the sweet scent of a bakery, then salt from a Chinese take-out that goes by in the night.

Violet uses three fingers to walk the distance across the map. Chicago is a thousand miles away, but it doesn't look so far on paper. As long as the car can go, so can we. It's thrilling, almost throbbing. Oscar says he's fixing the warrant on the robbery charge. Brownie and Gabby are taking care of each other. Violet is with me and Tuf is with Violet. My legs and arms are tingling as if I've just shot speed.

—That's the way things go, I say. Friends go old. We make new, then check in with the old, and that's okay.

—It's not okay, she says, but it's best to leave it.

She buries her head in the map and calls out the names of towns: Easton, Harrisburg, Pittsburgh and Columbus. With her fingernail, she draws an imaginary line across the continent until she gets to California and Los Angeles.

—You know where we are? I ask.

—How do you expect me to know? I never looked at a damn map before, Romey. You just head to a town and don't get lost. That's all I would do.

I pull over into a factory parking lot before the Holland Tunnel and turn on the dome light. The car behind us pulls in, too, and I look to see if it's a cop, but it's a dark sedan that pulls away in the opposite direction. I check the map. It's a chaos of roads and highways that lead everywhere and back again. When you learn to drive with a chauffeur, you never figure out where you are or where you're going. No need.

—How you expect to find the music, Violet says, if we can't even find our way out of the city?

I see the sedan in my rearview mirror. It's parked on the other side of the gray lot with parking lights on. The Holland Tunnel is a gaping black hole in the distance, and every car that slows down adds a little to my anxiety about the black sedan, and I'm staring at the map as though I'm looking for the help button.

—Let's just pick one going west, she says and hugs the passenger side door and eats chips more for the noise than for the salt. We've gotta go, she says, or we're never going.

I turn off the dome light and put the limo in drive. It lurches out of the parking lot to Broome Street before the Tunnel toll booth. I reach into my pocket for the first of Oscar's cash.

—It doesn't bother me, she says, this driving where we don't know where we're going. It's like taking a trick, and I know you don't like to talk about it, but I never know what I'm getting into. But it's got to be done, or I don't eat.

—That's all over.

—You think?

—I'm sure of it.

—How you sure, Romey? You don't know what's going to happen, so don't act like you do.

—Are you sure about this? I say. Because it doesn't sound like you're sure.

—It pisses me off, that's all. You thinking there are choices, clear and direct. It's like you haven't lived, Romey. Where you been living?

—There are choices. Everyone has choices.

—From my angle there's eating and sleeping, and the rest is just getting on with things. So we got to buck up and get this damn car going, because we sure as hell can't go home.

—You could.

—You're pissing me off, Romey.

—I guess I'm asking, are you sure about me?

—We got a limo and enough cash to get us out of New York. That's enough, and why do you have to go into this? We just get started and you get all futuristic on me.

We clear the Tunnel and spring onto a ramp with a bunch of highway numbers on big metal signs. I keep going straight until Violet tells me to take a ramp where she spots a gas station and fast food. We get off the ramp and stop at the first light. She jumps out and runs across the street to the station. We don't need gas, so I turn the big car around and park lengthwise along a guardrail, then wait about ten minutes until she comes back with a sack of snacks and drinks.

—Here you go, she says and she takes out a candy bar and gives me the bag.

—What's this?

—A gift.

I feel something square. I take it out, but it's in another bag so I take it out of that one and tear at the package until I see it's a CD.

—*Punk Bands of the 80's*, I read. What the hell, Violet, you see how much this cost? Where'd you get the money?

—I took it out of your jacket.

—That was gas money!

—So what? You don't want it? It has the Ramones and Culture Club and stuff. You want me to take it back? Is that what you're telling me?

She grabs the CD and peels off the plastic wrapper and pops the disk into the drive. She avoids my eyes, though I'm trying to burn hers with mine. A song by the Eurythmics starts beating out synthesized rhythms.

—I'm just saying we needed that money.

—I'll take it back, she says and pushes the eject button. I thought I was being nice to you, Romey. You're talking all this shit about me not wanting you. I thought we were on this big adventure.

She pushes the CD back in and hits the random button. The motor spins and from the dash speakers come rapid-fire drum riffs I recognize as David Robinson's, the drummer with the Cars. I maneuver the limo onto the highway and we listen without speaking. Route 78 bends south then west, and without really knowing whether it's the right way I take 95 north to get to 90.

After a few hours, Violet wants to take the wheel, but I don't believe she can drive. She tries to convince me that Brownie taught her last summer when he drove a taxicab. She tells me she has a license, but lost it, and I know she's lying, but we stop and I let her drive and she keeps it on the road and relatively straight. Trust has a frequency, I suppose. Two people trying to find the same wavelength, the same pitch, that elusive fundamental tone that puts the world in harmony. Nothing worse than the Eurythmics mixed with the Ramones, but if Violet can stop leaning on the pedal and keep the car on the road, I-90 should take us all the way to Aunt Hope, and that's better than no hope at all.

ELEVEN

November 2, 1985

Wonderful news, brother! The Dean of Royal Holloway College has discussed Justin's ideas with members of the Royal Society and now Justin is sure to be offered a grant. It also means we can stay together in London!

As soon as Frank told us, we grabbed our coats and ran with him like children to the street. We waved down a taxi and in the back seat Frank popped the cork on a bottle of wine he had in his pocket with a cup for each of us. While the cab was still moving, he poured one drink, then another, since we drank the first so quickly.

You heard me predict that Justin's ideas would change the world, Alberto, now others are beginning to see. We were in such good spirits when we arrived at the Fitzroy Tavern. This pub reminds me of the *Cafè a Anoria* near Rome. You remember the one with the stone facade and gray pillars topped by those horrible winged creatures? Such is the Fitzroy on the outside, but on the inside it is warm with a fire and crowded with students because it is so close to University.

The three of us settled at a small table near the back. Many of Justin's friends were there, so Frank ordered a round of drinks then stood and yelled above the crowd that Justin was destined to be a famous scientist! Everyone clapped and Justin's eyes sparkled. I wanted this evening to be wonderful for him because he has worked so hard, even into the nights. I told him I believe in my heart he will succeed and though everyone was looking I kissed him on the lips. Little did I know that someone was standing over us, watching.

Maybe I had too much to drink or I did not want to share this night with another woman, but as soon as Frank's partner arrived, I hugged Justin as if he could slip away. Silvie Nels was dressed in a long purple *vestito* with a scarf because, she was quick to tell us, she had just come from a dinner at Buckingham Palace. She stood above the table as if she was one of the winged creatures of the roof, but I must admit her beauty takes men's eyes away, including Justin's.

Frank ordered another round for us and a glass of wine for Silvie. She is descended from a line of Scandinavian kings and queens, he told us, who ruled Norway for centuries. He raised his glass and offered another toast to Silvie, who took Justin's hand, and though I could not decide which one was the cause, they touched too long.

It was becoming obvious that I was not a very important part of this party. Justin was almost giddy from drink, so he blurted something about my being his fiancé and I realized it was the first time Justin had introduced me as his *fidanzata*. I was so shocked, I could not speak.

So you are the violinist, Silvie said and I wanted to correct her, but Justin's eyes were so fixed on her *vestito* and her blood red lips, that I could say nothing.

There's a nomination in Justin's work, Frank said. I can feel it, Silvie. This is the one.

Then I could not believe my eyes, but Silvie tipped her glass on purpose and spilled red wine on Frank's white shirt. He pushed back his chair and wiped with his napkin, but the color spread like a wound.

He can be such a fool, Silvie said. Frank is always getting things out of order. The question is, will the bankers be intrigued?

If I have the money, Justin said, the equations can be finished and tested. You will have your product.

Frank dabbed frantically at his shirt. Silvie stared at me with her cold blue eyes. This fiancé of yours, she said aloud so others around us could hear, is he as weak as other men? Will the world crush him? Only a lover will know.

I looked to Justin for protection, but it was as if he had been struck dumb by this winged creature. Why would the world want to crush him? I said in a voice that even I could barely hear.

He is the most dangerous kind of man, she said. He thinks he teaches us a great truth. Think of what Einstein taught us, a great truth that gave us the nuclear bomb.

Justin will not make bombs, I said. He could never make bombs.

Frank put his arm around my shoulder. Don't mind Silvie, he said. All this talk of weapons, when we could talk of cures.

Good cop, bad cop, Frank and Silvie were experts. Over those many years of my childhood, I had seen them when they needed something from someone, a politician, a government official, anyone who stood in the way of progress for the good of the Foundation for Frequency Research. What they did not tell Justin and Maria on their night of celebration was that the groundwork for exploitation of the waveform hypothesis had already been laid.

According to grant applications filed at Royal Holloway College, Frank had convinced Leon Harrad that Justin's work merited funding. Silvie had contacted investment bankers in The City in London. Intermediaries in New York had used a copy of Justin's doctoral proposal to draw up position papers for individual investors.

All without Justin's approval or knowledge. Not that he would have protested. His student loans were mounting. He owed money to several laboratories for high-speed computer time. He was open for intervention and was practical enough to know that without the help of people like Frank Whirlpool and Silvie Nels, his ideas were too obscure to be of interest to bankers and financiers, especially his theories on three-dimensional time.

Let history decide if all of your ideas have merit, they told him. Let the markets decide which one holds riches.

It was the application of a particular facet of the waveform hypothesis, Frank and Silvie projected, that held the real potential. Investors could understand a simple concept, even clothed in the language of physics. If frequencies can be changed, and if people are simply composite frequencies, it may be possible to change the chemical make-up of the human body.

This was an idea that would resonate in the markets. If the elementary particles of our bodies are simply waves, with a specific wavelength and frequency, it follows that the wave structure might be altered. If Justin Bishop could find a way to change the frequency of the elementary molecules of our bodies, there should be a way to affect all kinds of processes, cell growth, reproduction, maybe the synaptic processes in the brain.

In the best of all possible worlds, Silvie's position paper for financiers had concluded, it might be possible to stop the spread of illness, accelerate the growth of healthy tissue, ensure the proper function of organs, or alter the genetic structure of a fertilized egg. It would be the beginning of a new age of human evolution not fathomed since the discovery of the helical structure of DNA.

Silvie and Frank filled Justin's eyes with visions of a new industry, a new world. It could be the start of an alternative health care revolution, they said, that would change the way we live. Even the way we die.

Letter continued…

Better watch her, Frank kidded Justin about the way Silvie was touching Justin's hand. She can be very persuasive. Indeed, better watch your soul.

Frank's face did not look as if he was joking, but Justin ignored the warning. He was intent on this woman who was wooing him in front of my very eyes. I stood abruptly and excused myself. My hands were shaking. I went to the bathroom and waited until the talk of bombs and chemistry might stop, but when I came out, Frank was waiting.

He said I should forgive their rudeness. Silvie was just looking out for all of our best interests.

I almost spit in his face, Alberto! I tried to move around him, but he grabbed my hand and pulled me to the bar. Have a drink, he said. Our lovers, he said, will do just fine without us.

I pulled away from him and stormed to the table. Justin and Silvie had their heads so close together they could have been one. I demanded Justin leave, but he acted as if he had not heard me, and she ignored me even more coldly.

Men love power, she said to him as if I was not even there. Ideas are power. If men have none of their own, they take the ideas of others. That is our advantage, she said. You will be leveraged by Royal Holloway to bring funding, but we must counter every attack Harrad makes to steal your ideas with an attack of our own.

This sounds more like war, I said as Frank also came to the table, not much like physics.

Such a contrast between two women, he said. How does your wave theory, Justin, account for two beautiful women so little alike?

Different frequencies, he answered and the three of them laughed like jackals. I put my hand onto Justin's arm and dragged him from the table. Then came the worst part, Alberto, the part that makes me think that all I had hoped for Justin will come to nothing. Though I was standing right next to him, Silvie stood and pulled Justin's face to her own and kissed him on the lips. With passion! The *donnaccia*! Money does not give her the right to interfere in love. This is no game, Alberto, but I swear I will not let that horrid creature win.

TWELVE

From a book the Whirl gave me for my sixteenth birthday, I learned a great deal about Fermilab. The particle accelerator is located southeast of Chicago on 600 acres of Illinois flatland. Tubing runs in a mound that cloverleafs for miles around a twelve-story A-frame that houses some of the greatest intellects in particle physics. It has always amazed me that, like an invitation-only party, this U.S. Department of Energy laboratory in the middle of the urban landscape sees hundreds of scientists performing strange experiments that, if put to a vote by the American people, would never be funded.

The stereotype of sedentary physics professors with patch elbows is lost as these sleeve-rolled, t-shirted techno-geeks take their seats behind terminals connected to some of the most powerful computers in the world. After spinning microscopic particles in wide circles to speeds approaching that of light, they smash them head-on into antimatter. The monitors light up like a Spielberg spaceship and the fortunate few feel a rush that only those involved in true discovery can feel.

—I got sixty more dollars, Violet says as she gets in the car and points toward a gas pump at the north end of the station.

I know how she got the money. I see the truck sitting away from the overhead lights on the diesel side of the station. It makes me sick to think of what happened inside that hooded bubble, but there's nothing I can do. I pull the limo in front of the gas pump.

I should have known it was coming. We ran out of money in Cleveland and the limousine has been running on fumes since we hit the border of Indiana. For hours, Violet had been spinning in desperate circles. The radio boomed and the windows were down and the hot wind jumbled her hair, but no matter how fast we went, sixty, eighty, one hundred miles an hour along the gray concrete highway, there was no way we could make it without more cash. I told her we could wait until Oscar wired us some money, but time has always been Violet's enemy. She thought I was just losing my nerve. I can't help it that she has so much nerve she can trade it for cash.

—Fermilab has buffalo, I say because I need something to say and I remember the pictures in the book.

—I thought all the buffalo were dead.

Violet has the kitten in her arms and is rubbing her lips across its fur. The hinged gas door is on the back of the car, so I stretch the hose over the trunk to make the nozzle line up with the opening. Violet puts Tuf into the front seat. She dips a squeegee into the dirty water and tries to scrub some bird droppings off the hood. Another four-door sedan rolls across the parking lot. It's the kind I swear I've seen following us ever since New York, but I can't see color so they all look dark. This one moves slower than the refuelers or the bathroom crowd. Chrome glints and tail lights flash like eyes, but I can't be sure it's more than a salesman who has lost his way.

—Why not cows? Violet says. Why not raise cows instead of buffalo?

—I don't know. It's the west, I suppose.

—They don't have cows in the west?

—That's not the point. They've got all this land above where the accelerator tubes are buried, so they planted it in prairie grass and they raise buffalo. Everything on the surface is normal, then beneath the ground they've got this bizarre Frankenstein thing going on.

—They could blow us to eternity, she says. That's what you told me.

—Not really, I say and jam the gas nozzle further down into the hole. I was just talking. If they could recreate the Big Bang, you know, through some sort of mistake, or a rogue scientist decides to test a dangerous theory, condense self-replicating matter out of nothing, we could maybe end up at the beginning of time. A mega-explosion, like at the beginning of the universe.

The limo has a huge tank. I crush the cold nozzle in my fist and lean with my back along the contour of the car's trunk. I look at the sky, but the light from the half moon hanging at the edge of the horizon keeps me from seeing many stars.

Anyway, it's useless to gaze at the sky in a city. No matter how much I tell Violet about the planets and the universe, it pales in comparison to the lines on the highway and the repetitive beat of Devo or Simple Minds. When I talk to her about science, her eyes glaze over and she turns up the music. In the glove compartment, we found an oldies tape that was probably the chauffeur's, mostly grunge and funk. When it was Violet's turn to drive, I used Danny's sticks to bang the rhythm on the dash until Violet's harsh stare made me stop.

—You don't have to do that anymore, I say as the gas pump jumps and clicks off.

I see the driver in the truck on the back lot jump down from the steps. He's got an obscene paunch that hangs over a silver belt, and I look away before I can record any more detail.

—You think they're gonna give us free gas? she says.

—We'll manage. You promised me you'd stop, I say and take a slip of scratch paper from my wallet with a phone number and flip it onto the trunk hood. You can call Oscar. I told you he'd wire some cash.

—I just might, she says and takes the paper and shoves it into the front pocket of her jeans. She wrenches open the passenger door, plops inside and slams the door. I use one of the station's paper towels to wipe my coat where some gas has sprayed from the nozzle. I go to the cashier and pay, then slowly walk back to the car.

—I just don't want you to have to do that, I say and squeeze behind the wheel.

—Let's drop it, Romey. It's done.

—If you're going to do shit like that, why the hell did we leave the Hovel?

—Just shut your mouth.

—The point is, I left, you didn't.

—I left, too, you bastard.

—You left what? I say. What the hell did you leave?

—My baby, asshole!

I think she means the kitten, but Violet's face is white as light. The truck driver comes out of the store. He has a toilet kit tucked under his arm and a cowboy hat in his hand. It's revolting, but it's even more revolting that I can never seem to remember that Violet had a baby.

—You said your baby was adopted.

—What of it, she says. I left it. That's all I was saying. You got anything else to say? Because if you do, then let me out right fucking here.

I try the key in the ignition, but my hand goes limp. A car wanting our spot at the pump pulls up behind, so I tense the muscles in my fingers and concentrate until the car starts. We pull from the station and I think I see a few stars in the north sky, but it's the reflection from the neon signs.

—You never say much about the baby.

—Nothing to say, she says.

—You ever see it? We could try to see it, if you want.

—It's a he. His name is Christopher. Besides, we can't even get enough gas to make it to Chicago. How we going to handle a baby?

I pull back onto highway 95 and fold into the traffic. Tuf climbs onto the back of my seat and tickles my neck with his tail. I'm getting familiar with the pale road, the white signs that announce places that mark our progress, but the repetitive white dashes that blur and disappear under our front hood seem no different since we left New York.

—It's another world, I say.

—What world?

—Fermilab, I say. You're going to be amazed, Violet. It's a place where things happen that no one ever thought could happen.

—You think?

—They're solving the mysteries of the universe.

—The universe is no mystery, Romey. The universe is shit.

—You're talking about New York.

—I can't believe how fucking innocent you are, she says. You know what makes the world go round, Romey?

—I'd say gravitation, but I have a feeling that's not what you mean.

—That's why you're innocent, she says and takes a long drag on the cigarette. You say something like that, Romey, and the rest of the world says money. You're lost in a book, man. It wasn't the fucking Whirl who was murdered last week. It was you. They killed you a hundred times over. Sometimes, I think what the hell am I doing with you in the first place? You don't know shit. Only you think you do. You don't do shit, but you think by driving this limousine into the damn sunset you're going to conquer the fucking universe. Well, it's not that easy. It's survival. You should look at yourself. It'd surprise you. It damn well would.

I stare at the road, but her eyes bore into the side of my head as if she's burying a spike. She wants me to fight, but I know it wouldn't help. Violet could take me in a thousand ways. There's nothing I could say that would rate on the scale of a lost baby. I thought we might be good together. I thought with the car doing eighty and the lights filling our heads, and Violet sitting there with a kitten like the girl next door, we might be happy, or at least calm.

—How long before we get there? she says.

—Gary, Indiana was the last big city. My aunt's house is near Fermilab. In a few minutes, we take a bypass around Chicago.

—I got family in Chicago.

—You should have told me. We could go there.

—It's out of the way, she says and rolls down the window and pitches her cigarette to the road. Just some cousins, she says. They live on the south side where there's all these factories and crap. I visited them once when I was a kid.

She turns up the radio and the limo dashboard shakes with bass. We swoop around an exit from I-90 to a secondary highway, then smaller roads to where Fermilab is shown on the map as a plot of open land in the middle of urban sprawl. We stop and get a map that shows Foxborough Road. It's getting dark and we can barely see the street names. We almost miss a sign hanging over the road, but at the last minute we turn left in front of a lighted guard shack.

A camouflage-garbed guy at the gate checks his book for Hope Bishop's name, then he asks us our names and makes a call. He comes back and tells us to pull to the side of the road, then he waves to another guard just finishing his dinner. I think about backing up and leaving, but the guard has a gun in a holster, and I thank God we don't have any dope, unless Violet sneaked some along without telling me. The guards do a quick search of the car and use a portable metal detector to check our clothes.

—Quarter mile, turn left, the guard says. Miss Bishop lives in the third house at the end of the street. She didn't sound like she was expecting you.

—She's my aunt. It's a surprise.

He waves us under the sign for the Fermilab National Laboratory, Department of Energy. In the street lamp's light, I see a field of prairie grass on the right and a smooth lake with some geese landing on the water. The pictures in the textbook have come to life. I can almost feel the tremors of protons racing around the tubes beneath the ground.

—Stand in the light, a woman's voice slips through a crack she's opened between the door and the frame.

Violet and I stand as straight as our tired bodies can handle. The limousine dwarfs the car in the driveway, a small convertible with its top down. I noticed the letters EV-1 on the side, and I know from reading old *Popular Mechanics* that it's an electric car from the early 90's. The passenger seat is stacked with books and papers.

The woman opens the door a little more. Wrinkles cover her face and her hair is held back in a scarf. In black pants and checkered shirt, she looks like a man, except for her breasts, which hang to her belt.

—I think I'm your nephew, I say.

She holds the door. Her look is something other than fear, but not far from it.

—Was Justin Bishop your brother? I say.

She opens the door a little more and stares at the wound on my head where Violet has removed the bandage. She fixes her eyes on my shoulder and the blue and red tattoo.

—Crab Nebula? she says and I nod. It's too late for this, she says and turns around, but she leaves the door open and disappears into the dark house.

Violet and I step inside and follow Hope Bishop to the kitchen. She stands at the sink and looks out an open window. I sit at the table with Violet, who is not helping break the ice because she's doing her nails with a broken file. Hope offers us coffee, then a beer. She starts talking in circles about babies and courts and how she hasn't had such a shock since her brother died. Then she gets some antiseptic and dresses my wound. The cold night air rushes through the window. The lights from the road illuminate the back yard. I see a patch of dark woods behind the house and a stretch of open field with a fence running bright in the moonlight. In the distance is the faint silhouette of an animal, maybe a buffalo, but it's standing so still I think my eyes must be playing tricks.

THIRTEEN

November 28, 1985

Has religion made such a fog in your head that you no longer remember me? You have not written or called for months, Alberto. Do you forget how we spent each hour together, how we roamed the hills hand-in-hand? You were the one twin who always spoke to strangers. Now you do not speak to me?

It is not that I want to hold you to me, brother, or hold you back. You have a new life in *Firenze* and I have mine. I just wish you could be here to see what Papà could not, that the world is much bigger than Mariano and our church at the foot of the mountain. Today we had proof I am not the only one who knows Justin's ideas are huge waves that crash on our myths and notions.

It was late in the afternoon. Frank Whirlpool had called in a panic. He told Justin to come as soon as possible to the headquarters of the Royal Society to meet with Dean Harrad. Justin was frantic. He paced back and forth while I tried to sew old clothes into new— Justin's worn brown coat, the black dress you remember from the summer concerts in Milan, my lace *camacia* with three burn holes from stray embers from Papà's pipe. From our neighbor on the second floor, I borrowed a blue striped tie.

Just as night fell, we met Frank and Silvie in the front hall of Carlton House Terrace near Buckingham Palace. It is a beautiful building near St. James Park. The walls are ornate with Greek facades and the words of famous scientists, such as Sir Isaac Newton and Christopher Wren, are chiseled with huge letters in the white stone.

While Justin and Frank planned what they would say at the meeting, Silvie took me aside. She insisted I see the famous library, more to keep me away from the two men, I thought, than any show of kindness. Yet when I found out the library is one of the greatest since Alexandria, I agreed to go with her. I feel rather ashamed that I do not trust her, but her red dress was tight and her blond hair fell like snow on her shoulders. In Justin's eyes, I must look plain in comparison, but I have music and that is something Silvie seems to admire.

You should have seen the library, Alberto, especially the music. There were rows of scrolls from early compositions and some original parchments of symphonies from the eighteenth century. I lifted to my chest a dusty volume of Handel's cantatas and I nearly lost my breath. I could not help thinking that all those notes were from inside his head and no other. It made me feel that one day I might, also, fill a few pages with a creation so beautiful.

I wanted to stay among those parchments forever, but Silvie said the meeting was about to begin. We met Frank and Justin and a man in a black tuxedo, who led us with great courtesy through the vast hallways and chambers. It was like walking through history. The man in the tuxedo pointed to the Baroque cornices with their gilded swirls, and the neo-classical columns, and sumptuous velvet curtains of the Victorians. On the walls were portraits of scientists in flowing robes holding antiquated instruments or thick books.

We soon came to a room with very high ceilings but no more light than was filtered through stained glass. Several old men lounged in deep, leather chairs and a few women played cards at a center table. Frank introduced us to an American, who woke from a sleep near the fire. I have forgotten his name but he is very famous, Frank told us, for publishing one of the first papers on the standard model of particle physics, where pieces of matter fit together like a puzzle.

Frank talked with the sleepy man for only a moment, then we left him to his nap. We stepped through a hanging of burgundy drapes and into a side room that was smaller and more ornate than the other halls. In a large, black chair near another fireplace, reading the *London Times*, was Dr. Leon Harrad. He shuffled his paper and tried to ignore us, but Silvie stood in front of him and lit a cigarette and blew smoke so that it swirled around his head.

What the devil! the Dean bellowed and his fat cheeks shook like jelly. Silvie told him the young man with the waveform hypothesis was there to see him, and the Dean reluctantly put his newspaper aside. He leaned on the arm of the chair so he could better see Justin, who wrung his hands and hunched his shoulders like a little boy.

And what do the markets need with a student barely out of diapers? the Dean started.

Then what occurred still gives me a chill, how they began to talk as if the universe was their private club and his theory was laying claim to the key. The more I hear of Justin's ideas, the more they make me think the world is a mystery about to be revealed.

I have since read Leon Harrad's papers and scanned his journals. The Dean was familiar with Justin's speculations and he was always ready to play devil's advocate. There was more to science than speculation, he said according to Maria's letter. Should science follow the markets, or should the markets follow science? Do you think your ideas, young man, deserve the attention of a serious scientist?

Justin weakened under the barrage. His face turned crimson. He would only mumble that it was for others to decide, not him.

If it is truth you seek, the Dean shot back, don't worry so much about the marketplace. Miss Nels and this fellow, Whirlpool, will take the risk. The markets are only one way to put a bad idea to rest.

Justin was right to be a little afraid. Leon Harrad had been a contender for the Lucasian Chair of Mathematics, which was held centuries before by the great Sir Isaac Newton. Justin knew the importance of this moment. He was fighting for his right to be heard by those in authority. His ideas, he knew, were too radical to assume quick acceptance by someone of the Dean's standing.

And the Dean, also, must have known this moment's importance. The world of science was changing, and ideas such as Justin Bishop's were tearing the old one apart. It was not so much that the new theories of the universe were adding to the bedrock of scientific knowledge. They were digging up the bedrock and creating a world of their own.

The further you go back to the beginning of the universe, Justin's paper drew first on contemporary theory, the more the rules of physics break down. The temperatures were so extreme and the energy so high, scientists believe these forces of nature could not have existed as separate entities. That means no particles existed. It was pure energy, without matter.

Yet instead of dealing with that issue directly, Justin contended, scientists were still trying to cobble the universe together with a particle theory, in which tiny bits of matter constantly break down or recombine in particle interactions. The goal of the standard model of particle interactions, as defined by physicist Steven Weinberg and others, is to split the universe into smaller and smaller parts that will, supposedly, give insight into how the universe is constructed. And that's the point that Justin made in his paper. Because particle physics is focused on a search for matter, there will be little progress in solving a mystery where the real culprit is actually energy.

As Justin laid out his theory that day to Leon Harrad, according to Maria's letter, the Dean did his best to appear disinterested. He folded and refolded his paper. He poured himself another drink of brandy. He *closed his eyes when Justin plunged into the details.*

And many details there were. An understanding of the waveform hypothesis, after all, required a recounting of the famous one-slit, two-slit experiments devised by Thomas Young just after 1800 and enhanced by scientists for the last 200 years. The results of these experiments are a conundrum, which no scientist so far had adequately explained. As Nobel prize winner Richard Feynman famously said, "Nobody knows how it can be like that."

In the two-slit experiment, individual bits of light called photons are shot, apparently like bullets from a gun, toward a wall with two vertical slits arranged side-by-side. When these photons shoot through the slits, they hit a screen behind the wall and create a pattern on photosensitive paper.

If the two slits are open, the electrons create a pattern on the paper that could only be made by waves. Like ocean currents washing through two open gates on a dock, a new wave pattern is created behind the gates. The waves from the one gate radiate out and interfere with the waves from the other gate. Where the wave crests meet, the pattern increases with intensity. When wave troughs meet, they cancel each other out. The result of the photons being shot through two open slits toward the photosensitive paper is a weak pattern at the edges and an intense pattern in the center. The interference pattern is predicted by the normal behavior of waves.

The problem comes when only one particle at a time is shot toward the two open slits. When these one-at-a-time particles mount up on the paper, you would assume some would go through the one slit and some through the other, and there would be no interference. You would assume a circular pattern, more like a target from individual particles than an interference wave pattern of dark and light bands.

Yet even though there is nothing for the single particles to interfere with, a wave pattern still appears on the sensitive paper! Either the particles are interfering with themselves, or they are conscious of other particles that will come later, or there is another, unknown phenomenon at work. This is the basis for the belief in the dual nature of matter. Photons shot as particles end up acting like waves.

This was why Justin's proposal was incredible to Dr. Leon Harrad. Justin contended that his waveform hypothesis resolved this contradiction in the particle-wave, dual nature of matter. There are no such things as a distinct particle or a particle-wave, Justin contended. There is only vibration and the waveform it creates in response to its position and momentum. There is only the energy of the photon, which travels as a wave and appears as a particle due to how we view the spacetime continuum. It is only the limitation of our measuring tools that creates the dichotomy.

Energy exists, Justin explained in his paper, as a vibration. This movement creates the first dimension of time, which is an oscillation of energy. As it vibrates, it forms a second dimension. We see this as a sequence of events that we know as sequential time. Waves are created from this vibration as they flow through time. Photons, or what we describe as light particles, are simply vibrations in a waveform. As they travel, they move through the universe in a way that we have defined as a wave of electromagnetic light. This is why some scientists think light is a solid particle and some think it is a wave, he contended. It is a vibration creating a 186,000 miles per second waveform that resonates as a particulate state of energy, a particle, a photon of light.

This was more than Leon Harrad could take. As far as he was concerned, Justin's ideas from there entered the realm of science fiction. Justin had devised the concept of a second and third dimension of time. His hypothesis, he noted in his paper, was derived from recent superconductivity experiments and Fourier analysis of frequencies of infinite height. There are at least three dimensions of time, he reasoned, just as there are three dimensions of space, the x, y, and z axes.

The third dimension of time, as Justin saw it, defines the characteristics, such as mass and spin, of the energy in the waveform. This dimension, Justin called resonant time. Together with the three dimensions of space, these three dimensions of time create a six-dimensional spacetime continuum. Many scientists have since speculated that there are actually many more dimensions curled up and hidden from our view. String theories first predicted ten, then eleven, then twenty-six dimensions!

Harrad reacted as most scientists at the time would have reacted. He laughed, according to Maria's letter. And now you've solved a mystery, he said to Justin, that has plagued the most brilliant minds on the planet. Bravo! Speculation is the pastime of fools.

Justin exploded. Any theory at a quantum level is speculation! Justin countered. And he was right, in a way. Why else would we have the mystery of Einstein's "spooky action" at a distance? Why else would a particle be able to detect what a twin particle is doing when they are in distinctly separate places? The Aspect Experiments using Bell's inequality theorem were said to have proven that particles behave non-locally. The American physicist David Bohm, in fact, believed non-local behavior is communicated on what he called a pilot wave. John Cramer at the University of Washington even believes that there is no reason why photons cannot go backward and forward in time!

If you give me the funding for my experiments, Justin told Leon Harrad, I will prove we can predict such events using the waveform hypothesis. The waveform determines the characteristics of matter, and matter determines how the universe appears to us. And this can be measured!

Harrad poured another glass, took a long drink, and said, You make me weary, boy.

That is what makes you weary, Justin said and pointed to the decanter.

Now it was Harrad's turn to explode. Enough insolence! he said. I'll take another look at your paper, if that is what it takes to be left in peace. Every time I go to my desk, another student has come up with a theory of everything. It's the madness of hope!

FOURTEEN

It's nine in the morning and the scent of bacon and eggs moves molecule-to-molecule under the door of Hope's extra bedroom. It was late before Violet and I made it to bed. After a couple of beers, Hope was over the shock of her long-lost nephew showing up and telling her the man who had fought her over adoption rights had recently been murdered. After a few more beers, she couldn't stop hugging me, and telling me how sorry she was that things had turned out the way they had, and how much I looked like her long-lost brother.

Hope had pulled an old suitcase from under her bed and showed us a photo of her and little brother Justin playing on a swing set. Another tattered photo was of her mother and father, arm-in-arm, on the front porch of this very house. At first, Violet went along with the homecoming, but as the night wore on her patience began to wear thin. It didn't help that Hope wouldn't let her smoke cigarettes in the house. Violet ended up taking long breaks on the porch, out of sight, out of mind.

—Here's another one, Hope says as I stumble this morning into the kitchen and find eggs still simmering on two plates.

—I forgot about this one, she says and hands me another

photograph. This is when Justin was seven. I had it in a book. Smell of bacon always makes me remember things.

Hope has on stretch pants that do nothing for her pear-shaped body. Her short-cropped hair and thick black glasses make her look as if she's a warped image in a concave circus mirror. Looking at dusty photos is a little too much to bear on this cold, dim morning, but she knows Violet and I have been arguing. It's Hope's way of mediating.

—He was tall for his age, Hope says. He had the cutest blonde hair in mounds of curls. They embarrassed him, I don't know why.

We finish breakfast while Violet makes some phone calls to her relatives in South Chicago. She comes in and stands at the screen door with her plastic sack tucked beneath one arm and Tuf tucked into the crook of the other.

—I'm leaving, she says. I'm taking the car for a few days, Romey. You won't need it.

What she's saying doesn't really register because I'm locked on another picture of my father and I can't tear my eyes away. I'm starting to feel things, my father's embarrassment over the curls, his worry about the stain on the knees of his blue jeans. In this heavy morning light, he seems more real to me, as if the scratch on his cheek and the scar on his forehead could hurt through time.

—You two have fun, Violet says and uses her shoulder to push the door open slightly so it bangs softly against the frame. I gotta get going.

—Well, you watch yourself, dear, Hope says. Chicago is not New York, but it's still dangerous. Never seen a peaceful city.

I look up from the photo, but now it's Violet who won't look at me. She pushes hard on the door, then skips two steps to the long grass that swirls toward the gravel drive. She gets smaller in the screen door's frame, so I jump up and follow her to the car.

—I'll go with you, I say.

—You got things to do.

—When will you be back?

—Couple of days, I told you.

I try to kiss her cheek, but she leans away. She puts Tuf on a pillow in the passenger side and stuffs her things through the opening for the glass panel. She climbs in and with the driver's door still open, she starts the engine and checks the glove compartment for sunglasses.

—You don't need to worry about the limo, she says.

—I'm not worried.

—You and Hope got things to talk about. I'm extra baggage.

—That's not true, I say. I'm just looking at some pictures. If you wait, I'll come with you.

—You got your business, I got mine.

—You're coming back, though? Promise me, Violet.

—You keep your promise, she says, and I'll keep mine.

She puts the car into gear and slams the door while I'm still trying to figure out what promise I made. Before I can ask, the limo lurches forward along the curve of the cul-de-sac. Her silhouette through the tint looks miniscule in the huge front seat. She stops at the main road and, though she has the opportunity to wave through the open window, she doesn't look back.

—I've something else to show you, Hope says and puts her arm around my shoulder as we watch the car disappear beyond the guard's gate.

—More pictures?

—I'm done with pictures, she says. I don't know what you know about your father, but I'm going to show you what the world meant to him.

Hope washes the breakfast dishes. I make the bed and try to pick up some broken potato chips from the living room carpet. She gives me an empty box and tells me to go out to the driveway and clear some clutter from the EV-1.

—It's one of the originals, she says as she pats the small car as if it's a show horse. They made EV-1's up to 1996. They were concept cars in the 80's. California was the first to legislate electric. Fella named Bill Lessing was on the original staff at Stanford. He gave me this one. You don't see any convertibles. One of a kind. He was sweet on me, I guess. I've had to refit the batteries with new cores a million times, but the car is a wonder of technology.

I circle the contoured vehicle and see a few small dents and imperfections in the aerodynamics, but it's a work of art. Across the main road, prairie flowers are stretched across linear mounds of dirt where the accelerator tubes are buried below in a huge cloverleaf. A lone buffalo stands near the fence munching on a roll of grass.

—Your grandfather, Hope says, gave his life for this place. Quit a cushy job at Princeton, but particle physics was his dream. Sometimes, I think how proud he'd be to see how the place has grown. They found the bottom quark in the seventies, you know. Then we found the top quark in the nineties, and that's something.

She opens the door and slips into the driver's side. The car is so small, I step over the door and plop onto the seat where the leather looks a little less faded from the magazines and clutter blocking the sun. She pushes a button on the dash but there's no sound, so I think it doesn't start, but she floors the accelerator and the car wheezes and backs up. We circle the cul-de-sac a couple of times *for fun*, she says, then the car hums onto the open road.

The twelve-story A-frame headquarters dominates the skyline. I'm hugging myself from the cool morning wind. As we get closer to the building, it makes me feel as if we're moving onto the set of a science fiction movie. With the flags of nations whipping in the wind, the huge triangular structure looks like an antique space station from a twentieth-century artist's mind. Fifteen-foot earthen mounds surround the building on one side. Hundreds of cars are parked in a blacktop parking lot that flares out from the front doors. Scientists with briefcases walk shoulder-to-shoulder with visitors with cameras and diaper bags.

—We're trying to figure out a new way to detect quantum tunneling, she says. A group of Swiss and German scientists at CERN in Geneva are collaborating. We've got some deadlines, but I can take a little time to give my nephew a tour.

—You're a physicist? I say and realize it never occurred to me.

—It's in the genes, she says, roots of the father, and all that. I try to earn my keep.

We park in a back lot, then join the steady stream of visitors as they funnel through the metal detectors and into the lobby. She shows her badge and gets a temporary one for me. We walk around Wilson Hall and she takes me to the top and we look out the window on the building that houses the linear accelerator.

—When voltage is applied at a certain frequency, she says, the proton passing through the electrodes gets accelerated to 200 billion electron volts. From there, it goes to that booster accelerator over yonder, which accelerates it to about eight billion electron volts. Then it goes into the huge, main Tevatron ring for further acceleration up to 980 billion electron volts. Sounds fast, but it's about a billion times slower than a simple particle travels when a star explodes. Still, it's enough to bash a proton into an antiproton and get all kinds of results.

We ride the elevator to the basement where the control room is located. She greets nearly everyone we meet. They call her by her first name and flash smiles of respect.

—We've been working for months on something that all comes down to one experiment, she says. That happened last week. We're still analyzing the data. The folks I hang out with, you'll see, are the experimental types, as opposed to the theorists. They spend their time trying to see if the recipe works, you know, rather than coming up with the idea of a cake. The field is exploding, astrophysics, string theory, supergravity, all kinds of new theories. Nobody can keep up, and the Internet has just made it more complicated. In the middle of the night, you'll see four or five postings with new equations and manuscripts. It's still one hell of a mystery.

We turn a corner and arrive at a room with a sign on the door that reads, "Authorized Personnel." She swipes her badge and we step into a large room with about twenty-five people with heads buried in computers or watching monitors in banks along the walls. Some of them are dressed in suit coats, others in t-shirts with graphics of black holes and matrices with snappy lines that make fun of physics, or those who don't know physics. Hope takes a chair in front of a terminal and motions for me to drag a free chair from the other side of the room.

—How much do you know about your father's ideas? she says.

—Just what Frank told me.

—Whirlpool, she says. I'm sorry about his death and all. I know you must have cared for him, but he was a promoter, not a real scientist. Justin was working on his own TOE, and that was more than Frank or his bankers ever understood.

—Theory of Everything.

—That's good, she says. Whirlpool must have taught you something. Only there's a difference between types of TOE's. Justin's work had a human element. Most physicists are deconstructionists, you see. They break things down. They try to avoid anything having to do with the human condition, which is too subjective for their taste. Justin was bold, maybe a little too bold. He went over the top on a few connections. He came up with a hypothesis that waveforms are the mode of the universe, which is reasonable, but he also thought everything that happens in this world can be linked to the waveforms expressing their nature. Whether it's spontaneous or causal, whether it's a waveform on its own or a waveform colliding with another waveform, that's just the way things work. It was how the universe was created, according to him, the way the heavy elements were formed, planets, mountains, life. All actions in the universe, including human action, can be directly related to probability waveforms being expressed. Simple as that.

—Frank said the theory doesn't get much attention these days.

—He's right, she says. The Nobel committee on physics had something to do with that. It made a big deal about it for awhile, then tabled the idea in the end. It was good enough for Justin to be invited to present a paper in Sweden. That's how he and Maria died. They were traveling to Stockholm.

She types her password. She concentrates on the numbers that flow onto the screen, then leans over to a person at the next terminal and says something in mathematical lingo that I don't follow.

—Now watch, she says. I shouldn't be doing this now. The numbers are not complete, but what the hell.

Numbers flow up from the bottom of the screen. Complex charts are constructed and disappear to be replaced by others. I watch the monitor intensely, but the minutes go by, then an hour, and as much as I try to prevent it, I start to drift and fall asleep in my chair.

—See that! she says and slaps me on the shoulder.

I jump in my chair. I don't know whether it's been hours or minutes. Several of the other physicists in the room are standing around us. The computer is still scrolling long columns of numbers.

—I knew it, she says. The little bastard showed up!

The others begin to slap Hope on the shoulder, and my chair is engulfed in a frenzy of congratulations and handshakes as if she's just found the key to life. As far as I can see, it's only numbers.

—We've been working on this algorithm for three months, she says as the group dissolves back to their computer screens. It's a new formula some theoretical came up with, she says, for identifying an instance of quantum tunneling. Did Whirlpool teach you about quantum tunneling?

—Not much. A little.

—It's a curious phenomenon, she says, an effect that was first seen in alpha radiation. Even though there is not enough energy for alpha particles to overcome the nuclear energy that keeps them attached to the nucleus, these particles still escape. It's called tunneling. This algorithm predicts the probability that the particle will be on what they call the escape slope, just for an instant. If it works, we might be able to predict when the electromagnetic forces from other particles will pull the alpha particle away from the nucleus. When it tunnels, in effect, through the barrier.

—How do you predict something like that?

—We're trying to get two atoms to approach each other with such momentum, she says, that there's a certain probability their electron clouds will overlap. Then the alpha electrons can tunnel through the barrier. But it's just a hypothesis. This data are preliminary. We needed to resolve the calculations for top quark interactions as a base factor for the momentum. Then we can program the computer for probability patterns and invest the extra power when it makes sense. You understand?

—Not really.

—That's good, she says. Once you think you understand, they say, you know you're wrong. That's the way with quantum physics. It's a crap shoot, but that's the way of nature.

She types more on her keyboard, then spins in her chair.

—Listen up, she raises her voice to the others. I want you all to meet someone. This is my nephew, she says beaming, Romeo Argasti. Justin's son. Romeo Quark Argasti, in fact!

There's another frenzy of backslapping and handshakes. The physicists and technicians come alive for a moment, then melt back to their terminals.

—Justin's a bit of a legend, Hope says in a whisper. That's the way we think about the theoreticals. Not that we believe them. The proof is in the pudding and these folks are in the thick of it.

Hope logs off the computer. She takes me to another room full of cabinets and shows me some files from Justin's experiments. She tells me more about waveforms and other ideas my father proposed about multiple time dimensions and composite frequencies.

—It's different from what Frank told me, I say.

—There's a huge difference between what Frank Whirlpool thought and what Justin Bishop believed. I remember when Justin came back from London to watch the experimentalists test his equations. He stayed up for four days straight without sleep until every bit of beam time had been utilized. Then he slept for forty-eight hours and missed the meeting when the initial images were supposed to be presented. Instead of giving up, he invited the funding committee for a night out on the town, hired two female escorts, who led the bastards back to Fermilab. He had a captured audience, if a little tipsy, for his final presentation on frequency modification.

—What happened?

—He got the funding, she says. They thought he was crazy enough to be right. It was 1986 and ideas about multiple dimensions were just beginning to take hold. Frank Whirlpool had a hand in getting him the funding, I suppose, but you would have been proud of your father, Romey. Just like he would be proud of you. He didn't give in for anything. He told them what he believed, as if it was God's truth.

—Did you meet my mother? I say.

—Never did. But I know he loved her. Nothing we could do to keep him from going back to her in England, even the lure of a professorship at Southern Cal. I could have arranged it. Bill Lessing could have swung it.

—My mother wrote chamber music for string instruments.

—She was a musician, I remember.

—A cellist.

—I didn't really pay much attention. Didn't think it would last, I suppose. Until you, that is. But if you're looking for more about Maria, Bill Lessing might help. He went to England to see the two of them. He was Justin's roommate when he worked on his master's at Berkeley. That's where I met him. Only male lover I ever had.

It throws me a bit, but I nod. We drive back to the house, cook dinner and watch a late movie. It's almost enough to make me forget about wills and dark sedans, if not murder. I'm starting to feel something for Hope and for Fermilab and this land of my father and my father's father. Yet it's limited, as if there was something here for me once, a family, a past, but it's almost gone.

FIFTEEN

December 9, 1985

Yesterday I tried to call Mamma in Mariano, but she would not talk with me. Has Papà shut me off from my brother, too? I am mad to know how it goes with you in *Firenze*. Have they cut your black curls? You must be their best student. Compassion is first truth of the Church and you have it in your bones.

Things are not so good for me in London. Today, I watched in frustration as Justin slumped in a kitchen chair and Frank Whirlpool lorded over him. Remember what Papà always told us, Alberto, leave a little winter fruit on the vine. This benefactor gives nothing and takes all. Frank pushes and pushes until Justin's head is far away, even from me.

It is an insult! Justin screamed at him. They will laugh at me. I will be the laughingstock of the scientific community.

I was on the couch with hands over my ears. The two of them were trying to write a magazine article, and Frank had just said scientists are as bad as lawyers. They create a language of their own, he said. They speak in code, as if the common people could never hope to understand. Or that, somehow, they would corrupt the search for truth with their imprecision. If you want to have an impact on people's lives, Justin, give the common people a glimpse of what your ideas could mean, then sit back and let them work.

I could not help thinking there may be a little truth in what he said, Alberto. Yet Justin was motionless in front of the typewriter. I know he was thinking of his father because it always makes him sad and silent. To Justin, his father is the best example of what a scientist should be, and Frank was going too far.

Department heads, Frank said, and deans of universities are simply gatekeepers. They feel they must control ideas. They believe they separate fact from fiction, but how can it be fair when old men only know old ideas? Do you think your father finished every detail of research before he acted? If your father was worth his salt, he turned his ideas into something meaningful before it was too late.

You know nothing about my father! Justin shouted and I knew Frank had finally done it.

I know he would have wanted you to succeed, Frank said. I'm not asking you to lie. Just give people a little of your theory and you capture the idea as your own. Follow every rule, every process, and you give too much away. If a theory resonates with regular people, other scientists will do the math. Why are geniuses, he said, so intent on giving away their gold?

Frank reminds me of Signore Vondricco, Alberto. You remember the mayor of Mariano with his bushy brown hair and bags beneath his eyes and, as Papà said, his fingers always in the pie. Frank wants us to trust him, but how can we trust someone who wants so much and understands so little. Sometimes, I wonder whether our benefactor knows anything of what Justin believes. There is a simple language of energy and waves that can change our lives. That is the simple matter of Justin's ideas. He shows how vibration is the motion of daily life, our thoughts and our actions. He gives the universe its simplest form, but Frank makes him the enemy of the world.

The scientific method can be a maze, Frank said. It was made to make people with ideas run in circles, that way people without ideas can catch up. For every Einstein published in a journal, there is a Tesla who waits for recognition. You can do better, he goaded Justin, better even than your father. Never think of your ideas as hypotheses, he said. Think of them as an industry!

The struggle between Frank and Justin began over an article for publicity. I realize, now, from my own struggle as child of two very different fathers, one birth and one adoptive, it was a struggle for control of Justin's ideas and, even deeper, a struggle for his soul.

The article for the popular press was Frank's idea. He knew the waveform hypothesis was of such a nature that it would never win acceptance by the scientific community in time for them to profit. He needed a pull from the people. He wanted the gatekeepers to worry about missing something important, the next big thing, before it could be stowed in dusty laboratories where innovation often waited too long for recognition.

It was a common circle of frustration. A truly new idea could take decades for even tacit acceptance. Powerful people held the key to funding and without funding there would be no experiments. Without experiments there would be no proven equations, and without equations there would be no acceptance from the scientific community. Millions of ideas, good and bad, die slow deaths, Frank told Justin, because talented people think the world will come knocking.

The world would ignore him, Frank warned, even disrespect him. Did he like to beg for recognition? Did he want his ideas to wait until another person might brings them to the public? The world needed changing and Justin had a world-changing idea. It would not be the equations that helped real people. Math would never cause people to rise from squalor. Progress needed to be of everyone's own accord, a realization, an epiphany of religious proportions.

When President Kennedy challenged Americans to conquer the moon, Frank goaded Justin, did the scientific community accept its practicality? Had the math been done? Justin needed to stir imaginations just as Kennedy stirred the soul. People will create the waveform with their thoughts and desires. Did Justin not believe in his own ideas? Yet Justin's fears about the scientific community were not unfounded. If he was not careful, his ideas would be rejected by those he most admired, the professors and scientists, those who remembered his father. To popularize an idea before it was proven would throw the timeworn process into confusion. Frank was asking him to reject the legacy of Descartes, Hobbes and Leibnitz, of Locke, Berkeley and Newton. There was a cause to every problem, and that cause could be isolated and equated. Justin thought he might as well post his ideas on UseNet and join the millions of crazies that think they've been abducted by aliens, or contend they found a secret code in the Bible.

Did Frank understand what the waveform hypothesis implied? Did he fathom its reach? Was Frank Whirlpool, himself, capable of epiphany? Yes, there could be a god, the God of creation, but the waveform hypothesis implied that what existed before the Big Bang was a possibility, a probability, a mathematical waveform. It was not the God people wanted. It wasn't visual enough, like a solid table, or heat in the air, or a divine being with a beard and throne. It was an abstraction, a swirling cosmos of infinite possibilities, and Justin realized most people would reject the vision of God on High as a simple, beautiful and omnipresent wave from which all things have been created. They would misinterpret the hypothesis as denigrating God to an equation, yet that was far from the truth.

The typewriter began to click, Maria thought, just as Frank was about to give up. Before the Big Bang, Justin typed, nothing existed except possibility. There was an infinity of possibilities, in fact, because there was no limit to what might or might not happen. Within this infinite possibility was not only the capacity for things to stay the same, but also the possibility to create something definite, something finite.

And this finite possibility was the recipe of the universe, the spontaneous creation, the Big Bang.

Would this language make anyone get down on their knees and shout to the heavens? How could Frank and Silvie make a product out of probability? Regardless of the mathematical challenges, he had to be able to explain his ideas in simple English. Why was he afraid to use words people fear? Physics was no longer afraid of theology, he contended, why should theology be afraid of physics?

Infinite possibility is the character of God, Justin typed. It has always been the character of God, but humanity in its infancy needed animation.

Justin grew more and more frustrated. He needed words that were understandable to the non-scientific, but what words?

The possibility for the creation of the universe existed before the Big Bang. There were infinite options. There could have been absolutely nothing created, or there was the possibility of a waveform with the characteristics of the Big Bang. If the possibility is looked at as a wave, which holds information, the singularity before the Big Bang, he surmised, was a frequency with infinite wavelength and zero mass. All the conditions of the universe were inherent in this original waveform.

It seemed useless, but Frank held fame and fortune like a razor sharp blade over Justin's head. Would he let the blade fall, or would he rise to the occasion and grasp its tainted handle? Despite what he feared would be a disappointment to his father and peers, he continued to write from his mind, if not from his heart.

Just as a photon seems to exist as a wave and a particle, Justin filled the white sheet, everything and nothing existed at the same time. In the beginning, before time, before matter, there was absolute freedom of action, or infinite potential. The singularity that created our universe was programmed by a waveform that held all the information of creation and expansion. The possibility, or God as we call infinite possibility, had the potential for infinite actions. Yet only our particular universe was created. That is, unless there are multiple universes, which there may very well be.

Now, it seemed even more useless to Justin.

There will be time for science fiction later, Frank told him. From this point, filling in the details of Justin's theory should be easy. After the Big Bang, the principles of the waveform hypothesis were simply what every physics book contained, but instead of the language of matter, they would be phrased in the language of energy.

At the beginning when the world was pure energy, Justin continued to type, a temperature drop caused a phase transition where gravitation waves condensed out of the unified wave. As temperature declined further, waves of the strong force condensed out to resonate as elementary particles. The spontaneous warps in the harmonic structure of the Big Bang resulted in wave clouds of particle interactions that resonated as atoms and molecules, which became the stars and planets. This is how the Big Bang and the inflationary expansion of the universe has been explained by a cavalcade of scientific icons since the beginning of the twentieth century. As the American physicist Alan Guth said, it was the "ultimate free lunch," and now the language of vibration and waves could give it ultimate meaning in our lives.

That was the beauty of Justin's hypothesis, Frank understood, and it was the power. Relativity and quantum mechanics could now be thought of as part of the programming. The original wave held the information that created the laws of nature, just as bits of DNA hold the color of your hair and the way you walk. The characteristics of the original wave included an initial warping in the harmony of the universe. The warping created the massing of waves at certain points, which created the look of the universe, with spiral galaxies and clusters of nebulous matter.

That these creative waves, indeed, existed from the beginning was verified by the 3K radio frequencies that Wilson and Penzias discovered in the 1960's. These lingering frequencies are one of the best evidences we find of the Big Bang. How could speculation or even more equations about the universal presence of frequencies do any better to define the first cause?

That's where Justin faltered. Once he left a consideration of ideas that could be backed by equations, the grounded scientist in him won over the cosmic theologian. He lost the center of gravity that had been pounded into him from the first moment of schooling. It was where he would personally have to embody these new ideas. It was where his hypothesis exited the realm of matter and entered the domain of energy. Like the faith that some hold for the soul or in the immaculate conception of Christ, verification of the waveform hypothesis eclipsed our normal frame of reference, and certainly the scientific method. To track one particle interaction required a computer. To track a secondary interaction of that same particle was problematic. To even imagine the chaos of multiple particle interactions required a leap of faith no less than what is required for a belief in love or Heaven.

Yet Justin could no more put the genie back into the bottle than stop thinking. His speculation was unending. The waveform hypothesis, to his creative mind, implied that energy is trapped in an additional dimension of time, a network of fields beyond simple vibration and beyond sequential time. It is a dimension of which we are not conscious, according to Justin, simply because we have never really conceived of it in our minds. Like relativity and quantum mechanics, this level of thought, he imagined, required a reorientation of the very way we think about the world.

Justin's ideas flew in the face of those scientists that wanted to do away with time. His ideas pointed to a third dimension of time in which energy is trapped in ways that create different parts of matter: quarks and neutrinos, atoms and molecules, the secondary substance of the universe. To Justin, it is this trapped energy that creates the four forces: electromagnetism, gravity, the strong force that holds the atom's nucleus together, and the weak force that governs beta decay. Energy oscillates and moves through sequential time, then it is trapped within another *movement of time that gives energy mass and spin and the characteristics of matter.*

In his article, Justin skipped lightly across this controversial concept. Three-dimensional time was not at the core of his industry. All objects are composites of particles and forces. All composites have a measurable frequency that determines their level of energy. Each particle, each atom, molecule and composite has a spectral signature that exhibits such characteristics as emission, shell level and composition. All composites, composed of different energies and different frequencies, can therefore be altered with inputs.

This is the simple idea, Frank understood, that could create a new way of living. Frequencies can be altered with inputs. Matter can be changed with the twist of the wave. It means the universe is changeable. It gives free will an extra power. It means that every time we get up in the morning, with our actions, our movements, our thoughts, we inevitably change the world.

Letter continued…

He manipulates Justin as a child, Alberto, rather than the *cittadino del mondo* that Justin is. I know why Frank does this. He is jealous. Justin has what a man like Frank Whirlpool will never have, a sense of purpose, a vision, a mind that works not only for profit, but also for love.

As Justin worked at the table, Frank sat next to me on the couch as if I were part of his realm. Justin will never believe me, but I know you will, because a priest should know and reject the desires of men. Justin is blind to Frank's ambition. He does not see Frank's desire to possess. People such as he and Silvie take from us the very air we breathe, since it is free for the taking.

I left the couch and went to hug Justin. Then I retreated to the bedroom where I found isolation, but no silence. I cupped my hands over my ears to keep from hearing their arguments. I pulled my pillow over my head and burrowed beneath the blankets.

Frank continued to bully him. Your words are too technical, he told Justin. Think of Maria, he said, the way she uses the language of music. Use words like pitch and tone, loudness and intensity. Speak to them of harmony, disharmony and syncopation. Instead of constructive interference of waves, you should say sympathetic vibration, or resonance, or beat. Use the language of music or religion if you really want the people to understand.

You mean the language of faith, Justin said. If I describe my ideas in terms of faith, they will be scorned by every scientist in the world.

Then let them scorn, he said. Faith is something you can take to the bank, Justin. People need religion and religion is always best in the language of music. Work on a way to link the vibrations of music to the vibrations of composites, and you will have all the funding you need.

Justin no longer argued. He said he was too tired to go on. He went to the couch and tried to sleep, but Frank did not leave. He acted as if he was still working on the article, but he soon opened my bedroom door. It scared me so badly my hands still shake, Alberto. I stashed the letter I had begun to write you under the pillow. I took my cello from the wall. I asked Frank to leave, but he sat on a chair at the end of the bed and watched me.

His cologne mixed with the smoke on his clothes in a putrid odor. He said my music was soothing, so I played badly on purpose, but he would still not leave. He asked me about my composition and I told him it was for my professors. I said he should leave, now, or we would soon wake Justin.

He only dreams of physics, Frank said. You and Justin are too much alike to be lovers. You want so much. Silvie and I are alike, too. We want so little.

I leaned the cello against the wall and tried to leave, but Frank caught my hand. His fingers touched my bare neck. It made my skin burn, not with passion but with anger. Justin slept as if nothing existed but the world he has created inside his head. He would not believe me if I told him. Only you will believe, Alberto, because you know this terrible world enough to reject it for the cloth. I miss you, dear brother. You are my protector and confessor, and I wish you could protect me now.

SIXTEEN

After three long days, Violet returns with a dirty car and nothing much to say about where she'd gone or what she'd done. The limousine engine is gasping like a tired horse and there's a silver scratch where somebody keyed the passenger side, but the limousine looks mostly the same. It's only Violet that's changed. I've seen her strung out before, when she messes up words and her pupils push all the white from her eyes, but this is something else, no slurs, no dilation.

—I don't know what's wrong with it, she says. I step on the gas and it acts as if it won't go at all, then it takes off like a bat out of hell. The car is a piece of junk, Romey. Oscar dealt us a lemon.

—Are you okay?

—I'm here, she says and gives me a hug so tightly it nearly stops my breath. Sorry about the way I've acted, baby. I'm home now, with you. I decided, Romey, I decided.

She gives me another bear hug and hangs on so long it makes me think she's never going to let me go. I don't smell smoke, so I figure it must be pills of some kind. Maybe amphetamines or a designer type, but not ecstasy because she feels warm like sex. I'm glad Hope is still at work. It makes me nervous, this new sincerity of Violet's. Sappy eyes are not something I can get used to quickly, but my heart melts like a sucker.

—How are you doing, baby? she asks. You and Hope got together on this thing about your mother? You find the music, Romey? Are we in the money?

I shake my head. She hangs to me like a leaf stuck before it falls all the way to the ground.

—All I got was stories, I say. There's a guy in San Francisco. Hope says he was my father's roommate. He knew my mother. It might be good to go there.

—That's good, she says. If this guy knew your mother, that's something. Can I crash, now, Romey? Maybe get some food?

She stumbles on the front porch step, so I slide my arm around her waist and guide her inside. I go out and rescue Tuf from under the passenger side. He purrs in my arms. I pour milk for him into a bowl and make Violet a sandwich with some leftover turkey. She gorges then her eyelids droop further, and I take her into the bedroom and put her and Tuf to bed.

—Sorry, Romey, she says. I don't know what's wrong with the car. I didn't mess it up, I don't think. Just drove it. Who'd know?

She sleeps for six hours. Hope comes back from the lab and, before she realizes Violet has come back, starts making a racket in the kitchen. In a few minutes, I hear the shower, so Hope and I go outside and take a look at the limo. She starts the engine then opens the hood as if she's been working on cars all her life.

—Vacuum pump, she says.

—I don't know much about cars, I say.

—You know anything about vacuum pumps?

—I know about vacuums.

—Just like your father, she says and flashes me a smile. I've got a friend who can help.

We lean over the engine. Grease and dirt are all over the chaotic run of metal and rubber pipes. Hope points to a pump on the engine block and asks me if I know how it works.

—Basic thermodynamics, I say. The vacuum pump draws gases out of the engine and this tubing recycles them through the engine.

—It keeps the fuel burning efficiently, she says. Or not, in this case. I'll call Gary Blevins. He runs a local repair shop.

—You shouldn't have to put up with us, Hope. If Violet and I are going to California, we should be leaving.

—Leaving? she says. Surely, not yet.

—I just don't want to be a bother.

—Don't you ever think that, Romey, she says. Not ever.

She closes the hood and uses her cell phone to call the shop, but not before I see her expression, which is one I never thought I'd see. It was a look of regret at the thought of me leaving. We go back inside and find Violet in the kitchen.

—I'll bet you're hungry, Hope says. I'll make some dinner. You make yourself at home, dear, and I'll take care of everything.

Violet's hair is wet from the shower and she's still in her panties and bra, so she shivers from the cold wind that blew in with Hope and me through the door. I take her hand and lead her to the bathroom where she can dry her hair. Instead she kisses me on the mouth and, as quietly as we can, we make love on the cold linoleum floor. Even scrunched up, it feels like we're back in the Hovel and we hold each other until we're calm.

—What do you think? she says as she sits up and leans against the bathtub.

—It was great.

—No, she says. About me deciding.

—Deciding what?

—About you, dummy.

—I thought you decided that when we left New York.

—Not like this, Romey. I thought about it a whole lot.

—You were going to leave me, weren't you? When you left for

Chicago, you might have left for good.

—Might have, she says, but it wasn't so good. It made me hurt, you know, hurt like hunger. I didn't think I'd ever feel that way, then you come into my life like a big geek. That's why I decided.

She hugs me and kisses me with a full measure of tenderness that I don't think I've felt from her before. I try to believe her. I try to kiss her to show I'm returning what she says she feels, but I know her too well and time is always a problem. For Violet, emotion is a fully spontaneous thing, the moment it exists is all there might be. But this time her eyes say something different. There's sadness in them as if the past lingers longer than she's let it before.

We try to make love again, but it's too soon and the cold from the floor has seeped into my skin. I shake my head and kiss her on the cheek. Then I see it. Right there on the sink next to her hairbrush and toothpaste, a jagged stone the size of a golf ball.

I stare at it without speaking, because I can't think of how a huge ruby could be here in Hope Bishop's bathroom. It must be a fake, but the light from the window strikes it and I see the light dancing inside like a jittery flame. The muscles on the back of my neck tighten and I slide from the bathroom floor with my back against the wall.

It's the ruby from the estate safe, or one exactly like it. The Whirl showed it to me enough times for me to know it's the same gemstone from the Foundation's frequency test. I could never forget the jagged edges and the perpetual fire inside, but it can't be same one. No reason it should be.

—Found it on the floor of the limo, she says as I reach to the sink and pick up the ruby. I was looking for an umbrella, she says, under the front seat and there was this beautiful rock. Must be worth something. It rained the whole time in Chicago. Did it rain here, Romey? It really poured in Chicago.

—On the floor of the limo?

—Yeah, she says. Jesus, you're looking at me like I stole it or

something. She reaches up and takes it from me, then tosses it up and
catches it in her palm. It looks real, she says, but it's probably fake,
something this big. I didn't steal it, if that's what you're thinking.

—I didn't say that.

—You didn't have to. I could see it in your eyes.

—Dinner's ready! We hear a yell from the kitchen.

We try to sneak from the bathroom to the bedroom, but we
meet Hope in the hallway.

—Yeah, we did it, Violet says. What's it to you?

Violet stamps to the bedroom and slams the door.

—She's a little tired, I say.

—Whatever you two got going, Hope says, it's none of my
business. I'm not a prude, you know. I've had my life and you'd be
surprised.

I follow Violet to the bedroom. I sit on the bed and watch her
finish dressing. She bangs drawers and throws her clothes onto the
floor. I tell her I didn't mean anything about the stone, but she
doesn't answer. We go to the kitchen where Hope has doled some
out-of-the-can beef stew onto three plates.

—Did you see your family, Violet? Hope says.

—None of your business.

—She's just asking, I say.

—That's right, honey, Hope says, just making conversation.

—Don't call me honey, or dear, she says. The relatives were there,
that's all that's important. They didn't remember me. It was as if they
hadn't heard of me, but that's the way it goes. Nothing to be sorry for.
If a family was meant to be together, it would be together, right?

—That's right, I say.

—Yeah, like you would know, Violet says. Some family you got
here, Romey. Trash all over the place. Living with the damn buffalo,
and this bitch who has never had a man and you know it.

Forks click on our plates. The wind rubs a branch against the kitchen window. I never should have told her what Hope told me.

—I've tried to be nice, Hope says and pushes her chair out from the table, but I guess I've had just about enough. If you don't like being here, honey, then you can get your little ass out to the street.

—She's just tired, I say. I pissed her off. It's not you.

Violet slaps her hand on the table and storms back to the bedroom. The door slams before her fork stops skidding across the linoleum. Beef stew sauce is dotted on the floor in a line, so I grab a napkin and try to clean up, but Hope stops me.

—Shit, she says. It's my fault. Should have known she didn't want to talk. You go to her, Romey. You love her, I can tell.

I give up the napkin and Hope starts cleaning the mess. I go to the bedroom and find Violet lying on her stomach with her face to the wall. I sit on the bed and put my hand on her shoulder, but she elbows me off.

—I'll sleep in the damn car, she says, so I don't have to hear none of this family shit.

—Hope is sorry. We'll get out of here, Violet. When the part for the car gets here, we'll fly. We'll take off.

She rolls over and looks at me. I've never seen her cry. A tear quivers in her eye as if it's about to roll off, but she wipes it with her shirt. She puts her arms around me, but not before I have a picture burned into my head of how she was lying on the bed, a little girl with hair sticking to her cheek. She holds me. I hear her heart beating. If this is love, then it's definitely what I want. Like making real love, it's as if time ceases and the universe is still.

—Want some wine? Hope knocks softly on the door. It's pretty good wine, she says.

—Not now, I say but it's too late because Hope opens the door an inch, then two. Violet and I split like opposite poles of a magnet. Hope opens the door all the way, hesitates, then comes in and puts two glasses onto the table.

—This will make you feel better, she says and shakes her head. I'm real sorry, Violet. I just can't stand you thinking I'm horrible. I didn't mean anything. I want you to know that. It's not great wine, but not bad.

She pours two half glasses, sets the dark bottle on the table and leaves still shaking her head. Violet wipes strands of hair from her cheek. We sip the wine and sit without speaking. We lie on the bed with our heads on the same pillow. As the sun goes down and the room goes dark, we wander into the living room and find Hope on the couch reading the paper and sipping from a tall glass of white wine, almost clear.

—Come in, Hope says and pats the couch cushion. The sun's going down. The sunsets here sure are pretty.

Violet sits at the far end of the couch and I sit next to her on the inside. Tuf takes a place on the windowsill, and the four of us stare out the window that overlooks the cul-de-sac and the dark fields of prairie grass that still vibrate from the last heat of the sun.

—You've had some rough days, Hope says. I know you have.

Violet crosses her arms, so I lean against her and put my arm around her shoulder. Hope pours us another glass of wine.

—We've got to think of things another way, Hope says. This is our time, you know. That's the way I think of it. It's the only time we're going to have here. No reason to argue, especially with family, and we're all family. Some of us just don't take to it so easily.

She lifts her glass and, as much as I can't believe it, Violet raises hers. Then I almost fall on the floor as Violet climbs over me and puts her arms around Hope.

—That's why I decided, Violet says and smiles more at Hope than at me.

The moon comes up as we polish off the rest of the bottle. We talk a little about our plans to leave the next morning, but mostly we watch TV. Like a family, I suppose, that knows everything about each other, even if when it comes down to it they're really strangers.

—I wish you had known Justin, Hope says. He may not have been right about everything, but the world was set back on its haunches when he came through. I'm sorry I never met your mother. A real beauty, they said, just like you.

Violet nudges me and giggles. I pick up my glass and down the rest of the clear liquid.

—Justin was about the only family I ever had, Hope says. Mamma was killed in a car accident in late seventy-eight. Daddy died of cancer in eighty-three. Justin and I were more or less orphans, like you. The lab took us in because of the respect they had for Father, but Justin left home and didn't come back until a few months before he died. That's when rumors of the Nobel nomination came in, and he was gone. He thrived on work. That's the high that really means something, when your ideas come out and begin to make your mark on the world. You can't beat that feeling. Justin wanted to feel that more than anything.

—Frank said he might have been a genius, I say.

—These ideas, she says, they float around until they collide with something else. That's what Justin said. He taught me a few things, and not only me, but most of those goons you met at the lab. Everything is connected in ways that all the computer power in the universe couldn't handle. It goes all the way back, if you want to think of physics, to Mach's Principle. The inertia of an object depends on its relation to everything else in the universe. We all sort of believe it, but we need to know how. That's what Justin did for us. He gave us something to consider, right or wrong.

—You miss him, Violet says.

—I do, she says, but I don't really think he's gone. Not Justin. I don't know how anyone could comprehend the beauty of physics and ever think when you die, you're gone.

SEVENTEEN

A vector is a math term that denotes a quantity of something that has a magnitude as well as a direction. An example of a vector is velocity, which has a magnitude equal to the speed traveled, as well as a specific direction of motion. On the other hand, if something has magnitude but no direction, it's called a scalar. As with time and temperature, a scalar is simply points on a scale with no direction. In theory, most of us try to live as vectors.

—They clipped the chains on the gate, Gary Blevins's voice rattles through the receiver. Never touched another car. Went right for your limousine, lickety-split.

At eight in the morning, Hope handed me the phone. Violet was still sleeping, so I took it to the bathroom.

—It's gone? I say.

—Not a trace. I came in at seven this morning and found the gate open and that big limo gone. That's all I know. I'm sorry, man.

—Did you call the police?

—I'm calling you first. Don't know your situation, but I did this job as a favor for Hope, now I've got a busted gate. You own that car?

—Sort of, I say.

—I thought as much, he says. Kids don't own limousines. Do you want me to call the police?

—No. I don't want any police.

—Yeah, well, I ordered a new vacuum pump. Hope is an old friend, so I'll do what I can. I didn't fill out any paperwork. The pump is coming in this morning, but I can send it back. I don't want trouble any more than you do.

—No trouble. Thank you.

I walk in a trance to the kitchen and put the phone into its charger. Hope is making breakfast. She knows what happened and starts to apologize, but I tell her it's not her fault. It might have been petty thieves, but that would be a coincidence and coincidences are simply probabilities, math problems with mind-bending coefficients. With dark sedans cruising for no reason and sober men always looking away, I can feel the amplitude of danger spike like a dagger.

Why shouldn't the bastards follow, anyway? Why wouldn't they interfere, Philip, Silvie, even Oscar and the family that was never around until the Whirl was dying? No doubt they all want me to fail. There's too much money on the line for me to be free of interference. The Whirl knew that's the way it would be. The day he wrote the will, he tied his fortune to me like a tangled anchor and threw me out to sea.

—You take my car, Hope says.

—I can't do that.

—Of course you can. I'm sure it would make it to San Francisco. Bill would love to see it again. You have to be a little careful with the convertible top and the batteries. Just juice it up every two hundred miles. Nothing to it.

—No way, Hope. You've got to work. How would you get to work?

—Listen, she says, I didn't do much for Justin while he was alive, so now's the time for me to do some good. You take that car,

Romey. Take it back to Bill Lessing for me. When your ship comes in, pay me back. Maybe one of those stainless-steel DeLoreans. Now wouldn't that be something.

It doesn't take much for me to take her up on the offer. The thought of henchmen and stolen cars is enough to make me want to be gone. Violet packs our things and we're ready by ten o'clock. I feel as if I've blown away Hope's peaceful life with a wave of chaos that began with the Whirl and ends up pulling everyone into its wake.

She shows us how to recharge the EV-1. We toss the bags into the car and put Tuf on the floor in a blanket where he can stay between Violet's feet. Hope stands with big tears that roll off her chin. Feeling sheepish, I lean against the car with the keys loose in my hand. She takes another look at the wound on my head, which feels and looks better thanks to her tending. She tells me to be careful and hugs me, then she hugs Violet who kisses her on the cheek.

We pull away from the house. Hope waves her arm, but before we make it to the stop sign she disappears inside the house. I know she's already thinking about work and the next experiment, and how she and the geeks at Fermilab might discover more of the mysterious world, like her father and brother in a family line of the gifted that seems to stop with me.

—Rev it up, Romey, Violet says. Doesn't it feel good to go?

—Better than standing still.

The highway goes up and down, left and right, and on and on into that infinite band of blurring white spots. We take Interstate 80 across Illinois to Iowa. Violet scores some speed at a huge truck stop in Des Moines while I use a service station's electric socket to charge the car. Through the whole of Nebraska, we don't sleep, but we stop every four hours to charge up and buy something to drink. We get all the way up 6,000 feet into the Rocky Mountains before we're exhausted. We pull into the parking lot of a state park in the middle of nowhere and try to sleep, but it's useless because I'm pulsing with speed.

—You asleep? Violet asks.

—I can't sleep.

—I don't know why we had to stop here, she says. Something's wrong with those trees, Romey. The leaves are screwing around, blowing all over. It's like they got arms and hands. Somebody could be in there and we wouldn't know it until it was too late.

She's hunched in a ball in the passenger bucket seat. Tuf is asleep on the floor. I'm propped in the driver's side with my knees pressed against the steering wheel. For three hours the sky has been leaking a misty rain, so we stayed in the car and tried to make love, but I twisted my back and scared the cat.

—The top is up, I say. The doors are locked. Everyone will think this is some kind of park vehicle. Nobody is going to bother us, Violet.

—You hear that? she whispers. It sounds like crying.

—That's a coyote. They call to the pack to tell their positions. They don't hurt humans, so you don't have to worry.

—Maybe people never live to tell. Shit happens, you know. You thought of that?

—No, I say, I never thought of that.

—Animals can smell fear. People know when you're scared, so why can't coyotes? It makes sense. All this stuff is out there, and we're here without a clue.

She rolls into the middle and reaches for me. I roll and hit the transmission hump with my side. She only wants to be held, so I hold her. It's as if we're back in the box at the Hovel, only instead of tall buildings all around there are black trees thrashing in a harsh wind.

—Go to sleep, baby, I say.

—You too, baby.

As the three-quarter moon peeks out of the clouds, the coyotes howl louder. In my wide-eyed stupor the trees become ragged silhouettes of creatures out of Violet's imagination.

—You asleep? Violet says again and I shake my head. Me either, she says. I was thinking how good it is, you and me here with nobody else around.

—It is good.

—What if Brownie hadn't introduced us? she says. You think we'd be together, Romey?

—We don't have to worry. He got us together.

—No, I mean like fate? You think if he introduced you to somebody else, you'd be with them?

—I think we have a choice. We can make things happen, or not. Who knows?

She turns her head so she can see me. A gust of wind jerks the tree limb that's closest to our car. Some leaves rip off with a snap and drift to the blacktop. Others stick on the windshield.

—That means you'll leave me, she says. Or I'll leave you.

—That's not true. It means we have choices.

—You have choices, Romey. You're the only one I ever met that has choices. Most people take what they can get. Whatever is dealt. You got it different. You'll find someone else, maybe better. That's okay.

—I love you, Violet. I won't leave you.

She puts one leg on the dash and twists her body over and away from me. Though she's making good into bad, the sound of Violet breathing makes me feel warm against the cold night. This is what people in a pack must have felt under the same cloudy sky for thousands of years. When you have someone, the night is warmer. Even millions of years ago it was the same. Yet billions of years ago, it was a very different place. People didn't count, didn't exist. It was before fate became supreme, or maybe because of fate, there were movements at a molecular level, primal connections between energy and matter, hydrogen and helium combining into heavier elements that blasted off into a trajectory that eventually came down to us, Violet and me.

The first law of thermodynamics says heat supplied to a system equals the change in the energy of that system, plus the work being done. Everything is conserved in the universe. Does that include love?

—This isn't right, she says and turns so suddenly she hits her head on the roof of the EV-1. It's easy to say you love someone, Romey, but I need something more.

—You mean marriage?

—Not like that, she says and rubs her head then moves it to her heart. I just need to feel it, you know, heavy right here.

Her hand is in a fist so I can tell she's holding something inside. I see the ruby through her thumb and forefinger. The moonlight splinters off the edges, and it occurs to me that even love on a mountain that seems like it could last forever, might be just as uncertain as love for pay.

After all, Violet is an expert. She's good at lying, always has been, even in the face of love. The uncertainty principle says if you know the mass of a particle, it's impossible to simultaneously know its momentum. The more you know about one variable, the less you know about the other. It's a law of the universe, a constriction. Yet it's also expansive as hell. It means that anything can happen. It's the method and the means for possibility. It allows for probability, where all things are possible before it all comes down to one. Fate is not as causal as it sounds. It's the spontaneous, infinite possibility at the start of every moment, every hour, every day. But where does that leave us? Leave me? If the ruby is from the Whirl's safe, how could I possibly know how it got here, now?

Violet puts her other hand on my shoulder and squeezes lightly. She curls a strand of hair over my ear. I'm not sure what she's thinking, whether it's about marriage vows or simply about tonight, but it would be nice to know, and safer.

—Why all of a sudden, Violet? You never mentioned marriage before.

—I don't mean marriage, she says. I told you. I just decided.

As much as I try, I can't take my eyes off the slice of ruby between her fingers, and she sees me staring. She opens her palm and hands me the stone.

—That'd make a hell of a ring, I say. Maybe that's what you need, a ring. Would that mean something to you?

The ruby is cold as ice. It's smaller in my hand than in hers, but it's still huge. Her ring finger is pointed at me as if it's accusing, then she changes it to her middle finger.

—You're a bastard, she says, like all the rest.

She takes the ruby, curls it inside a fist and tucks her hand under her arm. She turns her body away. We don't talk anymore. I can hear her breathing and it's a long time before it turns to unconscious sighs. Sometime later, I fall asleep too, but I dream I'm still awake and looking at the white sky, which wakes me up, again. It's about six in the morning and there's a hint of the sun making the sky a whitish gray. I slip out of the car as quietly as I can and find a place to pee.

The forest smells like sweetness rotting and it makes me hungry. I check on Violet. She's still asleep, so I rummage for food in the trunk, which is filled nearly full with the battery system. Violet's plastic bag of clothing falls open, so I stuff the shirts and underwear back into the bag. Inside a pair of socks is a hard shape.

I pull out a horizontal black book. A bank book. It's not like Violet to have a bank account, so I flip it open to the first and only entry. Ten thousand dollars.

—Shit, I say aloud and bite my tongue.

I stuff the book into the sock and pack it with the rest of the clothes. I close the trunk and lean against the car and spit at the squawking sparrows fighting for some trash by the curb. I stare inside the car at the sleeping heap Violet makes on the passenger side. The second law of thermodynamics states that no system is one hundred percent efficient. Everything is subject to external forces, every system is flawed no matter how beautiful, or innocent, or how much we want it to be perfect. That's just how the universe is.

EIGHTEEN

January 13, 1986

You must be furious with me. That is the only explanation for why you do not write. I know Papà has turned my brother against me, or maybe you are becoming a monk instead of a priest. Is that it? Have you taken a vow of silence, Alberto? More than you know, I am in need of your blessing because Justin no longer listens.

Tonight, though I told him over and over I did not want to go, he dragged me to the Fitzroy where Frank Whirlpool was waiting. The pub was so crowded we could only find a small table in a back corner where it was very hot. I sat between the two of them, my legs smashed together, but Justin did not see, or he would not see, that Frank was pressing closer than he needed to be.

This night is important to our future, Justin had told me, so I hunched my shoulders and stayed quiet. Frank ordered drinks and took some papers from his coat, then laid them flat on the table. It was a lease for intellectual property, he told Justin. It would give the Foundation, which Frank and Silvie own, the rights to Justin's ideas. It is standard language, Frank assured him. All Justin had to do was sign, he said, and the money will begin to flow.

Frank laid a pen on the paper and smiled as if he was asking for more than a signature. The waitress brought our drinks and Justin, I saw, was perspiring. Others in the bar were making napkins into fans. Justin loosened his tie and said we should find a place less noisy so he could think. I brushed the hair away from his eyes so he could better see what he was signing. The Fitzroy was packed with students and professors, but not one of them looked our way. They seemed to know what this meeting was about, everyone but me.

Silvie is going to bat for you, Frank said to Justin. She is putting her reputation on the line.

I should do more analysis, Justin said. Harrad may be right. I should see if I can test the hypothesis in the lab at Royal Holloway.

Frank stuffed the pen into Justin's hand. He and the Dean would have plenty of money to do all the experiments they wanted, but only after Justin signed. No investor in the world, he assured him, will be interested without release of the rights.

I whispered to Justin that he did not need to rush into anything, and that we should leave to give him time to think. You can always sign, I said, but you can never take back your rights.

Sign now, Frank said. Surely, you must have realized. The world changes too quickly, Justin. Silvie is working day and night to make everything right. Would you let us down?

Just say the word, I whispered to Justin and pushed Frank's leg away from mine. We can go. We can leave all this behind us.

As one does to an irritation, Frank turned his Cheshire smile to me. Is the world changing too quickly for you, Maria? Maybe you are the one afraid of what this will mean. No more small apartment to hide in. No more threadbare dresses for the struggling musician. Too much is riding on this project for you to have cold feet. Silvie has contacted people in London and New York. We thought you two were on the level. Until this contract is signed, we all could be accused of fraud.

The pub was silent as a mouse. Frank was speaking too loudly, and people had stopped talking and clicking their drinks when, as if a ghost had been summoned, Silvie Nels came through the door. She marched to our table and stared down the onlookers until they went back to their drinks. When she saw the paper and Frank's face so angry, she bent toward Justin.

Why have you not signed? This is not the time for games.

I pushed against Frank and struggled to free myself, but he put his arm around my shoulder. Justin's eyes were fixed on Silvie's as if he was in awe of her presence. It was all I could do not to slap every one of them, but Frank took my arm and pulled so hard I had to go with him or make things even worse.

Be still, he said as we sat at the bar and he ordered me a drink I did not want. Let's leave them alone for awhile, shall we?

They are alone too much, I said.

Do you believe in him, Maria? Frank said. Sometimes, I think you could care less about your boyfriend's ideas. Do you have any idea of the possibility they hold for ordinary people?

Then he told me what I could not believe. Silvie has already been talking with a company that sells pills. Frank said this company is interested in funding Justin's research, in buying Justin's ideas. To be able to alter a person's chemistry in a measured way, Frank said, may be one of the greatest achievements of this century.

Pills are not his idea, I told him. His ideas are much bigger than pills.

Imagine, he said, a line of supplements, like vitamin C or B, which can modify a person's energy. Do you realize what that could mean to people's lives?

This was Silvie's plan, he said. This company will build a tool to measure a person's frequency. A composite frequency, he said, to use as a baseline to measure changes after the person takes the supplement. I call them "Freq" drugs, he said and laughed as if Justin's ideas could be reduced to a joke. Yet I think this man is serious. How he spoke of the future could, indeed, snare the unwary. The drugs, he said, would work like a simple homeopathic remedy, but the ingredients would provide an alternate frequency, which would be prescribed to change a person's energy.

The pills, he said, would be sugar based with variations of spectral energies. The doctor would test the patient's reaction to them under certain conditions or diseases. No more dangerous than eating a good breakfast, he said. Think of it, Maria, a line of cures based on physics. Are you so protective of Justin that you would stop something that could help children?

I watched Justin and Silvie at the table. I wondered if she was giving him the same story about drugs and children. She was leaning closer to him than Frank insisted on leaning toward me. I did not believe anything this demon with the silver throat told me, Alberto. I just wanted to leave.

Watch them, Frank whispered. Justin is enjoying himself. Silvie can be very persuasive. Like all of us, he wants to control the future. He'll be the father of a new science. Frequency drugs are just the beginning, Maria. Justin's ideas can give people the ability to change themselves. It gives people control.

Matto! I said. You are crazy as a loon. You are trying to make Justin *matto*, too.

Frank turned my face with his filthy hand and stared into my eyes. You are jealous, he said. I should be a little jealous, as well. I know how you feel, not because of Silvie, but because of you.

Then in front of all those people, he kissed me like Silvie had kissed Justin. *Insolènte*! I slapped him and threw my drink into his face. I ran back to the table, but Silvie and Justin were no longer talking of business, but leaning even closer.

I saw the contract. A blue scrawl was still wet above the line. He had signed it. Without me! So I did not ask him, but grabbed him and pulled him to the door.

Can you blame me for fear, Alberto? These people want our souls and they will not stop until they have them. I work like mad on my music, as Justin works like mad on his ideas. Yet of my work, I can see no end. The music goes on and on with notes and melodies that build on each other without me realizing they turn in circles. These ones who prey on Justin might give us a new world, but how would a world they created be for good?

I yearn for what you must feel, my brother. Have you found solitude, and peace, and connections beyond our earthly bonds? Do you speak to God and does He listen? You are my only confessor. Speak to me, Alberto, because I am close to ruin.

NINETEEN

After three long days, the Rockies crash down and smooth into rolling hills and flatland. As we get to Sacramento, we spot our first seagull flying cockwing toward the sea. Through all the altitude and temperature changes of the tedious drive, almost as if it knew its birthplace, the EV-1 had raced across the mountains like a relentless stallion going home.

We cross the Golden Gate Bridge after midnight and park in back of the First National Bank. We slide down in our seats and sleep until the sun and traffic and Tuf's morning antics are too much to ignore. The skyline of San Francisco is a maze of splintering glass. Though it's not so unending as New York, this city is too big to ever find someone, especially by sitting in Golden Gate Park and watching the pilgrimages of old hippies.

—Let's find a phone book, Violet says. We've got to get moving, Romey. We haven't got the rest of our lives. You see that sun? I can see it moving.

We walk to the far side of the park and Violet clips a book from the booth near the women's bathroom. I go into a public bathroom and check the wound on my head. The gash is nearly gone and my hair is covering the rest, so you can barely tell I've been hit at all.

With Tuf between us, Violet and I sit on the soft grass and read through family names until we find two listings with the name Lessing matched to William. We only have twenty dollars and seventy-five cents, so I think about Violet's secret checkbook and become silent. She knows something is on my mind, but I can't say a word unless I want everything to explode. She gets up and runs to a payphone.

—Got it! Violet says as she hangs up the receiver. She knows him from college, Romey. She met the guy, but her husband's not related. Sounded just like my Aunt Louise, swear to God, I couldn't tell the difference.

—Who's Aunt Louise?

—I thought I told you. She works at a bank in Chicago. Right to my face, she called my father a son-of-a-bitch, just like that, without even knowing I think he's a son-of-a-bitch. Louise told me he's living in some crappy apartment in Connecticut. Doesn't matter, though.

—Why wouldn't it matter?

—Because my Aunt Louise is right. She gave me his address, but I didn't even write it down. He has lung cancer. Serves him right.

—You should have told me.

—You don't need to know everything about me, Romey. You don't.

She picks up the payphone receiver and dials the other William Lessing. Her eyebrows twitch and her lips curl. It's true. I don't know much about her. I remember that night outside of Chicago, how she stuffed Oscar's number into her pocket like she had a plan. And maybe she did. Was it Oscar who set up the bank account? Dark sedans can be everywhere. There have got to be a billion dark sedans in San Francisco alone.

—Is this Mr. Lessing? Violet says into the receiver. The one who knew Justin Bishop?

Violet nods, then explains a little about Hope and a little about me. Then her smile turns to a frown as she offers more information just to get an invitation. Finally, she writes directions on a napkin.

—We're in, she says and hangs up the phone, but the guy sounds like he's drunk. Don't tell me Hope's one fling was a loser.

We buy a map at a gas station and plot a course to Berkeley. We ask the old guy behind the counter about directions. He tells us it's a forty-minute drive to where Trumpet Street crosses Divine Avenue. It's an old neighborhood and an empty street that leads to a double house that looks like the before shot in a remodeling picture. Flakes of white paint have fallen over the wild bushes. A dented trash can is tipped at the end of the gravel driveway. The porch on the right side of the double is clean and organized, but the other is crowded with broken furniture and dead plants. Bill Lessing's house is the one with the junky porch.

—We called a little while ago? I say as two eyes peer out of a crack in the front door.

—That's an EV-1, he says with a slight slur.

—That's right. Hope Bishop told us you were on the design team.

—I thought you were a woman, he says and cracks the door further. You sounded like a woman on the phone.

—That was Violet, I say and wave to the car for her to come up to the house. Violet is my girlfriend, I say as he opens the door wider.

Violet leaves Tuf in the car and runs to the house. Bill Lessing is a short man with a t-shirted belly that tumbles over his belt. His thinning hair is tied in a ponytail and he hasn't shaved for days. His clothes look as if he's slept in them, and I try to imagine how long until I shake the thought from my head. He steps back and motions us in, but he stands at the door and looks at the car in the driveway.

—Lots of them still run, he says. It was a great car, a great car for its time.

The three of us go inside. Violet pinches her nose with her

fingers. The living room smells of dirty socks and booze. There's a half-packed suitcase open on the couch and clothes strewn across the floor. We follow Bill to the kitchen. He tells us to sit at the table.

—Can't say I remember Justin having a son, he says and shrugs. Maybe he did.

Violet and I sit, but the table is covered with unopened mail, beer bottles and paper plates with spoiled food. Bill offers us coffee, but we tell him not to bother. He takes a huge sip of his coffee and squints his eyes.

—I'd like to ask you about my father, I say.

—How old are you, twenty-one, twenty-two?

—Almost twenty. I was a baby when my parents died. I lived with my guardian, but he died, too.

—Let me look at you, he says and peers at my face with his beady eyes. Might be Justin's kid, I don't know. How is Hope?

—She's good. She lives just outside Chicago.

—Fermilab, he says. I was there a long time ago. Justin introduced me to his sister.

He moves a half-eaten sandwich off a kitchen chair. The smell of old food and sour beer is making me nauseous. Violet starts to peel the label off an empty bottle. I put my palms flat on the table and resist the urge to run out for fresh air. Entropy is all around us, a measure of the disorder of a system. It's the amount of energy unavailable for work as a result of the system's temperature, density and pressure. I think if I stay a minute longer, I might be drawn into this world of fat bellies and spoiled food.

Your father was something, Bill says after he puts his coffee cup down and takes a long drink from a near-empty beer. That's no bullshit, he says. We gave them hell, we did. Not like the kids today, with their bullshit manners. Neo-nazis and drag queens, the kids don't have anything to believe in. Not like Justin and me. You know how smart your old man was, kid? Smarter than me, that's for sure.

Smart enough to be dangerous. Intellect is despised in this country, always has been. Justin got himself into a little trouble, but that's no matter. The police made a huge deal out of it. The professors were jealous, that's what it was. They turned on him.

—You're saying my father was a criminal?

—Naw, he says. Don't take it like that. Justin kinda made loose with the law. A little hacking, that's all. Jesus, Justin's kid, right here at my table. I can't believe it.

Using his elbows, he rises from the table and lumbers to the living room. He takes a few shirts off the couch and puts them into a suitcase. Then he takes them back out and lays them on a chair. He pulls two beers out of the refrigerator and sets them in front of us.

—Hope said you were lovers, Violet says. You two made it in the old days, she told us.

Bill picks up a pipe from the counter and stuffs it with tobacco from a shiny pack. He lights it over and over as if it won't start, but smoke pours out like a chimney.

—You hungry? he says. There's a little place a couple of streets over. Serves a good hamburger for a little bit of money. I'm packing for Spain, but that's tomorrow. Hope and me, we used to go all over Chicago, jazz bars, dance clubs. We had a big time, but it's too late for that, too.

He pulls a jacket from the closet and fishes inside until he finds an airline ticket in the pocket, which he waves in the air. He grabs another beer from the refrigerator and tilts it upside down until he finishes half the bottle. He puts the plane ticket back into his pocket.

—Victoria Sanchez, he says, the rose of my elder years. A friend introduced us back in the fall. I'm leaving this dump. I'm going to Spain to meet her family. She's not much, a little plump, but what can I expect? That EV-1, that was my victory, hell of a car. It was an efficient design for the times. Now they've got hydrogen, but do they call me? Best automotive engineer in Palo Alto, and the phone is like it's disconnected.

Bill fishes in the closet and takes a large shoebox from the shelf. He carefully tucks it under his arm.

—Keepsakes, he says, nothing much, but it's got some things of Justin's. I'll buy you dinner.

I'm about to object, but Violet squeezes my arm. Bill leaves everything out on the table and the living room a mess. After we put Tuf inside with a bowl of milk and some canned tuna fish, Bill locks the door and fully inspects the battery compartment of the EV-1. The three of us squeeze into the front seat of his two-door Chevy. He takes a few deep breaths and shakes his head as if he's chasing away the drunk, and he seems to pull it off. Violet and I lock our hands together for the short, bumpy ride to a small Greek deli called Zorba's. We get there as the sun is dropping in back of the building and each car that goes by turns dark as a demon. We take a table near the front window and the waiter brings us water and menus. We order and tell Bill about how I was adopted and that my guardian was murdered. It's all outside his radar, all except the fact that I'm Justin Bishop's son and he was his best friend.

—Your father was a good man, he says. He had a rough start. Once he went a little too far with his hobby, broke into the National Science Foundation's mainframe. That was before the web, you know. Pure genius, the way he was able to do that. Just for kicks, he copied some data on black holes and let it loose on UseNet. They didn't appreciate the art of it.

—My father was arrested? That's what you're telling me?

—Shit, he says, it was nothing. Nowadays, the CIA pulls these kids in and accuses them of being enemies of the state. Bullshit. Then it was just scientists, the military and some college kids. They locked Justin up for a couple of weeks in a white-collar prison near Sundale. I'm telling you this because it affected him, and you should know. It knocked him back on his heels. From then on, he was straight as an arrow. He was the best, swear to God, but Berkeley freaked out over the thing. They didn't know what to do with the bad publicity, so they kicked him out. That's how he ended up at Royal Holloway.

—You ever meet Romey's mother? Violet says and I kick her under the table.

—Just once, he says. Justin did well at Holloway and it made Berkeley damn jealous. The physics department paid my way to London to get the scoop and lure him back. In 1985, rumors were flying around about big breakthroughs in string theory. He and Maria had an apartment near the university. She was a looker, believe me. You could be her son, now that I think of it. Good looking kid.

My hands clench. It is all I can do to keep my breath in rhythm. With Hope, the past collected in a jar like a motionless butterfly. With Bill, the past was exposed and hurting.

—Maria never quite got the hang of England, Bill says. Never made the cultural transition, I guess you could say. She didn't seem very happy.

He pries the lid off the shoebox full of keepsakes and empties part of it on the table in front of us. He picks through the mess of papers and badges, old driver's licenses, and several punched rail tickets to Los Angeles and Chicago. He uncovers a photo of my father playing basketball, and another of him with a couple of other guys at a bar Bill tells us was in downtown San Francisco.

—Here it is, he says and he holds up a paper that has my father's name on the front page. "Frequency Analysis of Composite Waves," Bill reads. Justin was working on the ideas before he left the U.S., he says. Berkeley wanted to lay claim, but the University of London had the publicity machine on full bore.

He hands me the paper. It's yellowed and has handwritten notes in the margins.

—It's the paper for the Nobel committee, Bill says. Maria

gave me a draft copy. She was worried. There were bankers sniffing around. Nobel committees don't like to be solicited, but that's just for the press. They're just like anybody else. They can be swayed, but Maria, she was worried. She thought Justin wanted it so badly, he might make a mistake. I knew better. Justin was fighting his way back from that prison crap. When I took a look at this paper, I found every fact dead-on perfect.

I try to read, but the lighting in Zorba's is too dim. I recognize some of the equations. The Whirl showed me a little of the math Justin had developed for the idea of dimensional time, which has since then been superseded by theories with multiple dimensions of eleven and even more.

—It's about energy-waves, Bill says, or particle-waves with DeBroglie wavelengths equal to Plank's constant. You'd have to be a mathematician to understand the details, but that's so small you can't really know for sure. You have to watch the effects from performing a blind experiment, and that's what Justin did. This paper summarizes his research at Fermilab. You can tell from the charts that the data was inconclusive. Never understood how Justin's theories even merited the committee's interest, but lots of these prizes are political. And there's lots of money to be made. From what I hear, people cashed in on Justin's ideas, big time.

We sift through the rest of the box, photos, receipts and tickets, but there is not much more about my father. Violet goes right for it and asks Bill if he knows anything about my mother's music, but he says he doesn't remember. Most of the junk in the box is about a young Bill Lessing, and it's difficult for me to believe he ended up like this, but any correlation, no matter how conclusive, is sometimes incomplete.

The waiter brings our sandwiches. I pile the keepsakes into the box and replace the lid.

—Hope called me when your mother and father died in that

plane crash, Bill says. There's another one who's brilliant. Hope was great. All these years of being around great people, and what am I doing? Marrying for money, ain't that a laugh.

He pulls the ticket from his pocket and stares at it a long time. He lights a cigarette, but the waiter tells him there's no smoking inside.

—You guys go ahead and finish, Bill says. Damn habit. Hope didn't let me smoke either.

He puts the ticket back into his pocket, picks up the box and goes to pay the cashier. Violet and I finish our fries. I take a last sip from my drink. Bill is already outside, so we head for the door to find him, but we hear brakes screech and tires squeal. There's a muffled crash and everyone, waiters and customers, rushes to the door.

—Excuse me, Violet says to a big woman blocking the door who doesn't move fast enough, so Violet squeezes around her. We land on the sidewalk, only to be blocked again by a crowd gathering behind stopped cars.

—Car came out of nowhere, a man says, and boom! Up on the sidewalk. I saw the whole thing.

My chest fills with butterflies. There's no sign of Bill. Violet pushes her way through the hunched crowd, and that's when we see him. Bill is sprawled on the ground. People circle around him, wringing their hands as if they want to turn back the clock, but can't. I drop to my knees beside him. There's blood coming from his nose. I smell alcohol mixed with hamburger meat and cigarette smoke. There's the scent of rubber and oil seeping from the pavement and circling around him like a shroud. He's as white as the Whirl was when he took his last breath.

—Call an ambulance! I scream. Somebody call for help!

It doesn't seem like anybody is moving. I see his shoebox has skidded across the road. The lid is off and some photos have spilled on the blacktop. The paper he showed us has a skid mark from a car tire, and the photo of my father playing basketball lies crumpled in the muck.

—Is he dead? Violet asks.

—Can we get an ambulance! I scream once more. Jesus, Bill, for God's sake, don't be dead.

The police come in a few minutes, but the sidewalk is still thick with people gawking. When the ambulance arrives, one of the officers takes Violet and me to a cruiser. I see two EMTs jump out with a pop-up gurney and rush to where Bill is sprawled. They check for his pulse. The older medic screams for more help. They put Bill on the stretcher and load him into the ambulance.

—We just met, Violet says to an officer. We don't really know him.

—Still, I'd like you to come down to the station. We've got a description of the car.

The officer calls in a report. Violet and I try to calm down in the back seat of the cruiser, but I remember the shoebox and jump from the car. The policeman yells at me, but I race across the street. I look everywhere, but I can't find it. I ask a couple on the street, another officer, a group of kids who flock from the surrounding neighborhood. No one has seen the damn box, so I check the ambulance. The back door is still open. I see them working on Bill. They bring out the probes and hit him with a blast of voltage. His body jumps and I'm about to vomit. The lights on top of the ambulance flash a chaotic rhythm. For a moment I see a red light pulsing, and I think it's the first time I've seen color in weeks.

I turn and see the police car with Violet in the back. Then the medics hit Bill again and, as I turn, I see his body jumps even higher off the stretcher. The color fades. The box is nowhere to be found. The watchers gather around the back of the ambulance. The light on top of the ambulance loses its pulse and slows to a lighthouse roll. I mash my fingers against my eyes as if I'm trying to dig them out of the sockets. The probe fires again, but I don't look this time. I stumble back to the cruiser and fall in next to Violet.

—Is he all right? she asks.

—It's no coincidence, I say.

—People get hit all the time, Romey. It's not our fault.

—It's not a coincidence, I say. It's probability, and that's the problem. I should have known.

The ambulance lurches through the crowd with its siren blaring. A police officer from another car comes over to our cruiser and stoops at the side window.

—They got a heartbeat, he says.

—No shit? says the officer in our cruiser. Is he going to make it?

—From the jaws of death, he says, then he notices us slumped down in the back seat. I'm sorry, he says. Are you family?

—Sort of, I say.

—Well if you believe in prayer, now's the time.

TWENTY

February 3, 1986

What do they teach at your seminary, Alberto, when it comes to new religions? I fear Justin is creating one of his own. His ideas not only have a way of explaining the most noble of actions, but also our subtlest of sins.

How can I tell the difference, brother, when the world is moving so quickly? This morning, it was Frank who put it in motion. He called to tell us the Fellowship Committee for the Royal Society would consider Justin's grant, but they wanted him at the Carlton House Terrace near St. James Park in less than an hour.

Justin began stuffing papers and notes into his briefcase. I helped him with his shirt and tie. My short black dress from high school with the small hole in the sleeve was all I had to wear, but I was glad he wanted me with him. We had been fighting over nothing, the way the couch is cluttered, the way he sometimes forgets I am here. I try hard to be patient as he builds this holy theory in his mind, but he must remember that all of us can not live and breathe his physics.

When we arrived at the Terrace, as they call it, Frank was pacing in front of the steps. Five minutes more, he said to Justin, it would have been too late. You think they suffer fools?

Justin's face turned red, then ashen. He said he thought he might be sick, so I helped him up the steps and to the bathroom in the lobby. As the minutes ticked by, Frank grew more impatient, but instead of making him angrier, it seemed to enliven him.

It is much better, he said to me, that Justin is afraid. He must understand how important this meeting is to his future.

He is just worried, I said. I should not have come. He worries too much about me.

Frank shook his head and took my hand. He cares nothing about you, he said. A boy like Justin is only concerned for his future, not yours.

I pulled my hand away and told him to stop telling lies, but he went on and on. He asked me if I thought about what being with Justin could mean to my life. He said I would be stuck at some college in the middle of nowhere with no money, no prospects.

I was terrified that Justin would come out and see us standing close together, but Frank would not let me alone. He touched my hair with his bony fingers. It was the first time anyone had touched me in weeks.

I should not have come, I said. You should have let Justin know earlier. That is why he is sick. He needed more time to prepare.

But Frank knows as well as I that it would have made no difference. One moment to the next is the same for Justin. He is in the future alone, but in many ways he understands the present more than me. In that conference room, Frank said, people would decide whether or not we will struggle for the rest of our lives. Why let your life, he said to me, be in the hands of others?

A woman as beautiful as you does not need them, he said. You need passions of the heart, not of the mind.

Then he kissed me on the cheek. Without the least encouragement, Alberto. It seems he thinks of me as someone who does not care for my own honor, but he soon found out! I slapped him as hard as

I slapped Victorio Remeri at school that day when we were barely fourteen.

Then, as if a devil was plotting, the bathroom door opened and Justin walked out as pale as Frank's cheek was red. I moved far away from Frank, but Justin had seen us together.

What is this? Justin said when he saw how flushed we both were.

Frank stepped forward and clapped Justin on the shoulder as if he was his oldest friend. The members are waiting to be amazed by you, he said. Remember, Justin, there will be few times in your life when how you handle yourself will be as important as this moment.

Justin stared from Frank to me. There was hurt in his eyes, but before I could say a word, Frank put his arm through Justin's, then the other through mine. He led us helpless like children up the steps to the second floor.

It is no time to be thinking of anything but your future, he said. What could be more important than the future?

Frank smiled at me as if he had proven the weakness of Justin's love. *Sfacciato!* I suddenly realized what he was doing. He was trapping me. Trapping Justin. This evil man was using the future to measure the worth of our lives, our love. How could Justin not see it? How could he not find this man ugly? If not for the way Frank treats me, then for the way he treats him.

Around the table that day in the headquarters of the Royal Society were five men and two women who ranked among the leading scientists in Britain. It was the end of old business and new business had begun. As with all meetings of the Fellowship Committee, the presentations were recorded. It was evident to me from the transcript that Justin was unknown to the members except for Dr. Leon Harrad, who had only that morning added the presentation to the agenda.

While a secretary made copies of the paper Justin had brought to the meeting, the Dean introduced him as a gifted doctoral student at Royal Holloway College. He gave a brief explanation of Justin's hypothesis on composite frequencies. Careful not to endorse the idea, Harrad turned the floor over to Justin, whose voice faltered as he began reading from his last-minute notes.

"I believe," he said, "there are at least three dimensions of time."

It was a bad start not only because of Justin's confusion over what had happened between Frank and Maria. He had also begun his presentation with the most controversial of his concepts. This was not what Frank or Dean Harrad had requested. The paper he had distributed was not what they asked him to bring. Frank had told Justin to present a briefing on composites and his ideas for measuring frequency changes, not his theory of time.

"The simple vibration or oscillation of energy," Justin continued despite the guttural sounds of Harrad's objection, "which is at the base of our atomic structure, creates the first dimension. This vibration, he said, I call oscillatory time. In effect, it takes a movement for the vibration to occur.

"The second dimension," he went on, "is caused by this vibration moving as a normal sequence of events. This I call sequential time, which is the type of time in common language. When you have a vibration and move it up and down, or back and forth, it moves also through sequential time. It creates a sinusoidal waveform."

"Is this part of string theory?" one of the members interrupted. "What is all this excitement about strings? It has my students in such an uproar that I can't get anything done."

"This is not about string theory," Justin said. "The paper you have in front of you describes what I believe are the three fundamental questions of physics. How does energy move? Is energy a wave or a particle, or both? And what makes energy display the characteristics of matter and force?"

"Are you sure this is not string theory?" the member persisted. "It sounds like string theory."

"I guarantee it's not about string theory," Justin said and his voice seemed emboldened. "String theory proposes that the fundamental elements of the universe are vibrating strings. My hypothesis is about three dimensions of time and the fields they create. How do the different particles and forces get their characteristics? How does one unit of energy relate to the rest of the energy in the universe?

"The third dimension of time," he continued, "is a resonance dimension that traps the vibrating energy to create a field. When certain characteristics are imposed by this resonance dimension of time, the energy displays characteristics such as mass and spin, at other times it becomes a force such as gravity. It depends on the character of the waveform."

"Why do we need another theory?" another member asked. "Doesn't string theory solve your problem?"

"String theory requires the concept of strings," Justin said, "a geometric invention that describes matter all the way down to the Planck length, 1.6×10^{-33} centimeters. It is not so different from the way we've always chopped matter into parts, only it's smaller, a hundred billion billion times smaller than the atomic nucleus. My hypothesis doesn't require the invention of anything, no matter how small. It is only about energy, an oscillation of probability, and how this vibration seems to move in the flow. It is about how energy creates different dimensions of time in its wake. Therefore time is not something of substance, but rather a mathematical medium of vibration."

"You would have us abolish time?" Harrad asked.

Frank Whirlpool must have been squirming in his seat. This was not the part of Justin's theories that he wanted the Fellowship Committee to hear. The concept of three dimensions of time was too speculative. It would get in the way of the actual waveform hypothesis and its implications for the possibility of altering human behavior.

"In a sense," Justin began again, "time is the result of energy existing. In the beginning, there was only the probability of energy. When the Big Bang occurred, energy was created. Time was a marking of the *movement of energy. From that time on, all energy has been conserved and is intimately connected as waveforms that resonate with each other.*

"As you know from textbook physics, composite waveforms result from the constructive or destructive interference, or superposition, of waves. Energy waveforms, no matter how complex, exhibit measurable characteristics such as frequency and wavelength. Other characteristics are beyond our measure, such as what resonant features make a proton different from an electron, but they are still characteristics of the waveform. The only thing holding us back from this simple realization is the way we think of and talk about the universe as something solid."

"Now you would have us change our language?" Harrad scoffed.

"At least a change in language would let us think about what we are actually saying," Justin said. "We need new ways to comprehend the universe. These ideas about waveforms are not really new. Philosophers from the beginning of history have been struggling with how to explain this exchange of energy, especially its non-local and spontaneous nature. When we look to other cultures, we find words that address the needs of the new physics, but many are too abstract to be considered scientific. The Buddhists have the Tao. The Hindus have the Brahman. The Jews, Christians and Muslims have the emanations of God in the form of divine prophets, Christ and Mohammed. Philosophers have idealism and metaphysics, even deism.

"We scientists rely on reductionism," he said. "Our culture has yet to deal with the simplicity of the new physics. We have words such as frequency, wavelength, causality and spontaneity, but these words still have no meaning to the average person. We may ask if we are on the same wavelength or describe when two people have the same thoughts as being of the same frequency, but we do not go far enough for us to really understand how intimately connected we are to the universe of energy. We are energy and all energy is interconnected."

"What do you suggest?" Harrad asked. "You would like us to throw over the wisdom of the centuries for this theory of everything?"

"It's not so different," Justin said, *"from the way we have always incorporated new words to explain new technologies. Take zero as an example. For thousands of years, the Greeks and other ancient cultures did not have the language of zero. It was a huge cultural gap that prevented advances in science and commerce. When Arabian scientists introduced it to Western scientists, the way was paved for immediate advances in science and business."*

"Then what sort of language would you suggest?" the Dean scoffed.

"Just de-solidify our current language. Use the language of energy. The physics community has been reluctant to escape the bonds of mathematics because it is the only way they have found to describe the world. Yet without a debate in a language we can all understand, we're trapped in a Newtonian world. We need to pass this knowledge along to the other disciplines. Unless we do that, our concepts of energy will be bound by useless attempts to fit it within the framework of matter. And that, from the time of Einstein, has been counterproductive to progress. With the language of energy, we can begin to realize how energy waves superimpose as interconnected waveforms. Only then will we begin to understand ourselves."

Letter continued...

The meeting was most uncomfortable. Justin was very nervous so his voice nearly failed him. Frank sat next to me and tapped his foot on the floor as if he was measuring the beats in Justin's voice. For nearly two hours, Justin talked while the Dean and the other members of the committee took notes. Once Justin had settled down, he did better and it began to look as though he was the teacher and these old men and women were the students.

I was proud of him, Alberto. There were many questions, but the members' stone faces began to crumble as they realized what he was saying. When Justin finished, the chairman thanked him and motioned for us to leave. Frank took our arms and pulled us out of the room.

You knocked it out of the park! he said to Justin as we ran down the steps to the daylight.

They only looked bored, Justin said.

Scientists such as these, Frank told him, would not be so gracious. They would have stopped you in the beginning. The gears of the machine are grinding, he said. Silvie is making things move quickly. These people have as much to gain from your theory as we do, maybe more. They'll make Stockholm aware of your research, he said. Very few scientists win a Nobel Prize for decades after a theory is conceived, but these ideas will cause controversy. Ideas have power, and power can make you rich!

The three of us floated down the steps arm-in-arm. Frank was between Justin and me, but Justin paid no attention. You see why I am worried, Alberto? Should the leader of a new faith ignore the demons created in its wake? I need your counsel, brother. If I am to reject this new religion, I need to know if you still find solace in the old.

TWENTY-ONE

The San Francisco police station is packed to the metal detectors with characters of all sorts and conditions: a seventeen-year-old girl for car theft, a middle-aged transvestite in ruby heels, an old lady with a mink coat who shoplifted a leather purse the size of a backpack. Though I'm just a witness and not one of the accused, I still plead my story to a disinterested man with a badge that gleams like a gold tooth.

—It was no accident, I say for the fourth time.

—All I see is a hit and run, the lanky detective says. If you know something more, you'd better say it and stop with the mystery.

The rectangular window on the interview room's wall is tinted. The tile under the table is scuffed. I wonder about those who were here before me and those who will be here after.

—If you're right and the guy dies, he says, it's manslaughter, hit and run. Withholding information could make you an accessory.

Another officer raps twice on the door and comes into the interview room without waiting for an answer. She's the policewoman who came in before and told us Bill was alive and being treated for internal bleeding at San Francisco Community Hospital. She hands the detective some papers, whispers something I can't hear, then leaves us alone.

—What the hell is this? the detective says. He slams the papers on the desk in front of me. A closed felony charge from New York City? he says. You failed to mention that.

—Can I talk to my girlfriend?

He lights a cigarette and looks right through me. A round clock with a hesitant second hand ticks aloud each increment until ten long minutes go by. The same officer opens the door and motions the detective into the hall. I rub my nose and stare at the tinted window where I can feel eyes watching. I push my stringy hair over my ears. When the detective comes back in, he's flipping a new printout.

—You must have a damn good lawyer, he says.

—I didn't do anything.

—This whole thing smells. First there's a warrant on you for grand theft, then somehow, like you got an angel on your side, it's pulled back by the district attorney. Now you turn up in San Francisco in the thick of trouble with a convicted prostitute you say is your girlfriend. If you're on the level, kid, you better take a look around.

—It wasn't just a hit and run, I say again.

—You give me something to go on, a name or a motive. Otherwise, there's nothing we can do but kick your butt to the street. Now, get lost, kid. I got things to do.

I bust out of the goldfish bowl and pick up my coat at the front desk. I see Violet smoking a cigarette near the bathroom. Her left hand is smacking her leg in time to some music she's thinking, but it's slightly offbeat and disjointed, as though she's thinking of other things and the music has fallen behind.

—Romey! she screeches as she sees me. Her pupils are dilated. This place is screwed, she says and hangs on to me. Bill's going to be okay. That's what they told me. I'm glad. He's just a joke, but he doesn't deserve to die.

I go to the desk and ask for some help in getting to our car. The sergeant arranges for a cab, but we do a change-up on the driver so he takes us to the hospital. It's three in the morning. The volunteer at the desk won't let us go up to Bill's room, so we take a couch and act as if we're sleeping until he forgets we're around. We eat a couple of donuts and do some coffee from the machines, then we sneak past the desk and ride the elevator to the fourth floor.

Bill is bandaged on his head and torso. He's watching television with earphones and has an IV running down his arm. He smiles when he sees us and we hug him like he's an old friend, until he cringes with pain.

—Sorry, I say.

—Don't worry. It passes. They've got me on some good drugs.

—I'm sorry about getting you into this.

—What are you talking about? he says. It was an accident. I wasn't looking. I got whacked a little, but I'll be fine. They say I'll be out in a week. No internal bleeding, so I'll be fine.

Violet sits in an armchair at the end of the bed. I look out the window on the streets of downtown San Francisco. He shows us his right side with the broken ribs, and his leg that's scraped from top to bottom, but he's alive and knows he should be dead, except for luck.

—It's strange, he says. Everything shut down. I didn't feel any pain. They tell me they hit me with the electric paddles. I have the burns right here, he says and lifts his shirt to expose the burnt circles on his chest. It was dark, he says, then all of a sudden it was light like daylight, except I was still out for the count. Very strange, I can tell you. If I didn't know better, you know what I mean. But that's crazy. Must be the drugs. I watched it on TV once, but I know it's crazy.

—You were gone, Violet says, no doubt about it. The cop said as much.

—A second chance, he says. I'm thankful.

It's the middle of the night and the painkiller is dripping from a bag into the tube, but his eyes are gemstones, as if he's emitting more light than reflecting. He's alive and that's more than I can say for the Whirl. Frank Whirlpool said he wouldn't die and did. Bill Lessing could have died and didn't. The difference is just in the physics, I suppose, electrons and molecules that feed on stray photons and molecules of oxygen and hydrogen.

If death has a cause, life should have one as well. Death must be more than a wet breath in and a dry rasp out. While the Whirl is resting in his grave, the electrons are busy transposing and decomposing in the physical mortality of cause and effect. Yet Bill Lessing's electrons are bouncing off this hospital room's walls like super balls. His energy is vivid. I can almost see the virtual particles condensing and disappearing as if to taunt all the energy conservation laws we humans can devise.

—We better let you sleep, I say.

—You got a place to go? he says.

—Don't worry about us. You just get better, Bill.

—You stay at my place. I'll be in here for a few days. It won't matter.

—We'll get along.

—Listen, Romey, he says and tries to pull up, but the pain prevents him, I owe your father a debt. He took me seriously. He was my friend. You can't just walk around the city, not Justin Bishop's son. It's the middle of the night.

I shake my head no, but Violet takes my arm and pulls me to the hallway. The nurse is busy doing paperwork at the desk, so we duck around the corner.

—Romey, she says, I'm sick of sleeping in that damn car and we haven't got any money.

—You mean, *I* don't have any money.

—What the hell do you mean by that?

—Nothing, I say. You're right. We should get out of here.

—And go where? We've hit the end of the country, Romey. So let's face it, we're nowhere.

We go back into the room. Bill asks for his coat, which is dirty and bloodstained, but it's hanging in the closet. I hand it to him, but he can't do anything with his banged up hands.

—You looking for the ticket? I say and he nods, so I reach into the pocket and hand it to him, but he doesn't take it.

—I can't go now, that's for sure. It's nonrefundable. I've been thinking about this. You take the ticket, Romey. You go see your mother's family. I'd be grateful, actually. It wasn't to be, Victoria and me. You'd be in Spain, not Italy, but you'd be closer to what you're looking for. Closer to your mother.

—The ticket is in your name, Bill. That won't work.

—I got a contact, he says, a former student who works for the airlines. He arranged a trip to the old CERN laboratory for my class a few years back. He'd do it for me. It's something I can do for an old friend you've made me remember. Maybe I'll forget Victoria. She doesn't need me. Maybe I'll go see Hope when I'm better. Who knows?

I hold the single ticket in my thumb and index finger and raise my eyebrows at Violet.

—Don't look at me, she says. Anyway, I've been thinking about going back. You said it. I should check on my baby. Not make trouble, you know, just check in.

—Maybe see your father? I say.

—Just take the damn ticket, Romey.

It doesn't take me long to give in. What else am I going to do? I get him some water. Violet sits on the window ledge and stares at the lights on the street below. Bill calls his former student from the airline, who wakes from a deep sleep. He says he can cancel Bill's ticket, which will open up a seat so he can issue a new ticket in my name. There will be an up-charge, he says, so Bill gives him a credit card number and it's arranged.

—Your ticket, Bill says, will be waiting at the airline counter for tomorrow's boarding. It's set. Nothing to it.

He tells me to get his house key from his pants, so I do and sit for awhile at the foot of his bed. Violet curls in a chair at the other corner of the room. We wait without talking until Bill goes to sleep. The nurse comes in about seven o'clock in the morning and kicks us out of the room. We don't wake Bill, but leave him a note that we wish him well. I have the same feeling leaving him as I did when I left Hope. I thought it was family, but maybe it's just a connection to what lies outside ourselves.

Violet and I walk in the morning light that's just beginning to outshine the streetlights. It's not far to Trumpet Street. When we get to Bill's house, Tuf jumps into Violet's arms as if we'd abandoned him to the wolves. It takes us only a second to know why he's freaked. Drawers are open that we remember were closed. The closet, which I distinctly saw him leave open, is shut tight. The unopened mail on the table is in organized stacks that the disorganized Bill Lessing could never have managed.

I pull the drapes over the windows and peer outside through a gap, but there's no traffic on the lonely street and no one lurking in the bushes. We sit for a long time on the couch without talking. We fall asleep for a few hours, then about noon Violet risks a run to the corner market and gets some cereal and cat food. Occasionally, we look out the window to check a sound or see a car at the intersection as it goes by too slowly. Violet smokes cigarettes and studies the map for how she's going to get back across the country.

We try to make love for what might be the last time, but we can't do it. Too much unsaid, so I try to sleep, but I can't do that either. When it's time to leave for the airport, I realize I'm leaving the one person on this earth I love, if not trust. My way goes to a place where love doesn't exist, never has. At least that's the way it appears to an orphan whose family had too many years to show it, and didn't.

We leave the key on the kitchen table and lock Bill's house. We fire up the EV-1 and pull away from the rundown double and I try to imagine Bill coming home. Was his elation just temporary, or will the second chance change everything?

—This is screwed, Romey? Violet says. Like we don't give a shit.

—Do you give a shit?

—I told you, she says. I decided. It seems that you've got the problem, not me.

—I need some time. I know some things that I wish I didn't know.

—You know nothing, Romey. You may think you do, but you don't.

We park the car and she walks with me to the baggage counter. Violet has tears in her eyes and it throws off my resolution. I wipe her tears away and keep the moisture on my finger. She turns and shakes her head and I watch her walk away without emitting a single sound of the chaotic argument that goes on in her head. I think she's going to come back, but she doesn't. I lose sight of the white hair with the black roots grown long, but her clicking heels still echo.

I toss my backpack onto the conveyor. I'm a bit queasy and my legs are weak. I realize I forgot to say goodbye to Tuf. The officer nods me through the metal detector, and I walk toward Concourse B. People are moving around me, against me, perpendicular. All are strangers, kids with popcorn and ice cream, business people with briefcases and computers, lovers arm-in-arm as if they're the only ones in the airport.

Then, I see him. A man with a bald head and huge nose, a sport coat with a white dress shirt and wooden heels that pad on the tile floor in fast repetitions.

—Philip!

The man doesn't turn, but quickens his pace. I try to run, but the perpendiculars are fixed and I knock over an old woman's luggage. I make it to where I think I saw him disappear, and I do a three-sixty to see if he's changed direction.

—It was him, I say to myself, and a man pushing a woman in a wheelchair looks at me as though I'm part of the show.

The airport surges with people that look like others I've seen before. The intercom announces my seat block. I shuffle along with the line and board the plane. My skin is clammy and loose as if it's draped over my bones. Bill's accident could not have been a coincidence, because the Whirl taught me not to believe in coincidence. Math can't reason with it. Philip knows where I am and where I'm going, and that means anyone who wants to hurt me knows where I am. And they can easily hurt me, I know, just as they hurt Bill Lessing, anywhere, any time, on or off a plane. What the hell do they think I'm going to find?

TWENTY-TWO

We plunge beneath the clouds to a view of the rocky, bungalow-encrusted coast of Portugal. I see the beginning of the long earthen fingers that reach across to Spain and on to the mountains of northern Italy. Below the plane's tilted wings is a trembling ocean that curls in troughs and crests all the way back to the shoreline of America. There is little to console me in the homeland behind or the ancestral land ahead. I'm a stowaway, a pretender in the seat of a good-hearted engineer with a new debt of life to pay. A million connects and disconnects push and pull me in a closed-loop circuit that wires my future, just as it has my past.

—We thank you for choosing Atlantic Airlines, the pilot's voice pierces the pressurized air. We hope you fly with us again.

The plane hovers weightless over the runway. The wings wave one way then another as a gust of wind takes us prematurely down and the plane hits the concrete once and bounces. The shock throws everyone but me into animated tension. I'm fixed on the skyline of Madrid and a cluster of ancient stone towers and tiled roofs. The brakes screech and the plane skids to a stop. Despite the warning sign flashing, passengers pop their seatbelts long before the doors burst open. I jostle with the others down the aisle toward the cockpit and down the steps and on to customs.

—*Buenos dias.*

I nod at the officer. His lips curl down. Things more important catch his eye: three women in Arab dress, a little kid traveling alone, a family of Nigerians that walks so close together that they bump like a pinball game. Dark complexion, black hair and deep-set eyes, the Spanish customs officer looks more like me than most of the people in America.

—*Hagan el favor de mostrarme sus pasaportes,* he says. *¿Cuánto tiempo se quedará aquí?*

—I don't speak Spanish, I say and hand him my passport.

—How long will you stay?

I place my return ticket on the counter and push it to him. It's the first time I've really thought of the future since leaving San Francisco. I've been thinking mostly of the Whirl and his flaccid face on that deathbed, and the attack on Bill, and my anger and love for Violet. If all went well, she should be in Nevada by evening. I explained to her twice how she must stop every four hours and recharge the batteries of the EV-1, but I know she won't remember. She'll be stranded and alone, but why should I worry about her? It's others who get hustled, including me.

—Is that your only luggage?

I nod. His focus leaves the pinball family and he concentrates on me.

—And you're staying a month? he says.

—I have relatives in Italy. In Mariano.

He shakes his head and asks me how much money I have and I tell him fifteen dollars. He sniffs and shakes his head again, then hands my passport and ticket to the uniformed guard at the end of the turnstile.

—*El inspector tiene que revisarlas,* he says and the guard takes my arm and pulls me to a room at the side. They check me with a handheld metal detector. A dog sniffs between my legs. They take me to a smaller room and dump my backpack on a table. They lay each item on the counter until a man in a dark blazer interrupts at the door.

—*El muchacho es bueno, yo conozco su familia.*

The guard growls and tucks my things back into the backpack. He stamps my passport for one week, not the customary month. He points for me to follow the man in the dark blazer. I follow him from the room and down the long concourse. We emerge at street level. From the blur of daylight, I hear a voice call my name. The blazer hears it too, and he yanks me through the crowd to a short man dressed in a light jacket.

—Romeo! he says and embraces me. Good to see you, Romeo!

I'm sure I've never seen him before, and how could anyone know I was here? The light jacket thanks the blazer, then this man I do not know hustles me willingly toward the doors.

—You are Romeo Argasti, he whispers, are you not?

I nod. He is balding and so fat I think if he would fall over he would just bounce back. When we get across the street, he stops and looks behind us. He seems relieved. He extends his plump hand and I shake it. He smiles broadly, but looks from side to side as if we are doing something illegal, and I am sure we are.

—I thought I might have the wrong plane, he says. Alberto figured you would not make it through customs. Big hassles, now. They think we should not travel. No?

—Who are you?

—A friend of your Uncle Alberto. I am Luis. He sent me to get you. Someone contacted him from America. Bill something, I did not get it so clear. Alberto will come tomorrow. He lives in Zurich. You stay with me. I spent some time in America, you know, in Philadelphia, Pennsylvania. My sister lives there with her husband, who is the brother of the guard who got you out of the airport. We will thank him later. I have a car. You come.

I follow him between parked taxis and vans as his portly sway whisks the dirt off their sides. A car cuts in front of us and I nearly lose sight of him at the entrance of the parking lot, but he comes back, grabs my hand and pulls me to where his car is parked on the curb.

—How was your flight?

—My Uncle Alberto, you said?

—Yes, Alberto, he is a good friend, a priest in my church before he was transferred to Zurich. He wants me to look out for you. He says you have trouble, but I don't want to know. You just stay with me until Alberto comes. I pay him a favor.

We pull from the curb and he gives some Euros to a woman in the booth, then he squeals from the lot. Once we're in traffic, he slams the accelerator. The buildings around the airport go by in a flash. My uncle Alberto is a priest, that's news. I think of the names of the relatives I know about, my grandfather Sergio, my grandmother Elana. My chest twinges with what I think might be a form of genetic pride, but since I've never had such a feeling before, it doesn't seem real. What if Bill had second thoughts and called them only to warn them? Warn them about me.

—After a long flight, you need a drink, heh? I buy you one in my bar, no charge, you see. That is where you will sleep. I have an extra bedroom and you will be fine. Alberto will be here early tomorrow.

The place Luis owns is on the first floor of a corner building where cars and motorbikes try to pass each other in a game that Luis wins. We park and enter the bar through the back door. The Ventura is a small, neighborhood bar and grill with men and women that look married or soon will be. Luis gives me one drink, then another, and I sit on a plastic barstool and stare into the horizontal mirror at my face, which looks as though I've had no sleep for weeks.

—When was the last time you were to Mariano? Luis asks.

—I've never been there, I say. The only other time I was in Europe, I went to England with my guardian, but never to Italy.

—You will like Mariano. It is quiet as a ghost, but where there is family, well, you know there is always too much noise. My family is in Barcelona. They live in the hills and that life was not for me. You like the city?

I answer his questions, but I don't really think about what I'm saying. It takes one more beer to feel queasy, and as much as I try to prevent it I'm close to tears and telling him my story with few omissions. In a foreign land, acquaintances become friends too quickly.

Luis puts me to bed on the second floor in a dank, dark room with a single bed. The ceiling spins a little, but I know the room isn't really moving. It's me. Momentum equals mass times velocity. The change in the momentum of a vector is equal to the impulse it receives. An impulse is the force acting on the object during a specific time interval multiplied by the average force over that same time interval. People don't live in a vacuum. There is always force and time flowing by us, constructive and destructive, connecting and reconnecting, but it's the liquor that makes the room spin.

I sleep through until almost noon. I take a bath in an ancient tub that's rusted and cockeyed on the floor because the lion's feet are slightly bent. I say good morning to Luis and walk up and down the crowded streets of Madrid until I get rid of my hangover. Alberto comes at two in the afternoon. He doesn't look like a priest. Dressed in full leathers with chaps and a thin black coat, he has a motorcycle helmet tucked under one arm. He wraps the other around me in a bear hug, then releases me and slaps me on the shoulder.

—My God, look at those eyes. Maria lives! he says and then hugs his friend Luis. You have taken good care of him?

—He drank a little, Luis says and shrugs.

—Say something, nephew. What do you think of Luis? What do

you think of your Uncle Alberto?

I can't do anything but self-consciously smile and stare because he takes off his jacket and I see the black shirt and white collar. Luis brings us two beers and the smell of hops makes me nauseous.

—You look like a good boy, Alberto says as we sit down at a back table and eat. My sister did well. Almost a man, you are.

—How did you know I was in Spain?

—Your father's friend in San Francisco. He called and told us you would be on the plane. He was very concerned. He told us about the murder, Romeo, that your guardian was poisoned. I was sorry to hear that. May God bless him.

—His name was Frank Whirlpool, I say, but I called him the Whirl.

—He took care of you. That is a great gift. The news of your coming has hit this family like an earthquake, Romeo. We haven't seen you, you understand, because of the way things were.

—How was that?

—Very bad, he says and takes a long drink from his glass. Americans do not realize the way it is in Europe. Illegitimacy is not uncommon, but it is feared. There is too little land. People are always fighting for a little bit of dirt and stone. My father would never think of contacting you. He still lives in the old Church, and the Church still lives in the past, Father forgive me.

—Because I'm a bastard? I say. Is that what you mean?

—Many kings and popes were illegitimate, he says, so it is not as terrible sounding as you speak it. A family fears the unknown. Who will inherit? Who will take care of the parents? We do not have so much as Americans. It is not that way in your country because everyone is rich, maybe? To me, you are my twin sister's son, my nephew. I will take you to my father, and I will fight for you to be taken into the family. Would you like that?

He sits back and looks at me as if he's checking for familiar signs, the color of my eyes, the pallor of my skin, a distinctive wave in my hair. He was my mother's twin, I realize, but it doesn't register anymore than if my mother had no brother at all. It was my mother who wasn't flesh and blood, so how could a twin be any more real?

—Because my parents weren't married? I say. That's why you never tried to see me?

—We do many things that should not be forgiven, he says. It makes me ashamed. Your parents were not married, but sometimes I wish my parents had never married. I would not have to put up with my father, your grandfather, but of that you must learn on your own.

TWENTY-THREE

Alberto hands me a helmet. It is just after daybreak of a new day and the church bells across Madrid have calmed from their hourly oration. He kneels beside his motorcycle in the parking lot of the Ventura and checks the oil, then he kicks the back tire. I think about telling him more about the murder and the frame, and about Philip at the airport, but I haven't figured out how to make the high-pitched racket of America sync with the barely audible timbre of Madrid.

—A 1990 Moto Morini, he says. A classic, you know, for alpine riding, as the Transalp Honda. You know motorcycles?

I shake my head and run my palm across the smooth contour of the Morini's glossy gas tank. A front cowl curves around the bike like the chest of a proud horse. The motorcycle's frame runs in an arching spin horizontal under and over the massive engine to the center sprockets of the rear wheel.

—We could have sent your luggage by carrier, he says as he straps my small bag to the back of the cycle, but you have so little, maybe this is just as good. He launches a leg over the beast. We buy you some things in Mariano. Hop on, Romeo. Overhead valve, V-twin. Are you afraid?

I shake my head, but I am a little in awe of both the bike and this new uncle who is a priest but who does not act like one. It occurs to me that I have at least a quarter of the same genes as Alberto, and each time I look at him I see another familiar gesture or expression that connects us to some ancient family tree. He dons his helmet and only his nose protrudes. I lift my wobbly leg over the back seat and bounce to a stable spot behind him. He starts the Moto Morini and the roar is a rocket's. I put my hands on the chrome sidebars that run along the seat. Alberto waves goodbye to Luis and we are off with a G-force that almost leaves me behind.

—Make sure you hold on tight! he yells above the noise of the engine. Some of these roads are rough.

I hold on even tighter and the world becomes a warm streak as the motorcycle weaves across brick and stone and blacktop roads. We leave Madrid behind and, according to signs I decipher, we take the highway toward Barcelona. The land is thick with trees and wide with newly tilled fields, and people along the road wave to us from trucks and bicycles. Because of me, he tells me, we stop more times than he would alone, but we still have too little time to talk. I am desperate to know about him, about me. It has only been four hours and my butt feels like it's on fire, though pain is little to pay for such a whirlwind introduction to family.

—Do you know much about your mother? he asks in a park outside Barcelona.

We have stopped in the afternoon sun to eat sandwiches made from beef and dry bread. There is a church at the end of a stone walkway that reaches up into the sky with a looming tower.

—I have a photo, I say and show him. She was a musician. That's about all I know.

—It's a shame. He looks carefully at the photo. She was wonderful, he says. She was a siren. When Maria played the cello it sounded like the angels singing. Nothing mattered to her but music, not the words of others, or the ways of the Church. That is what caused the problem, you know. It is why my father never speaks of her, or you.

—Why would my grandfather hold that against me?

—The ways of the family go back to Constantine, he says, and even before. Traditions were carved into the walls of the catacombs. Sergio lives in the shadow of his father and grandfather and back through time. There is pressure for eternity, as if everything is fixed. Maria had no sympathy for tradition. First she refused to take communion. Then she decided to live with a man before she was married. That was something my mother and father could never accept. I was surprised a little myself, I am ashamed to admit.

Alberto gives me the photo and I stuff it into my pants pocket behind the empty wallet. The road in the highlands narrows until it becomes a thin ribbon of blacktop through Marseilles and Monaco. Before nightfall, we stop and take a warm swim in the velvet Mediterranean where the trees along the water give some privacy. We stay the night at a monastery in Imperia near Genoa.

In the morning, I can barely think of another day on the hard Morini seat, but Alberto's encouraging smile is enough to convince me. We fly along the coast to Genoa and La Spezia, then inland to Sarzana, and through the highlands of Tuscany toward the village of Mariano.

—You pay your respects, he says and pulls the motorcycle off the road.

To the right is a mild hill with a short wrought iron gate and behind it a graveyard. The sky is as clear as Violet's eyes, and I realize I remember them with less detail than before. It scares me. I want her to be here with me. I want to tell her how proud I am of having such an uncle, and I want her to give me strength as I walk to the grave of my mother.

—Maria rests among the Argastis on the hill, Alberto says. My brother Favio who died at birth is here. As is my aunt, your great

Aunt Floria, and Lavinia who was the only famous painter to come from Mariano since before the time of Garibaldi.

My feet are anvils. I plod up the hill behind my uncle. Stone markers are encrusted with lichen, and broken stones lean against others. Near an olive tree is a small gravestone in front of which Alberto drops to his knees and touches his chest in the sign of the cross. No lichen or moss mars the obelisk. The word *Pax* is chiseled above the name so deeply that a little dirt has caught in the letters.

—She was so good, Alberto says, his cheeks on fire. I miss her. Even now, I miss her. She was wronged.

I kneel beside him. The stone is chiseled with the name Maria Elana Argasti. I want my eyes to cry like Alberto's, but they're dry as dust. Below my knees is a ghost, transparent in death as she was to me in life. Not far below this ground is what is left of Maria, now wrinkled flesh and crumbling bone. Alberto puts his arm around me and his emotion is like a child's from whom something profound has been taken. The branches on the olive tree droop against the sky. I touch the marker where the word *Pax* is etched. The stone is hot from the sun. I touch the ground and find it cool and dry.

Alberto's arm slips from my shoulder. He stands and says he will wait by the road. I want him to stay. I want him to be my priest. I want to confess that there is too much distance between the living and the dead, that I do not feel my mother's presence and the face that stares from that picture is fixed, nothing so moving as this swirling ground.

Alberto leaves me alone. I stay bowed before the gravestone. Below the roots and rock there is a box with my mother's remains, and I form her image in my mind, her eyes, her hair, her mouth and nose. Her eyes are dark like mine, her hair long and flowing. Is she as beautiful in death as she was in life? Is she smiling now that her son has finally come to see her?

I pull the tattered photo from my wallet and place it on the ground in front of the marker. She stares at me with her glossy smile as if she knew, someday, I might be looking. The afternoon sun pushes down on my head and scorches my neck. My heartbeat slows to a throb that syncs with my breathing. I stare so hard at the picture that I bore through it into the ground to the casket and the face that no longer smiles. My knees dig into the rocky soil. My cheeks burn from the wind of the ride. The black and white photo lies on the ground baking like bread. I run my fingers through my hair, which has been mashed from the helmet so that it curls upon curl like a twirling rope.

I have heard that hair still grows on the dead, so I know my mother's is far too long. I have heard that electrons from one person mix with the electrons of another. The current in my spine surges down my arms and legs to the tips of my fingers and toes. There are pocked marks on the dry ground beneath me. A huge drop explodes on the photo, and I wipe the wet from my eyes.

The sun slips behind a cloud and the heat dissipates. Not knowing if I will ever be so near my mother again, I stand weak-kneed and walk down the hill of my ancestors to where the priest waits with lips turned down. Alberto's face is as pale as mine feels. His hair is mashed curl upon curl. He dons his helmet and hands me mine. Just before the motorcycle roars away, I glance up the hill and it occurs to me how just it is that, despite the objections of the living, the dead still go on.

TWENTY-FOUR

March 15, 1986

First you leave me, Alberto, now it is Justin's turn. Why did he go at this moment when everything hangs in balance? We fight too much, but does that give him the right to abandon me? I am alone in this wretched flat. I sit in the dark with his lingering scent.

It will take less than a moment to do the test, he told me, but if that is true, then why will he be so long in America? If it takes less than a second to smash one proton into another, why did he go for three months? He has too many distractions. Silvie, he tells me, is with him. He had the nerve to say she is there because she needs to understand more about the physics, but he must know how it makes me feel. Why does he let these outsiders conspire to destroy our love?

In his last letter, he told me I should savor my time. He said I should concentrate on my music, forget about everything else, even about him. He uses my music for his own purpose. From the time I wake to the time I sleep, I work on the string quartet, but not for a moment do I stop thinking of him and his physics, praying for him and his memory.

How could he imagine I could ever forget? If only it were

possible, Alberto. You remember how it is with me. If Justin thinks I could so easily forget about love, he does not know me. I am with him in spirit, his companion in form, spending what I have left of courage to give him more.

I could blame his indiscretions on the long hours he keeps or the hounding of his father's success, but he should know there is a bond between us. We are two notes fixed in a measure. As he pursues his theories of time, he forgets how we make the future, just as a song runs through us from past to present. Like you, brother, one who refuses to even give me the solace of a letter, Justin risks losing the present. He does not understand how history runs like poison in our veins. We must constantly reorder the disorder of our song. I remember Papà's stale breath and the smell of wine turned to vinegar. I think of how saintly Mamma looked lighting the candles around the image of our Lord. You know as well as I do that she will suffer for Papà's disorder to the end of her days.

I had hoped not to trouble you, Alberto. You are starting a new life and should not be burdened with my unrest. Yet I must turn to someone, confess my blunders to another.

It seems I have fled my sins in Mariano only to land in the arms of another sin just as vile. An unwanted visitor came this evening, but I swear I did not ask him to come. For all the world, I would never have asked him to come. He is a person who acts as if he respects Justin, but who secretly disdains him. He acts as if he loves me, but he disrespects everything and everyone.

I thought it must be a mistake. He knocked so softly on my door that I decided someone must have lost their way. You will be angry, brother, but at first I was excited that someone had come, so desperate was I to leave my cello for a human voice.

I ran to the door, but when I realized it was Frank Whirlpool, I held the door closed. He said he needed to talk. Through the door, he said he had news from America. I was in my purple robe and told him it would be improper for me to let him in, but he would not go away. He said he was exhausted. He said he had not felt well for days, but I still should have made him go.

You know, Alberto, it is against my nature to turn away even a dog. He pushed through the door. He hugged me as a friend. He told me he was lonely and having trouble sleeping. He handed me his coat that stank of alcohol. He said he had been working too hard and had not eaten anything for days. I told him he should stop drinking and then he might sleep.

As you read this, my brother, you must be growing angrier, but I put a pan of water on the stove for tea. I could feel Frank watching me, as he has watched me before. He began telling me about his life. He was married once, he said, when he was a young man, but it lasted only three years. He said I reminded him of her. He told me her name was Karen and that she made him feel warm, the same way I made him feel.

The water came to a boil. I poured two cups of tea. He pushed the drink back on the counter and put his arms around me. I pulled away, but he would not stop. I slapped him and he slapped me. I tried to scream, but he put his hand over my mouth. I could barely breathe, so I took the cup of hot water and threw it in his face!

A neighbor pounded on the floor above us, but Frank still would not leave. He pleaded with me to forgive him. I think of you, he said, when I am lonely. You must be lonely, too.

Then tell Silvie to come home, I said. You will not be so alone.

You could not be that stupid, Maria, he said. Surely you know. Why do you think they went to America when there are plenty of laboratories in England? Justin has no idea what he has in you. Young men never know.

He touched my cheek. It felt like nettles. I said nothing, Alberto, but you must know that I nearly fainted from his poison. I pushed him as hard as I could. I ran to the bedroom and tried to close the door, but he held it. I pushed harder and the door pinched his hand. When he screamed, I let the door free. He grabbed me and kissed me so hard that my lip split against my teeth.

When he saw my blood, thank God, it stopped him. Blood is the most fearful of sights, even to a drunken man. I slammed the bedroom door and locked it. I pressed my ear against the crack. I could hear him taking a glass from the cabinet and pouring from the bottle of whiskey Justin keeps for company. He came to the door and, again, asked my forgiveness. My robe had torn open and I wondered if he had seen me. I wrapped it tighter and held myself against the door. Go away! I shouted. You should not be here.

They are lovers, Maria, he said in the devil's voice. We can have our revenge. Unlock the door.

I slid to the floor. I clutched my robe around me. Frank's lies oozed through the cracks in the door. I waited forever until I heard the door to the hall open and close. I could not tell if Frank was gone or if he was just trying to make me a fool, so I waited as the clock chimed eleven times on the hour. I opened the door. The room was empty. I bolted the front lock. I could still smell his putrid tobacco and liquor. I could taste the sweet blood from my lip. That is a mix of the senses I shall never forget.

TWENTY-FIVE

Mariano folds with the valley into the mountains of Massa-Carrara. The highland forests give way to the endless rows of grapevines on the lower hills of Lucca. The motorcycle loses its smooth gait on the uneven lane that rolls up and down toward a single ornate steeple with a tall spire and cross. Alberto grasps the clutch and lets the engine lose several octaves. Lining the narrow streets by the church are rows of stucco houses. He runs the Morini in first gear. The air is thick with a mingling of feces and fruit. Stray stones get caught beneath the motorcycle's tires and shoot like bullets against the short fences that line the road.

An old woman runs out of a small house. Alberto pulls in front of the gate. As she draws closer, I see tears streaming down puffed cheeks. She wipes a huge bubble away with the tip of her apron. I jump off the bike and this old woman with deep wrinkles and a pale flowered dress, this time shifted image of my mother, hugs me for a long, long while. Elana Argasti's body is a pool of water. I nearly swoon from the smell of garlic.

—*Mamma*, Alberto says, *tuo nipote, Romeo.*

—*Io sono nonna*, she says and hugs me again. Alberto tries to translate for me what she is saying, but he can't do it nearly so fast as she speaks.

—She says your face reminds her of Maria, he says. It makes her cry. She is glad you came. She wants to know if you want something to eat.

—I'm fine, I say.

—There is something you should know about your grandmother, he says. When she tells you to eat, you eat. She thinks you look thin. She accuses me of starving you. *No, Mamma!* It is good to see her so happy.

We enter the doorway through a wooden frame thick with vines and flowers. She takes my hand and pulls me to the kitchen. She moves a chair and makes me sit. She flutters about like a bird, and Alberto says she's obsessed by the worry that I could wither away before her eyes.

—*Dov'è Sergio?* asks Alberto and she answers him. He is at church, Alberto tells me. I told you so, he says. Mamma tells me he was in the fields, but he wanted to go to confession. There are only two things in the world for Papà, wine and confession.

Alberto sits across from me at the table and picks up the local paper. My grandmother pours olive oil into a pan and dusts in some herbs. She cuts up oranges and apples. She uses a wooden spoon to push herbs in a sizzling pan. Her faded dress is covered to her ankles with an apron that has a pattern of chicken heads. She concentrates on her cooking, and her eyes almost close, but when she looks my way they spring open, and I know she sees in my look another long dead.

—You like lamb? Alberto translates without looking up from his reading. She will cook you a feast. She says you will be glad you came. Maria would be proud. You have her face.

He puts down the paper. I follow his eyes to his mother who has walked away from her smoking pans and leans against the sink.

—I wondered how long it would take, Alberto says and goes to her and gives her a shoulder massage and says something in Italian that sounds very soothing.

Elana returns to the pans. I eat a mixture of lamb, egg and greens that tastes like a meat-filled omelet. It's delicious. She gives me wine and the second glass goes to my head. It's nearly three in the afternoon and the sun has gone behind the hill to the west. She goes to a drawer and pulls out photos of Maria as a child. Pudgy as a baby and thin as a teenager, Maria soon loses any shape but the curving form of the cello, which must have never been far from her when a camera was near.

—She has a letter, Alberto says. Maria wrote lots of letters, but most are gone.

Elana hands me an envelope. It is wrinkled and dark with age. I pry open the flap that has resealed from being pressed in the pages of a book. The words are in Italian, so I can't read anything but the signature, which says "*Amore, Maria.*" I hand the letter to Alberto.

—"Dear Mamma and Papà," he starts to read, but stops for a moment, and I think he is going to cry those unabashed tears, but he is only waiting for Elana to stop shaking.

—"I often think of Mariano and the farm," he reads. "I fear this country will never feel like home. Justin has gone to America to do research and I am working hard at University. Soon you will hear what I am playing, because I am saving money for the train ticket home. I hope you will like my music. It reminds me of what the organist played at Saint Jerome when I was little. When I play it, I think of our village and the red tiled houses that shimmer in the sun."

Alberto stops for a moment and clears his throat. My grandmother sits in a chair beside me and puts her hot arm around my neck. The house is silent except for the occasional sound of a car or the telltale clashing of a bicycle chain.

—"I have something to tell you when I come home," he reads,

"but I must tell you in person. I will try to be there in the spring. Try not to love me too dearly. I may disappoint you. I wish my life was my own, but I know what I feel and what you feel are connected by more than memory. No matter what happens, try to find forgiveness in your heart."

He hands me the letter and I stare at the scrawling ink and the smudge on the left side, which I realize to my horror is the stain of a tear. Elana's or Maria's, it's from a time before I was born when tears were shed because of my coming.

My grandmother kisses me on my forehead and wipes her eyes with a hand towel. She begins to clean up the kitchen. I walk around the house for no other reason than to feel solid ground beneath my feet. Everything is too much in motion, the convulsing of time, the flow of family, the forming of one gene from another through generations. What is this pull I feel to Elana? How can I be more at home in this old woman's arms than I've ever felt anywhere before? I can feel my own mother moving, not smiling or anything so garish, but simmering with a genetic link between Elana and me. What force is this beyond the four forces of physics, a tug between parent and child, family and clan, human and nature? How powerful and intelligent are these electrons that spin around protons and neutrons in remarkable waves of energy and matter that echo past and reach into the future. I always thought we voyage across this universe alone, but nothing could be further from the truth.

The afternoon hours drift away. I sit at the table and watch Elana prepare vegetables for this evening's meal. A little after five o'clock there is a ruckus at the front door. Elana wipes her hands on the apron and hangs it on a hook behind the door. Alberto is already at the front door and argues with someone in a sweep of Italian that has no pauses, only jabs and waves of the hands. Elana joins in the fray, and I stand by the sink and think of all the places I would rather be than here, waiting for the man whose name is never used in passing.

—He is very tired, Alberto says as he comes back into the kitchen. He needs some time to rest. You want some more to eat? Have some more to eat. There are apples and a pear.

I shake my head. The thought of more food makes me queasy, as does Elana's screaming. The shouting soon turns to whispers that rise and fall like the hills I see through the window. The cut-up fruit that Elana stacked on a plate by the sink is going to waste. The apple is almost black; the pear has hardened. I hear the heavy boom of stocking feet on the plank floor. The sound stops at the door and there is loud breathing, but I cannot make myself turn to greet its source. There is a grumble, not a voice.

—*Papà* wants you to go with him, Alberto says over the shoulder of my grandfather.

I turn and am surprised that Sergio Argasti is short and slight, and his face is covered with a careless, white beard. His right hand curls with evidence of stroke. The stooped man turns and Alberto nods that I should follow. My feet move as if by command, and I follow through the front door and out to another building attached to the house by a fence.

My grandfather opens the door and lets me go in before him. He switches on a light. He arches his back as if he will stand erect, but it is too late in the day and he must be tired from working in the vines. The room is small. There is a bed and chest of drawers with cobwebs that stretch from the ceiling and walls. A nightstand with books is covered with dust. A cello with no strings is on its side in the corner. Music books are stacked on a bookshelf next to a music stand that serves as a place for a bow with frayed strands.

—*Mia rosa*, Sergio says in a voice like rocks shaking in a box.

On the stand is a page of music. My pulse pounds like a tom-tom as I push cobwebs away. It's a Vivaldi score, preprinted music. My pulse disengages from its race. I pick up the lined paper and hold it so Sergio can see.

—Do you have any of her music? I ask but he shakes his head to tell me he doesn't understand. For the cello? I say.

—*Violoncello!* He points to the one in the corner with no strings, then some music books in a small bookshelf by the bed. I take out a book of songs with a dark binding that is torn a bit at the edges. I sift through some loose papers and flip through the other books. I feel like a grave robber, but my urge is not about wealth, but that these things touched my mother's hand.

—Do you have any of her music? I resort to using my hands to mimic writing music. Do you know of any music?

—She could play like no one else I ever heard, Alberto says as he steps in from outside. She got the talent for both of us. I remember her playing with this window open. As we worked in the fields, the music would drift up the hill. When the plane went down, Papà tried to rent this room, but no one would take it. Everyone remembered Maria. This room never changed, and my parents are too old to change it, now.

—*Lucifero!* Sergio suddenly waves his hand around the room and talks fast and angrily. I stumble on the bed frame and nearly fall, but Alberto catches me.

—He is *matto*, Alberto says, a crazy old man. He sees devils. Since the stroke, everything bad is the fault of the devil, even the sun when we need more rain.

Above the dresser is a mirror with three photos stuck in the side of the frame. One is Elana and Sergio at their wedding. One is Alberto and Maria when they were seven or eight. They were laughing and playing on a swing. The other photo is of Maria alone when she was ten or eleven. She hides behind the cello.

What trajectories of particles combined to change a smile into fear? The way she holds that cello reminds me of the way you hold a rope when it's all that keeps you from falling. The bumping of particles, the combination of atoms, the forming of molecules caused by the forces of electromagnetism. Is that what it takes to create a string quartet? Or is there a slight diversion, a changeup from what was before to what is after? Like the singularity before the Big Bang, when all the matter and laws of the universe were held in a state of immobility, timeless, breathless, was there a point where my mother escaped the causal world and let the spontaneous world reign? How did she create the music of angels?

Sergio has stopped ranting. My eyes move from the photos to the mirror, and I see the reflection of my grandfather behind me. He is trembling, his deformed hand is at his face and he scrubs his stubble cheek. As if there is something I can do, I turn to reach for him but he bolts out of the door.

—I'm surprised, Alberto says. He rarely lets anyone into this room. He sits here sometimes, alone for hours.

Alberto turns off the light. Elana waits by the door of the house. Sergio stands near a water well built up to knee-level with round stones. My grandmother asks me to stay the night and Alberto unlashes my small pack from the Moto Morini. The sun is gone and we stand in the dark.

—*Uno notte*, Sergio says.

—One night? Alberto translates. You stay as long as you want, Romeo, and to hell with him.

My grandfather walks to the house and takes a cup from a hook by the door. I watch him shuffle to the well, pull the bucket toward him, dip the cup and take a long drink. Elana holds me to her chest and pulls her pale dress around me in a warm cocoon. There is running water in the house, but I wonder if the water from the well is somehow better, maybe cooler, at least after so long a day in the fields.

TWENTY-SIX

A train rumbles into the station along the tracks where Alberto and I stand. I clutch the envelope Elana gave me before I left Mariano. There are no sheets of music inside or answers to questions that mothers should have time to reveal to their children, but it is something of a clue. Faded and smudged from handling, the return address is still readable.

—You have any money? Alberto says.

—Fifteen dollars.

Alberto and I left early this morning, long after Sergio and Elana had gone for their weekly trek to the market in Massa-Carrara. Rather than hear my grandmother's relentless pleading, Sergio had let me stay for three days more and would have let me stay longer. I made the decision to leave of my own free will, but it was difficult. From each dawn to dusk, I would walk with my grandmother or uncle on the cobbled streets of my ancestors, where I was introduced to friends and neighbors as the long lost son of Maria.

On the last day, it had rained a little in the afternoon and villagers took full advantage of the lull in fieldwork. Mariano came alive with the opportunity for celebration, and I drank sweet wine made from red grapes picked from the hill above the house. I ate bread and vegetables from the garden. When the rain subsided, I walked alone to the hill and stood next to my ancestors' markers, the sentinels that guard my mother's small grave as if they could, somehow, do for her in death what they could not in life. I was sorry, too, that I was not there to protect her and for her to protect me.

For hours I sat on top of the soil above my mother and experienced the woozy dreams of suffering until darkness covered us both. As I walked alone down the hill to the house, I realized how these few short days had teased my empty history with the cause of family. It was almost enough to forget my place, or lack of place, but there was far too much unfinished. There was more to find than my past. There was murder and until I found some answers there would be no rest for my mother, or me.

—This will get you as far as London, Alberto says and hands me a ticket. You can sleep on the train.

—I'll be fine. I thank you for everything.

He puts a rolled-up wad of Euros into my palm and closes my fingers. The speaker announces final call.

—I don't know how I'll repay you, I say and he hugs me and shakes his head to say there is no need. I lift my pack and am about to leave when he turns me around and kisses me on both cheeks.

—You should know something, he says.

Alberto takes my arm and pulls me aside, and we let other passengers go by us. The last whistle blows, but the linemen are still standing at the newsstand talking with a fat vendor in a ball cap and tweed jacket.

—When she needed me, my uncle says, I was not there. All those years ago through our school days and summers, your mother and I were always near. Twins and never apart, people would say, Maria and Alberto, but I listened to my father and that was my mistake. I ask your forgiveness, Romeo. She wrote me many letters, but Papà had the Seminary stop them from getting to me. I knew what he was doing. I could have called her. It might have helped, somehow. When she died, I could have fought for you, but I thought she had done wrong, and I was doing right. It was terrible what I did to my sister, and to you.

I shake my head because I can think of nothing else to do. That was a long time ago, I say weakly.

—I cannot understand, Alberto says, how I was left on this earth when she was so talented and beautiful inside. Our father betrayed us. Maria did nothing to deserve his anger, but because I was ignorant I helped my father in some stupid hope that I would be worthy of Heaven. But Heaven is only fear, God forgive me. It means nothing when one is dead on Earth.

—Don't worry about it, I say because he insists I say something, hear my voice, her voice. And somehow what I say must be adequate, because he leaves me with a dim smile and without another word.

Eight hours later, I still see his reflection in the train's dirty window, white collar and wavy hair. I feel sorry for this priest who thinks Heaven is only hope. What point is there to wearing a collar if it doesn't protect you from fear?

The border of Switzerland goes by in a flash. The train's engine drags the heavy cars kicking and scratching into the heights of the Alps. Propped in the cold compartment, I watch the brilliance of Mariano dim in my head to a tired glow, but the constant station stops and the lights of Geneva and Dijon keep me from sleeping. Day breaks as the train reaches the outskirts of Paris. By late morning we plunge into the dark tunnel and through the catacombs beneath the English Channel. I close my eyes until England appears in the window's blur. The countryside is not nearly as bright as the sun-blasted fields in Tuscany, and by the time we reach the grimy slums of London, the sun is on the wane.

I flag a cab outside Victoria Station, and the driver goes out of his way to find me a cheap hotel in Soho that still has a vacant sign. It's a small room and the mattress is filled with balls of matted feathers, but there's a phone in the hall and at the front desk is a directory of the neighborhoods of London. If I could only talk to Violet, I reason, maybe I could forget for a moment about Alberto and Mariano and my mother's lonely grave.

—I'd like to make an international call, I say.

The operator searches the number for Oscar's law offices on Thirty-Seventh Street in New York City. Maybe a lawyer has ways to find her. He could make sure Violet's all right. I dial collect, and as the phone rings I realize how few times in my life I've had to call anyone for help. Everything in my childhood was planned. Limousines waited; hands held mine as I crossed the streets. The Whirl's staff passed me along the chain of responsibility like a tag team.

—Boyer, Fine and Roberts, the receptionist says.

The operator explains the collect call and asks the receptionist if she'll accept the charges. She does and puts me on hold. Then a different woman's voice comes on the line.

—Romeo, is that you?

—Silvie? I say.

—Where are you?

—I need to talk with Oscar, Silvie. What are you doing at his office?

—Oscar is in a meeting. Where are you? We've been worried sick.

—I need to talk with Oscar.

—You don't know what you've put us through, she says. You've been a very naughty boy. You stop this nonsense and tell me where you are.

—Silvie, put Oscar on the line.

—You thankless child, she says. Tell me where you are. You'll bankrupt the estate. It costs thousands of dollars each day you delay.

Is that what you want? For Frank's estate to be taken by the courts?

—It's not my decision.

—That's the problem, dear boy. It is your decision, but we can remedy that easily.

—By signing away my claim, you mean?

—Tell me where you are, she says. It's too complicated for a boy to understand. I'm asking you, Romeo, for the family. Philip needs your signature on those papers. You're killing him. Reporters are asking questions he can't answer. He needs funds for his campaign. You have no claim. An adopted child has no right.

—That's not what Frank said.

—Frank, she says, was losing his mind.

—Because he wanted you out of the Foundation?

—That's no business of yours. You need to sign the papers.

—I won't do it.

—Sign the papers, young man, or . . .

—What? You'll do what, Silvie?

—I'll take you to court.

—That's not what you meant.

—You make me so angry, she says, I don't know what I'm saying.

—Put Oscar on the line.

—There is nothing you can do, she says. This piece of music is a fabrication. Something in an old man's mind. It was nearly twenty years ago. It was the last wishes of a demented old fool. Can't you see he's sent you on a fool's chase?

I slam down the receiver, then I pick it up and start to redial, but stop. Why would Silvie be in Oscar's office? I should have known a lawyer wasn't to be trusted. Playing both sides is the double-edged sword of modern justice. Once Oscar sees I'm failing, he'll go where the money is and that's far from me.

I leave the hotel without returning the directory to the man at the desk. He scowls at me as I bolt through the door. It all comes back now, the poison, the frame and the fact that for all those years the Whirl withheld information about my mother. Could it be anything but a setup, but a setup by whom?

I buy a map at a small grocery store. The street address written on the envelope is near the central campus of the University of London. I take a subway to the block where the building is located and walk to a small brownstone of four floors. It's getting very dark as I climb the concrete steps and open the front door. The lobby is very small. There's a door on the left, a narrow stairway in the center, and a door on the right with "Supervisor" printed in bold letters.

I stand in front of the stairs. I feel a chill, but it must be my mind making things up. Physics is science, I've got to remind myself, but what is stranger than relativity or quantum mechanics? They've been here, Maria and Justin, and my eyelids won't stop blinking. There's a tremor on the back of my neck that pulses. My hair rises in an electrostatic field, and I can't help wondering if electrons can linger after almost twenty years. Do remnants of the past dwell as ghostly particles? My parents walked these steps and carried groceries to the third floor. They stumbled on the carpet and paid the rent. Except for time, there is little to separate me from them, and that's enough to make me pound on the building supervisor's door as if there's a fire.

TWENTY-SEVEN

March 30, 1986

My hands are trembling, so forgive my scrawling. What happens to one twin, we said as children, happens to the other. Have you ever felt such terrible pain?

It is two weeks since I last wrote you, Alberto, since Frank Whirlpool came to me that first time. I still taste his horrid breath and see his red eyes that taint every color. I must tell someone, without telling too much. It must be you rather than Justin, because of him I despair.

That horrible creature came a second time. I should have known he would not stop. Frank is a man who is not satisfied until he has taken all. I should have fled the first time he came, but this city without Justin is endless streets of unfriendly doors.

It was one o'clock in the morning. I was not yet asleep, but it scared me from the deepest of dreams. I went to the door without bothering with my bathrobe, thinking I would send whomever it was away. The building soon shook with his pounding. I pushed against the door. I threatened to call the police, but he only pounded harder. The neighbor at the top of the stairs opened her door and yelled for quiet. I could not let my problem spill into the hallway, so I opened the door a little to plead with him to stop his pounding.

I know this will hurt you, Alberto, but I must tell someone. Frank Whirlpool did not leave. I made a terrible mistake. He pushed hard on the door and I fell back onto the rug. He stumbled in with a putrid wind of smoke and whiskey. He was even drunker than before. I imagine what you must think of me, brother. My bathrobe was in a pile at the foot of the bed. I crawled for it, trying to cover myself with the rug, then a pillow from the couch, then the throw from the table, as if modesty could tame a wild creature.

You must not think of me as evil, Alberto, or as a harlot. I do not deserve it. I tried to scream for the neighbors, but I could not open my mouth. I curled into a ball. I could see him, but he could not see me. The lights were still off, so he stumbled until his eyes adjusted to the light. Then we stared at each other until the noise of night dwindled. I heard him breathing. He sounded as terrified as me.

That is why I thought he would leave me alone. If he sees how he hurts me, if I do not fight him, he will leave because of my crying. Instead, he reached for me as one reaches for trash. I tried to run to the other room, but he caught me and we fought until my fingers could scratch no more.

He locked my arms to my sides. He spoke in a quiet voice, thinking it was a song, but it rumbled like a growl. He told me I was beautiful. He said he loved me, but I spit in his face and it made him furious. He called me a whore, and I told him I hated him. I said that I loved only Justin, but it only made him angrier. I pulled my arms free and slapped him and bit him. Then he slapped me and dragged me to the couch.

I pleaded with him, Alberto. I begged him. I screamed again, but my cries were as weak as breath. He began to put words in my mouth. He said I loved him. He was the devil himself with his lies. He said he could see in my eyes that I cared for him but I have nothing for him but loathing. He kissed my lips and, when the bleeding came again, it enraged him all the more.

I remember little but this, I swear to Jesus. I am sure I fainted. Even if I did remember, I would not write of it, sweet brother. Your pain should not be as piercing as mine. Frank Whirlpool left me in shame. I was reborn as sin. He will die as our Papà will die. In my eyes, he is already dead.

I am far from you and home, Alberto. It is a cold evening, but I keep the window wide open. I sit in this unholy place where Justin left me and another man passed judgment on my soul. You are the anointed one in faith, brother, but I take little solace in religion these days. It speaks too boldly of the blood.

Justin, for me, is the anointed one in this earthly realm. I am a slave to his mind. I try so hard to believe in the justice of physics, but it falls short of the way Christ spoke to me as a child. I am desperate for that purity and peace. The Bible has been sitting too long without reading. The *logos* is all that is left of my theology, the essence of Christ, the breath of God. I want to see eye to eye with my savior, but all I can do is cry.

My greatest fear is that Justin will not recognize me as the woman he loved. Sin lingers in guilty minds, but why should I be guilty? It was Frank who sinned. If all this physics is true, then Justin should forgive me. He will feel the pain I feel. He will shower me with energy. This is the true miracle of Christ. No rosary could have such power.

For days, I have not eaten a bit of food. I wonder about you, brother, why I do not hear from you. I sit on this bed and stare out the window to the statue of St. Andrew. I fold my arms around my body and rock to the noisy rhythm of traffic. The thought of you praying in the Chapel of Our Mother in the beauty of *Firenze* has helped me these terrible nights. As for me, I find it difficult to pray. I reserve the right to hate, at least for awhile. Insanity comes to my window like an invisible bird. It flies to the foot of my bed and smells like the scent of tobacco and drink that is on everything, the couch, the rug, the cup where the demon put his lips.

Sometimes, I think I hear it at the door. My bones creak with fear. It is only through the glimpse of eternity that you and Justin have given me that I do not quit and fly away with this bird.

TWENTY-EIGHT

—I didn't work here back then, he says. I came two years ago, when my wife got a job at Hospital. I'm sorry, but there's nothing I can do. Good day.

The supervisor starts to close the door, but I stop it with my foot. He's an Irishman who lives in the apartment on the first floor with his wife and boy. He has no interest in helping me. I can understand why. The past means nothing to men with little boys and futures.

—Please, I say, does anyone still live here who might have known them? I'm sorry, but I need to know.

—Get your damn foot out of the door, or I'll call a bobby.

I pull my foot back and apologize. I tell him I'm trying to find something about my parents and his anger subsides.

—Maybe someone has lived here that long, he says, but I wouldn't know.

—Maybe the old super, his wife calls from the kitchen. Tell him to see the old super. Give him something to do, other than bother us, it would.

—You won't get much from Blakely, but suit yourself.

He points to the door on the left of the stairs and tells me the man he replaced still lives in the basement where an old storage room has been converted into an apartment. The stairs are wide and steep. The sides of the runners are clogged with tools and empty bottles of soap from tenants using the washer and dryer that occupy a long hallway lit by a bare bulb.

I knock at a paint-flaked door on the right and stand staring at the balls of dust and slick grime that coat the basement floor. There is a strong, cold wind coming from the exit door at the end of the hall. The hole in the lock directs a thin horizontal beam that's the only clue there's still daylight outside.

—Who's there? A voice barks through the thin crack where a man opens the door and stares out at me.

—I'm looking for Mr. Blakely, I say.

—New super is the one you want. You want a room, he takes care of it. You want something fixed, he fixes it.

—Nothing's broken, Mr. Blakely. I just want to ask you a couple of questions.

The door creaks open a little more. I see a hunched over man with two sweaters that overlap.

—Yeah, yeah, he says. What is it now? I'm watching the tele, can't you see?

—I wondered if you knew a couple who lived here about twenty years ago.

—For Christ's sake, you're talking daft.

—Justin Bishop and Maria Argasti.

—Who is asking?

—My name is Romeo Argasti, I say. They were my parents. They were both killed in a plane crash.

Mr. Blakely takes a look at my earrings and shakes his head. He leaves the door open and walks with difficulty to his chair, which is huge and covered with a blanket and a thick, quilted throw. I step in and close the door. The room is cluttered with magazines and newspapers. As with the basement hallway, there's a moldy odor that must have a half-life and never goes away.

—Maria Argasti and Justin Bishop, I say. They were kind of famous, at least my father was.

—They died, you say?

—In a plane crash.

—My mind's not gone completely. I remember them. It was sad, it was. They had a little one.

—A baby.

—Mrs. Donnely kept the baby. You the baby?

—I was born just before they died.

—That's a shame, he says, sure is, a baby with no parents. I guess that's not so bad. No parents any good these days.

—You remember them?

—Sure I do. I remember them all. They were bad at leaving that damn window open, running up the heat bill. I had to tell them, but mostly they were quiet. You think your parents would like all that nonsense on your ears? And that tattoo, bloody Christ?

I take a deep breath. The old man uses both arms to launch out of his chair. He limps to the wall and pulls a set of keys from a nail driven into a long wooden panel by the door. He sits on the ottoman and begins lacing his boots. He blows his nose on a large bandanna, then goes out the door, expecting me to follow.

—The ones that were in there lately are gone, he says. Moving out, 3B. That's what the new super said. They'll leave the place a mess. That's what always happens, then we got to clean it up as if we're the bloody maids.

He holds onto the handrails and pulls his way up the steps, and he gasps for air when we reach the third floor. He jangles through his key ring and opens the apartment door wide.

—Are you sure? I ask. I don't want to disturb anyone. I only wanted to see if you remember anything about my parents.

—We're not disturbing anyone. I go anywhere I damn well

please. They haven't taken that away.

Boxes half-filled or closed are stacked and scattered around the room. The television is unplugged and the antenna dangles from the wall. A couch is pulled at an angle to match the end table, which is covered with paper plates of leftover Chinese food.

—A damn mess. I told you so.

—This was my parents' apartment?

—3B, it is. I remember your mother kept calling me because the drain wouldn't work. We had a problem with that drain until I called Ed Shibley and he fixed it good. Genius. Haven't had a problem since, but I always thought your mother called me because she was lonely. Wanted to talk to someone besides the tele, you know. Good looking woman, she was. Anything of your parents is long gone. Not sure if there's anything in the left-behind room.

—What room?

—It's been too long for that. People leave things they don't want or can't move. We keep some things in the basement in case they come back, but they usually don't, so we pitch the stuff every couple of years. Not a chance anything of your parents would be there now.

The window is slightly open and a breeze is blowing the curtains. I look over a rusty rail that surrounds a small platform that leads to the emergency stairs and down to the street, which is swarming with pedestrians. A church is in the distance, beyond a park. They must have looked on the same street a thousand times. I turn back to the dark room and I can almost see their ghostly images sitting on the couch, watching through the window at the cloudy skyline of London. I walk to the kitchen table where an open box of spices and dishes from the cupboards is ready for packing. In the bedroom, the bed is unmade and the mattress has stains, but it can't be from my parents' time, too new.

—I feel like a robber, I say.

—You got something to hide?

—Coming in with these people's things all over the place. We probably shouldn't be here.

—Just boxes to me, he says. People come and go. I thought you wanted to know about your parents. This is their flat. This is where they lived. That's all I know.

He moves a stack of books from the floor to the table. He flips the lid on a large box on the counter. A small chest sits beside it, ready to be packed, and I see that the drawers are open and filled with rings and necklaces. Mr. Blakely tries to shut a drawer, but he accidentally bumps the chest.

—Damn! A ring rolls across the table and falls on the floor. A necklace and broach tumble to the counter. He stoops to pick up the ring and says, They're probably not worth a thing. It's been forty years since rich people lived here. Even when your mother and father were here, the place was already going down.

My legs feel weak. There is nothing in this place but echoes. We step into the hall and Mr. Blakely locks the door. We plod down the stairway to the basement. When we get to his room, he gives me a piece of paper, and I jot down the address and phone number of my hotel.

—Could you call me if you think of anything, I say. I'm looking for a piece of music my mother wrote. Anything at all, just call.

He nods and I grasp his shaking hand. I walk up the steps and emerge onto the busy street. What was I thinking I would find there, anyway? Some message from the dead? Something from an empty apartment where the years have erased all trace of them except for ghosts inside my head?

I use the last of Alberto's Euros to take a cab back to the hotel. I'm exhausted. The lights are off in my room, and I lie motionless on the bed. The air around me is dense with an ocean of fields, falling and rising, my mind playing tricks on sleepless eyes. The darkness is soothing after the bright street of pointless rooms and nameless people. The dark is something I'm comfortable with, a matrix with lines crossing in a four dimensional pattern, waves jittering across the room, meeting other waves and combining into larger waves so that the room is completely filled.

I lie for hours in this darkness of made-up memories. I can't possibly remember my mother rocking me, my father gazing down on me with pride, the fold of family that started and stopped so quickly it didn't really exist. Virtual particles condensing out of nothing, electrons colliding with other electrons, atoms forming from collaboration and conquest, molecules bubbling to the surface only to be caught in the tension. I feel as if I'm under water, swimming, drowning, rolling through the ether in the fold of a spacetime made up in my mind.

I sleep in my clothes, and it's a deep sleep. I dream of Mariano and Alberto, Sergio and Elana. As if I'm one of them, I feel the push and pull of family. I dream of Violet and Gabby and Brownie. I remember the long days of childhood in the shadow of the Whirl, when Bam! Bam! Bam! there's a pounding on the door so loud I jump from my bed like a cat surprised.

—Open the door.

I rub my face, then shake it to see if I'm still dreaming.

—This is the police. Open the door, Mr. Argasti.

I look at the clock on the bed stand and see it's nearly nine in the morning. I've been sleeping ten hours.

—We know you're in there, the voice says.

The pounding grows louder. In socks that catch on the sandpaper floor, I slide toward the noise. I lean against the door and peer through the round brass peephole and see two policemen with stripes on the cuffs of their jackets.

—What do you want? I say without opening. I notice the chain is not latched and try to latch it, then stop. I look again and they seem legitimate, so I unlock the door and open it slowly. The bobby on the right pushes it open further.

—Mr. Argasti?

I open the door and step outside. The one on the left flashes his badge.

—Are you Romeo Argasti? the other says. Can we come inside and ask you a few questions?

I step back into the room and the policemen follow me. The one has unnerving eyes that never leave me. I turn on the light and open the window curtain. I make an attempt to smooth the bed where I've tossed in my sleep. The first bobby walks to the kitchen table. His back is to me, but he sifts around in something square I can barely see through a gap between his arm and side. I step toward him to see what he's looking at, but the other bobby takes my arm. The first one sifts through a box of jewelry.

—And what do we have here? he says.

I blink. It's the small chest from 3B. My heart skips a beat, then bounces like a ball.

—That's not mine.

—I imagine not, he says. We'd like you to come to the station, Mr. Argasti.

—That chest wasn't here, I say.

—Indeed, he says. It goes with us now, same as you.

—You ask Mr. Blakely. He's the old supervisor at this building where my mother and father lived. He'll tell you it's not mine.

—You keep saying that, and we totally agree. Breaking old habits is hard to do, and it seems you've had your share of habits. First you clip some items in your own country, now in ours. We've checked your record, son. Come quietly. You don't have to make this hard.

TWENTY-NINE

You can't get away. For better or worse, everything is connected. When I was old enough to listen, the Whirl let me in on what physicists have been quietly debating as the question of the century. Does one electron know what another is doing, even though the two may be a billion miles away from each other? Non-locality is "spooky action at a distance," as Einstein quipped. According to some, it is instant communication, not just faster than light speed, but instantaneous between any two points of space in the universe.

The double- and single-slit experiments, it can be argued, saw the birth of that question. Then in 1932, Einstein and two colleagues devised the EPR thought experiment intended to show the absurdity of quantum inconsistencies. In 1952, David Bohm attempted to explain non-locality by forwarding the idea of "hidden variables." Two decades later, John Bell devised his Inequality Theorem, which the Irish physicist never thought could be tested.

Yet in the 1980's, Alain Aspect's experiments in Paris showed as definitively as it may get in theoretical physics that instantaneous, non-local communication does occur. Through a polarization technique, these experiments proved that what happens to electron A must also happen to its twin electron B, no matter how separated in space and time.

For my situation, non-locality was never considered. To the London Metropolitan Police, there was no need for a non-local conspiracy. No need even for a robbery charge. Over a week before, the customs officer in Spain had taken a look at my money and stamped my passport for a one-week visa, and according to the police I had overstayed my welcome. Deportation took less than twenty-four hours, no questions asked. I was put on the plane before I could convince anyone it was spooky action at a distance and I had nothing to gain from stealing trinkets. The flight from Gatwick Airport to Kennedy International was compliments of British Customs.

—You don't know when to quit, do you? Oscar says.

The lawyer ushers me out the front door of the U.S. Customs Detention Center on Staten Island. It was less a jail than a holding tank, with a few indignant white faces contrasted with the simmering throng of non-white. My short-term cellmates were Seresh from India and Itibe from Sudan. Seresh's face was so hot it looked white; Itibe's had a phosphorous glow that must have looked to those who could see true color a cool, radiant blue. They spoke enough English to tell me they saw me as part of the threat, a temporary tourist in the wrong neighborhood. White or blue, it was all I could do to keep myself from slamming their instability against my own. The whole detention scene was kinetic energy about to blow, and I was a black body experiment absorbing all the frequencies of the spectrum.

—I guess it's time, I say.

—You're lucky to be alive, Oscar says. You don't realize what you're dealing with, and with whom you're dealing.

I throw my bag into the trunk of his limousine, a brand new Lincoln Continental. The leather seats are little consolation for the hours spent on the wooden benches in the Detention Center, but to have been in England so close to where my parents had been was worth a little indignation. I was in the apartment where they created their great tsunami of music and physics, and for the first time in my life, I was feeling less like an orphan.

—Back to the estate, Oscar says into the intercom and I see through the glass panel the driver nod his head. Philip and Silvie are waiting for us, he says.

—Good. I can tell them to go to hell.

—That would not be advisable.

—They set me up again, Oscar. I'm tired of getting framed and having people screw with me. Frank is screwing with me. Silvie is screwing with me. And that Philip is a fucking lunatic.

—Unfortunately, he says, raving about it won't help anything. The police are investigating, but they aren't any closer to knowing who poisoned Frank. That means the killer is still on the loose. You should know when to quit.

—Does it matter who actually did it? They all wanted him dead.

—We may never find out, he says.

—Philip was in San Francisco. He tried to kill my father's roommate, I'm sure of it. Bill Lessing was a friend of my father, but you know that, don't you. You know everything about this, Oscar, don't you?

—What are you talking about, now?

—Why was Silvie in your office when I called?

—When did you call? he says.

—Now *you're* screwing with me.

—You're talking nonsense, he says, but at least you're beginning to understand the gravity of the situation. When it gets through that thick head of yours, you'll quit. Then everyone will stop screwing with you.

The Lincoln jostles with the other cars for position in the middle lane of the turnpike. The car weaves along the Atlantic coast on a long, gray snake of a highway that leads from New York to New

Jersey. We don't say much more on the long ride. Oscar combs the *Wall Street Journal*. I fall asleep and wake up just as the car loops around the coiled off-ramp to the secondary highway that winds to the estate.

—It's time you started thinking about your future, Oscar says as he puts the newspaper on the seat between us. Philip is consolidating his wins. He's taken steps to circumvent your claim. He's made some progress.

I rub my eyes and open the small refrigerator door beneath the seat. There are several beers, a bottle of wine, two waters and a cranberry juice. I grab one of the waters and slam the door.

—He's filing a lawsuit, Oscar says, but that's manageable. It's the sly ones you have to watch.

—You mean Silvie, I say. She threatened me, Oscar. When I called you from London, she threatened me. Not directly, but I could tell what it was.

—Frank had to know this would happen, he says and shakes his head. More than anyone, he knew Philip and Silvie wouldn't go along with the will. You need to sign that agreement, Romey. We've got to put a stop to this before things go completely wrong.

I think of Seresh and Itibe sitting in the Detention Center without a lawyer to make things right. By now, they must be shooting alpha particles so far and wide that even the automaton guards must be getting their drift. That's the problem with negative energy. The hotter they make you, the higher the frequency and the more energy you emit. People go on a slow burn as if all the negative energy they bring on others will do anything but dissipate themselves.

—I heard from your old girlfriend, Oscar says.

—Where is she?

—Stephanie is in New York.

—Violet, I say. You mean Violet.

He opens his briefcase and pulls out a folder labeled "Phelps."

I see a school photo of Violet. She can't be more than twelve or thirteen. She has braces and a ponytail.

—That's her real name, he says, Stephanie Phelps.

—I don't want to know, Oscar, and I don't care what you've dug up on her life. I just want to know if she's all right, so tell me.

—Did you know she grew up in Queens? Her father is a computer scientist at IBM. He lives in Armonk near the headquarters.

—He's dying, I say. He lives in Connecticut, not Armonk. She told me everything.

He tries to hand me a printout with her police record, but I won't take it. He sifts through the documents in the folder.

—Birth certificate, he says, school records, a court document that details her convictions on vagrancy and prostitution, it's all here.

—You gave her money, I say. You paid her to leave me.

—I don't know where you get these things. If she left you, it was on her own, though I won't say I'd be sorry to hear the news.

—I saw the bank book. You gave her ten thousand dollars as a payoff.

—You must be joking, he says. Your girlfriend tricked me out of a limousine and that was enough. Even if I wanted to pay her off, why would I risk that kind of paper trail? I'm an impartial lawyer, not a contestant for the estate.

—I'm going to see her.

—You need to forget about her, Romeo. How much does she know about your situation? About Frank's wealth? The layout of the estate?

—Don't even think it, Oscar. She had nothing to do with the murder or the safe.

—Her father won't even acknowledge her, he says. Her mother was a dancer, but she died about seven years ago. That's when Stephanie went with her father. It's right here, he says and taps the folder with his finger. Your friend had an illegitimate kid when she was thirteen. She gave up the baby and hit the streets. Not a pretty story. I feel sorry for her.

—I'll bet you do. You felt so sorry you paid her ten thousand dollars.

—You think for one minute I would risk getting mixed up with that kind of trash?

—Damn you, Oscar! I say. You're over the line.

—I'm not the only one.

—It doesn't matter what she's done.

—It would, he says, to a judge. You stay involved with Stephanie Phelps and that's another reason to sign the papers. No judge in the world is going to give you the time of day when you're cavorting with a street prostitute. It shows an amazing lack of character.

—You're working for Philip, I say.

—I'm not working for Philip. I promised Frank I'd look out for you. That's what I'm doing. Whether you like it or not, I'm your only friend.

—Bullshit.

He stares ahead. The estate is in view. The stone turrets and tree-lined lane are much the same, but the entry from the street has a new guardhouse and a guard who, until he recognizes Oscar, hassles the limousine driver.

—Romey, I wasn't just Frank's lawyer, Oscar says. I was his friend. He thought of you as his son. That's why I'm saying the time has come to quit. I wouldn't put it past Philip or Silvie to have murdered him. You'd be right to walk away. As your lawyer, I'm telling you it's time to quit. If you play your cards right, you could get a couple of million out of the deal.

—And be the good orphan, I say. Take the money and get lost. Say to hell with Frank's murder. Just fade into the woodwork, like the insect I am.

—Look, he says, I'm trying to do the best I can for you. Frank would have wanted you to have some of the money.

—That's not what he was after. He set this whole thing up for a reason, Oscar. He knew he was going to be murdered. He told me as much, but I wasn't listening. I'm listening now.

The car pulls beneath the canopy at the front door of the house. The DNA field fence has been fixed and the shutters on the upper floor windows have a new coat of paint.

—Frank is dead, Romey.

—He didn't believe in death, Oscar.

—That's a hell of a thing to say, he says. Sometimes I can't understand you. Just let me take care of things and let the dead be dead.

THIRTY

April 25, 1986

There is nowhere in London, Alberto, like Massimo's Market in Massa-Carrara. The grocery on the corner of my street is out of *pomodòro*. I am tired of this country of people who care so little about life that they leave their shelves empty.

I cooked *ratatoulle* tonight so I could remember when we were young and went with Mamma to pick out firm tomatoes and fresh mushrooms. Even good memories do not bring peace here. Justin is asleep with his dreams of pride. Between bites of warm pasta, I told him a great truth and an even greater lie. There is no longer any doubt. Twice, the test has shown positive. This is something I can tell you, brother, but promise me even more silence than what you promised the Church. The nurse at the clinic says I am almost two months pregnant, and how I wish it were just two days.

Justin deserves the truth, I know, so I gave him a truth of omission. He is not at fault, nor is this baby, but I am chained to a sin that chokes us all. Trapped energy, as Justin puts it. The baby forms in my womb as if it were meant to be from the beginning of time. How will I tell it about the world if I am bonded to a lie?

I am no longer sure of anything. It has been this way since Justin came home from America. His eyes were puffy and he had lost weight. I remember the way he looked at me before he left. He said the winter blush on my cheeks made me even more beautiful than in summer. In his first letters from America, he said that he loved me and thought only of me. He said he was sorry for the way we parted, and that the only thing he had in America was work. That was an omission, too.

Now he is glad to be home, he says. It would have been better if he had stayed in America. To forget a lover for even a moment is the greatest betrayal of all. I know this deep inside. I made the mistake of forgetting my savior for just a moment, now there is little left of God.

I am afraid my love for Justin goes the same way. I had everything planned, the wine, the dinner, a speech I practiced in front of the mirror with closed eyes. I relearned how to make his favorite side dish. When I picked him up at the airport, I put on makeup and practiced my smile. Which Justin would I see first, the man who sent me love letters, or the man who left me alone?

We hugged and we cried at Heathrow. I withheld my troubles, though they consumed me like a sickness. He told me a thousand stories about America, about his sister Hope, about the protons at Fermilab that spun so fast they made him dizzy with life. I stared at the new speckles of brown among the blue in his eyes. Was he unfaithful? Did I detect Silvie's icy touch on his skin?

Did he detect Frank's horrid hands on mine?

As ever, Justin is deep inside his mind. He has gone well beyond protons accelerating through tubes. He is alone in his dreams of discovery, though he tries to explain them to me. He has a new way to describe the world, the way we are born and die. We are the same waves of energy that began at the advent of time. We are vibrations of matter on a trip through space for millions of years, combining and separating, constructing and deconstructing, creating and destroying.

When he talked, it made me a little afraid that he already knew about the baby. We are not conceived, he said, but formed in the same way the stars and planets are formed. We do not live, but transform over and over, second to second. We do not die, but continue as energy that is free to form again. Human life, he said as if he was speaking about what is growing in my stomach, is a state of energy, which is transforming and ultimately conserved.

As is love, I wanted to tell him, but of that I am less sure. Justin and I will never be one, no matter how much he imagines and how much I pray. It would take me falling in love with him again, and he with me. When he talks of the future, there is no hesitation or apology, only purpose. He needs his energy for ideas. That is why I did not burden him with the whole truth. I need him to think only of physics. Would he match the weeks he was gone to the term of my pregnancy? Does he remember how little we made love before he left? I did not want to lie, Alberto, but the world has grown too confusing to be left alone.

For his part, Justin performed admirably. When I told him about the baby, he shouted for joy. He said he would never leave me and our life together is fixed. He said we should not only be proud of the baby, but also in creating a new form of life. The tests at Fermilab, he said, were a small step to a world that is much better for all of us, especially for the new generation.

I wished I shared his glory, but he had a life without me, and I had death without him. He asked me why I looked so unhappy. It is just normal, I told him, for a new mother. He said we would go somewhere together, take a holiday before the baby makes me too big to travel.

We have money, he said, because Frank has given him another check. Justin said that we should marry and tell Mamma and Papà. He joked about the baby's name, girl or boy. He wants to give honor to the great mystery of physics, he said. Nucleon, Quark or Hadron, as if anyone will understand this tribute to the universe. Does he not see the forces mounting against this innocent child? Who better than Justin should understand these waves that from the beginning of time are reconstructed from our deepest fears? The womb of a sinner is no forming place for the next generation of stardust.

We will be a family, he said. My baby will have art from you and science from me. He will be a musician with a physicist's eye!

I was nearly caught up in his delusion. It is one of our greatest desires to create life in the manner of God. I told him I needed rest. I locked myself in the bedroom and played my cello as if I was performing for a perfect world. Justin knocked on the door and asked me if he could watch me play. I told him I was sick, that the baby was making me ill. That is not far from the truth. *Mi manca il coraggio.* My courage fails.

THIRTY-ONE

Oscar and I slip from the back of the Lincoln and walk to the main door of the manor house. The west meadow near the drive has been paved to accommodate more cars. A guard at the door wears a short jacket with the Whirlpool name. A gold lion's head has replaced the bronze knocker made from Werner Heisenberg's shoe. Nothing to remind us that the more we understand one part of the mystery, the more uncertain we are of another.

—Philip is in the receiving room, says the guard as he nods to Oscar.

—You've done one hell of a job with security, Sam. The fellow at the gate did a full license check. It's very comforting.

We go inside and walk to the north end of the house. Oscar raps on the wooden door two times quickly, pauses, then taps a third time.

—Ahhhh, good, good, Philip says as he opens the door wide.

His bald head skews the light from the crystal chandelier. He's wearing a dress shirt with an open collar and I see his tie is tossed in a careless manner on a chair with his suit coat. Silvie floats from the other side of the room.

—Wonderful to see you, dear boy, she says and kisses my cheek.

It seems only yesterday that I saw you in the cradle. Won't you have a drink? The burgundy is very dry. Philip is a connoisseur of wine, you know, the least of his talents.

She picks up a silver tray from the table and offers me a glass of what I see only as a black liquid. I decline, but Oscar takes a glass and sits deep on the end of a black leather couch. Again, Silvie tries to hand me the glass, but I ignore her and sit on the far cushion. The lawyer smells the burgundy and smiles as if poison would never occur to him, but I know better. He puts the glass untested on the table.

—Romey just landed at Kennedy, he says. Nasty business, this deportation.

—I should call the Ambassador, Philip says. I'll give him a piece of my mind, Romeo. You must be furious.

—You think? I say.

—Thank God for family, he says. Am I right?

—Even when there's no real family, Silvie says and flashes her pinched smile. For all the trouble you've caused, dear child, you have accomplished one thing. You've got Philip looking after your best interests.

—That's right, Philip says and with a handkerchief he wipes his forehead. Frank took you in, so I've done the same. I've decided to do right by you, Romey. I owe it to the memory of my late brother.

—To Frank, Silvie says and swirls the black liquid around her glass and downs it with a gulp.

—I have something to propose, Philip says. He lopes to the bar in the corner and pours whiskey into a short glass.

—Listen closely, Romeo, Silvie says. He's chosen to be magnanimous. Philip could leave you with nothing, but how would that be, to leave a poor orphan with nothing? Almost as unjust as a poor orphan who gets everything.

She slips around the end of the couch so she's in back of me. A chill reaches down my shirt to freeze my spine. It's all I can do not to jump up and run. The urge to escape is powerful, but I know there's only one way out, down the throats of these murderers.

—How would you like to be rich? Philip says as he drinks his whiskey and pours another. He stands near a window with its beam of sunlight that bores a gaping hole into the top of his head. You won't have to find, he says, or do anything. This music of your mother's, it could be anywhere.

—Or nowhere, Silvie says.

Oscar reaches down and opens his briefcase. He pulls out two papers and puts them on the couch between us.

—You've seen this one before, he says, and points to the document to disclaim the estate. The other is a contract, he says, with a dollar amount that Philip is offering. At his request, a contract specialist has reviewed the documents. They will hold up under the most intense legal scrutiny.

—Five million dollars, Philip says, transferred to any account you name, Romey. Any bank, any country, you just name it.

—More money, Silvie bends and breathes next to my ear, than someone of your background could ever hope for.

—Especially, Philip says, someone who insists on living as you do. In a commune, isn't it? Now you can do what you want, live like a vagabond.

—Run with the whores, Silvie says. Violet, isn't that your friend's name?

The chill has maneuvered from my spine to my legs and toes. Silvie puts her hands on both my shoulders and begins to massage.

—Philip is offering you enough money, she says, to take Violet away from harm, somewhere you can live happily ever after. What do you say?

—I'm not signing anything, I say and push Silvie's arms away from my neck.

—Dammit! Philip says. You've had your fun, boy. This is the big world, Romeo. We have expenses. There are bills to pay, loans to negotiate. You have no understanding of what it takes to be a Whirlpool.

—I don't want the money, I say.

—Take the damn money! he says and lunges to the couch and spins the contract so it faces me.

—Don't be a fool, Silvie whispers. That's more than enough for an adopted boy. You should be grateful. It's not as if you were really Frank's child.

—One of you is a murderer, I say.

—Oscar, take note, Philip says. The little bastard is slandering me.

—One of you killed him, I say, and now you're stealing the money, just as Frank knew you would. That's why he made a new will. That's why he came to see me. He knew it was the last time.

—Suicide, Philip says. Surely you've told him, Oscar.

—We haven't discussed it, he says.

—There was no murder, Silvie says. The police think Frank did himself in. It would be just like him to leave us with a great mystery.

I can't move. It has me thinking, this lie they speak. In another life, the Whirl might have committed suicide, but not this one. His death was murder no matter how the police collaborate with the murderer, or murderers. I've got to escape, somehow break from these liars before their lies never let me go. Alpha decay. As Hope told me, it's when a radioactive particle, with the help of uncertainty, breaks the strong force of the nucleus. The particle can tunnel its way out if it's on the right slope at the right time to have its momentum break the bond. I've got to tunnel out like the weak particle I am.

—All this nonsense, Philip says, is giving the papers a field day. I'm getting killed in the polls.

He stands like a barrier in front of me. The veins in his face show through his pale skin. Silvie weaves her way to the front of the couch and stands next to Phillip. Her eyes are black slits. Oscar takes the glass from the table and doesn't drink, but he spills a little on his pants. If I'm going to tunnel, I know it's got to be now.

—This madness must stop, Philip says. You're an orphan, for God's sake.

I launch my body from the couch and bust through the middle of them. Philip spills his drink on the carpet. Silvie hisses an oath. At the door, I turn to face them.

—Maybe I wasn't his son, I say, but he treated me like one. I'm going to find out what his will was all about. He loved me. That's what pisses you off. Frank loved me, at least most of the time.

—That's it! Silvie says. I wouldn't have thought it. You poor, grieving boy. We should have realized, Philip. We've got to be a little more understanding.

—Ridiculous, Philip says. I'm meeting with the Governor in two hours. Tell him, Oscar. It was your job to get him to sign. Now do your job!

Oscar's face turns as dark as the burgundy. He doesn't look me in the eye, but he picks up the papers and holds them aloft.

—Without money, he says, you haven't got much choice, Romey. I wish I could tell you different, but that's the way it is. I'm just thinking of you.

—You're as disgusting as them, I say. I'm leaving.

—Not before you sign, Philip says, or you'll get nothing.

—Then we all get nothing, I say and I spin to leave.

—Romeo! Silvie shouts. You should know this about your *beloved* guardian.

It stops me. Her words snake across and curl on the wooden floor around my feet. The room echoes from her shrill voice. One or the other, my momentum or slope, must not have been right.

—He hated you, Silvie says. He hated your mother. He hit her. Did you know that? Frank hit your mother, just as he hit you.

My legs are like trees fixing roots. Silvie's lips turn up with a half-smile.

—This is revenge, Romeo, she says. Your mother rejected him. When he died, he pitted you against us, against a force that will defeat you, hurt you.

My feet won't go. I'm trapped in an invisible force that winds in tight lines that knot at my knees and wrists. It might not be a lie. The Whirl was always playing games, good love, bad love, but any love he gave had strings as long as this field that winds at my feet.

—Frank is laughing at you, Silvie says. You fell for it, you and your mother.

—That's enough, Oscar says. Let him be.

—You hear me, boy? she says. Why should Frank have cared about you? After all, you weren't really his child.

I turn and take one more step toward the door, but my legs start to fail, then her voice gives me strength. I start running. I don't stop until I've taken the long hall and pushed out the front door to where the Lincoln still waits. I jerk open the door and tell the driver to go, but he only puts up the divider. Oscar soon catches up. He's panting hard as he drops into the seat.

—Are you sure? he says.

—Let it go, Oscar.

—Five million is a lot of money. It may be your last chance. You've threatened them and that's not so good.

—You're in it with them.

—That's not true. I simply checked their documents.

—It doesn't matter, I say. I'm going to find out why Frank did this, Oscar. Maybe he hit my mother, just like he hit me, but all of those bastards can kiss my ass. I'm going to find out why he's putting me through this hell.

THIRTY-TWO

The Lincoln decelerates from the eighty-five it's been running since leaving the estate and exits onto a twisting concrete avenue in New York City. Oscar still won't look me in the eye. It's not, I know, that he likes Philip and Silvie any more than I do, but they'll soon be his clients. When I lose the game, in fact, he wins again. He's got to have that in mind, just as I know that refusing their offer might have been the biggest mistake of my life.

The limousine pulls in front of a carryout near the Hovel. Oscar starts to say something diplomatic, but I cut him off, jump out of the car and without looking back sprint to the Indian grocery. I buy beer and a bag of groceries and walk fast to the old warehouse. As I climb the metal stairs, I hear the familiar bantering, so I take two steps at a time until I reach the third floor.

Brownie shares a roach with Lacky Giovano. Sarah Connell and Gabby are sitting together on the floor. They're all loaded, but they jump up and gather around me and hug me like I'm long lost family. Brownie hands me a bottle of whiskey. I take a drink and begin to shake off the chill I've had since Silvie's hand was on my neck. There's danger in the Bowery, no question, but it's the kind that comes at you from the front, not from behind.

I stoop to the concrete and spread the groceries into a circle. Some of them, I know, have not eaten well in weeks. I watch them closely, their smiles and laughter, and they watch me. I can see in their eyes that they wonder how I can give away a bag of groceries without eating some. It makes them distrust me, but I'll never be one of them again. You can't lie forever about who you are. As much as I hate the thought, I've been around people like Silvie and Philip since I was born. I've been exposed to their hate and anger too long for it not to have warped me. I'm more like them than Brownie and Gabby, and that's why I have no appetite.

—Romey! Violet bounds up the steps, gives me a huge hug and wets my face with kisses. We hold each other until the others start to heckle us.

—How are you, baby? I whisper.

—You're the one who's been to Europe, she says.

—I got kicked out.

—No shit. You got kicked out of a whole country? What'd you do?

—Stayed too long.

—The bastards got to you, didn't they? You tell me, Romey. I'll kick their asses.

I pull her over to the window where we can be alone. Her eyes have gone wild again, the pupils so large and dark they remind me of an eclipsed moon.

—Forget it, I say. I don't want to think about anything but you, Violet. I want to know you've been all right. That's what I want to hear.

—Nothing to tell, she says and puts her arms around me. I came home. Sold the damn car, that piece of shit. It might make Hope a little mad, but she'll get over it.

—How's the baby?

She shrugs and leaves me and stoops to where the groceries are almost gone. She takes a piece of bread and finishes it in a few bites.

—I didn't do it, she says. Couldn't see him. Not the baby's fault. It's the damn adoption parents. They think they know me. I stayed with my father a few days. My aunt wasn't bullshitting me. He's not dying. He's got cancer, sure as hell.

—In Armonk?

—How you know that? She looks at me with surprise but not suspicion. He's not the same as before, she says, but he's still a bastard. He makes me think too much. I don't need it.

She puts her arms around me and kisses me. I smell reefer, but it doesn't matter. She told me the truth about her father, and that's a start.

—I've got to ask you something, I say. There was a bank book.

—What bank book?

—When we were in the mountains. I accidentally found it. Oscar says he didn't give it to you.

She pulls her hands from my waist.

—So that's why you've been such an asshole, Romey? You don't trust me?

—I didn't know what to think. How did you get that kind of money?

—What the hell, she says, you got all the fucking money in the world.

—Just tell me, Violet. Why can't you be straight with me?

—They paid me, goddammit! she says. You want the truth, Romey? That's it. They paid me for the baby. So what?

Words gag in my mouth, so I spit out a gasp.

—I've been trying to figure you, Romey, Violet says. It's all been because of that damn bank book. You think I'm screwing you. That's why the change of heart.

—I'm sorry, I say. I didn't know.

—You should have asked.

I reach for her, but she pulls away. She walks slowly to the stairs. Then she stops and runs back and throws her arms around my shoulders. She says she's sorry, too. She tells me she had no address, so the money went to her Aunt Louise in Chicago. She reaches into her bag and pulls out the bank book and shows me it's all there, ten thousand dollars.

—I tried to buy him back, she says, but they didn't go for it.

—I'm sorry, I say. I shouldn't have asked. It's none of my business.

—I'm going to save it, she says, for when he gets older and needs it for college, or a trip, or something that matters, but that's a long time.

I kiss her. I tell her I should have trusted her, over and over until she gets angry. I don't ask about the ruby. What's the point? It's just a stone, worth something and nothing more. Whether she found it under the seat of the car, or on the street, or in her hand when she wasn't looking, matter is here one moment, gone the next. It's only the intent that remains, the decisions we make to escape the past and run toward a future that we fear for no other reason than the present is too hard to understand.

—You're right, Violet. I should have asked.

—Damn straight, she says. Whatever happens, from now on, we've decided. That right, Romey?

—That's right. Damn straight.

THIRTY-THREE

August 13, 1986

I called you, again. I leave messages at the seminary. I understand why you do not want to live in the same world as me. You think I am compromised by my sinful nature, Alberto, but it is only by others who are posing as saints.

Today, Justin asked me to put on a nice gown, but he would not tell me where he was taking me. It was a surprise, he said, but he did not know how much of a surprise it would be. In his ignorance, he conspires with our enemies. The evening became a sordid play with players that do not speak to one another, only to me.

An evening out with Frank and Silvie is just what you need, he said. It will bring you out of yourself.

When will men learn how to listen to their heartbeats instead of their voices? All evening, Frank did not look at me, but his eyes could not divert his thoughts. I stared at him with all the hate I could muster. If he thinks I will let him forget, he is just as ignorant as Justin pretends.

Silvie sat on her chair as a queen on a throne, and her smile tells all. She knows everything. Any woman would know who sees how I stare at her lover as if he were dead.

To Maria, Justin gave a toast, the love of my life and soon to be the mother of my child.

I could not stand it. I excused myself and fled from their stares. In the bathroom, I ran cold water on my hands until I stopped shaking. When I returned to the table, their silence was even more painful than their voices. I tried to eat, but the food was bile in my throat. I left again, but even cold water could not help. The baby's feet were kicking.

I heard Frank at the door. I could hear him breathing, see him pounding, feel him pushing in. Just as he opened the door, I threw up in the sink. I leaned against the wall to keep from falling. Frank tried to help. He asked my forgiveness, but I tried to hit him. I told him what I wanted to believe, that God would never forgive those who by all rights should burn in Hell.

The baby kicked harder. As if it knew its father was near, it punched my stomach. It made me want to hurt Frank as much as he has hurt us, but all I could think to do was take his hand and force it against my womb. With vomit still in my mouth, I spit in his face, God forgive me.

Frank pulled his hand away and wiped his face, but he could not rid himself from shame. Others were coming. They had heard my cries. Justin grabbed me and held me. We got our coats and, without explaining to the others, we left the restaurant.

Is it the baby? he asked as the silence in the taxi grew too long. It must be making you nauseous, he said because that is what he has read in books. It must be making you nervous, giving you doubts about the future.

That may be true, I thought, but it is not the whole truth. It is not the baby's fault. The lie that I told is growing and making me sick and separating me from Justin. I have stopped talking to him and to everyone else. I spend all my time thinking about the baby and withdrawing in music. I now know what this composition has been trying to say. There is a way through to love, but it goes below the anger and hate to where we all are the same. The only sin in this world is that our short lives are wasted seeking redemption, when seeking redemption is a backward path that leads away from love.

It is a sobering thought that flies in the face of all I have learned and cherished. Where does a world without redemption leave us, leave me? Where does it leave Papà and Mamma and the billions of others who live under the darkness of sin? Does it leave the world without hope, Alberto, or does it leave a world without sin?

For me, the only way through this confusion is through musics. I have found a name for my string quartet, my brother. I named it after the most rebellious of your thoughts. The *logos* is the warm breath of God, as you whispered when we were young, and this idea is what enables me to breathe. It lets me see the healing nature in what Justin believes. His physics seeks the *logos*, our most fundamental nature. It is that which has always been and will always be the spirit, the surge of free energy through the universe, wreaking havoc with those who stand still and allow fate to rule.

We can choose our path, he has taught me. I try to keep this always in my mind, but it is elusive. The waves of energy can destroy or build inside us as a great ocean ebbs and flows. My music searches for the simple notes that will build a huge wave so resonant it will give us a chance to glimpse the harmony that is God.

Tell me I am wrong, dear brother, or right. Your priestly silence is too much to bear. Remember how much I need your voice. You should not excommunicate the one with whom you shared the womb. While you stay solid on hallowed ground, I am in motion and drifting away.

THIRTY-FOUR

Sitting pretty in her first-class seat on a flight to London, Violet is a rags-to-riches queen dressed in silk pants, a blouse with a flared collar and thick-rim glasses that solve a nearsighted problem I didn't even know she had. I traded my jeans for leather pants, a linen coat with big pockets and two gold earrings to replace the silver ones the guy who pierced my ears gave me for free.

When I threatened Oscar with filing a complaint with the New York Bar Association for his double-dealing with Silvie and Philip, everything suddenly changed. The lawyer gave me twenty thousand dollars of his own money and called the British ambassador to fix the robbery charge. Now, Tuf is stowed in a gilded cage below deck, which the attendant at the airline counter assured us is heated for pets. A stewardess with blonde hair and a thick southern accent is fawning over us in our padded seats, saying we're the cutest couple she's ever seen.

In Texas, she says, the next thing we would do is get married. So she brings each of us a fluted glass of champagne just to introduce the idea. We sip on the drinks and eat individually wrapped treats. Trepidation is hundreds of miles behind and Violet can't stop smiling from the way her world is now clear skies and first-class drinks.

—Do you think, Violet whispers with a little slur, that if the stewardess knew who I was she would be so nice?

—I'll bet they get prostitutes in here all the time, I say.

Violet spits a laugh and spills her drink, so the Texan brings us a rag so we can dab the cushion.

—Only the rich ones, Violet says and laughs again, but this time she holds her drink in equilibrium so she doesn't spill. Whores like me, she says, we take the bus.

—I'll bet that one across the aisle, I say and point to an old lady in a fur who has been staring at us since we lifted off, is a high-priced one.

—Too old.

—Retired, I'll bet.

—Shit, Violet says, no social security for hookers, Romey. We're like them elephants, you know. We go alone to some graveyard where nobody can see us or be bothered. That's okay, elephants are cool.

She takes a long sip of champagne to cover a glitch in her smile. She hits the button on the side of her seat and floats back like an astronaut.

—Anyway, I say, that's in the past. You don't have to worry anymore.

—That's right. I got you, and you got money, she says and clicks her glass against mine. Not bad for a street sheet.

I push my button and settle back to match her declination. I'm in the window seat so I stare through the glass at the clouds and sky. We land at Gatwick Airport in London just as the sun goes down and I show the customs agent five thousand dollars in hundred denomination bills. No problem getting a full-month visa. Stay as long as you want!

Tuf arrives at the baggage area on a flat cart, so we free him from the cage and hop a cab to a big hotel near the University of London. We pay cash for the room, bed the kitten on a pillow in the corner and fall asleep with nothing on but dreams of how things could stay as nice as this, if we just have some luck.

—Now, what'd you say your name was?

Mr. Blakely goes back inside his basement hole and gets his glasses from the coffee table that's stacked with dirty cups and saucers. It's late morning and Violet and I just walked two miles through old London to the apartment building. Violet was excited to see the sights: Parliament, Big Ben, Westminster Cathedral and especially the old ladies with umbrellas who pulled their grocery bags on wheels. Only trouble was, every time Violet saw a cat, she would run after it until it escaped her clutches. She's worried about Tuf, but we left him curled up sleeping soundly in the hotel room. Just a feeling, she says, like eyes staring at you from behind.

—Romeo Argasti, I say to Mr. Blakely. I came here two weeks ago. The new supervisor told me to come down. You remember? I wanted to know about my parents.

—You're the robber, Jesus, he says, Holy Mother.

—No, no, I say and try to calm him. It was just a mistake, Mr. Blakely. I'm not a robber. The police department apologized.

—Apologized?

—That's right. It was a mistake. You took me to the apartment, remember, and we didn't take a thing. You were there with me. I'm no robber.

—Maybe they apologized to you, he says, but the new super reamed me out royal. A jewelry case, I think it was. Got me into all kinds of trouble with the bastard.

—I didn't take anything. Believe me.

He shines the lenses on his glasses. He puts the frames on and stares at Violet for most of a minute. He leaves the door open and limps back into his dark apartment and sits in the overstuffed chair with magazines and newspapers spread around him like he's potty training.

—I knew you didn't steal, he says. Them blasted bobbies never believe old people. I figured it was for the insurance. People do all kinds of things for money, then blame it on me. Prejudice, mind you, it's not just for the blacks and browns. Wait until you get older, you'll see prejudice.

—Could you show us the room where you keep people's things? The left-behind room, I think you called it? I know it's been a long time.

—You want to steal something else?

—He didn't steal anything, Mr. Blakely, Violet says and reaches down and touches his hand. It's just a loose end that he's got to tidy up. He's an orphan, you know. If you could see your way to show us the room, I'd appreciate it, I really would.

—Some people just don't come back, he says and stares where Violet's hand is touching his. Damnedest thing, he says. They leave everything, books, couches, all kinds of things. You'd think they were feeble-minded or something. Mostly, it's stuff people leave behind because they don't want to haul it away. No use for it, myself. Except this one, he says and pats the arms of his chair. This is from 2G about fifteen years ago. Still a good chair.

With difficulty, he pushes with both hands until he's upright. He lifts the keys from the hook beside the door. Then he backs Violet and me into the hall and locks the door. We follow him further into the darkest part of the basement. We pass several doors that look as if they've been kicked at the bottom or furniture bashed into them by accident. The last door on the right is oversized and I'm not really sure what color it is, but it looks like a door that should be gunboat gray. Mr. Blakely turns the key in the rusty lock. The huge door swings out on an angle to the frame. A mouse scuttles between Violet's feet.

—Just like home, she says and tries to kick it with her foot, but she misses.

—Damn rodents, the old man says and steps inside the room.

Cockroaches, lately, but the new super says there's none here. That's a hoot.

He searches for the light switch, which turns on a bare bulb in the middle of a cavernous room piled high with tables, chairs, couches and trunks. He moves slowly down an open aisle to the back where the furniture is yellowed and stripped of thread by several generations of rodents.

—I guess we haven't kept up on it very well. Like I told you, the super throws everything out. If there's anything going back as far as the eighties, he says and points to a cluster of boxes that lines the wall floor to ceiling, it would be over there in that mess. I've been meaning to get around to this, but I haven't had time, and the new super wouldn't stoop so low.

A couch standing on its end keeps the pile from tumbling over. Two crowned-back chairs, one turned upside down on top of the other, have a note attached. "Mr. Dominick to return, Friday, Sept. 23."

—That was about seven years ago, Mr. Blakely says and swats the note. I used to clean this room regularly, to make room for more, you see. But the other damn fella doesn't keep no personal effects. Just pitches them without a care.

Violet and I sift through boxes and notes, but there is nothing labeled Argasti or Bishop. Most of the boxes are filled with old kitchen utensils and appliances, or books and magazines. I'm about to give up when Mr. Blakely pushes with his feet a dirty box that is coming apart at the seams.

—That's where they were, he says and points to the marking, 3B. Don't know if this box was your parents', now, but that was their number.

I stoop to the box and peel the flaps. There are magazines and books, two ashtrays, and several pots and pans. Violet finds another box with the same number. She pulls dried pens and dusty pencils from an empty jar. I see a binder with the papers falling out where the three-ring fastener is pulled apart.

—Jesus! I say. Violet scrambles over to me as I pull from the binder several sheets covered with mathematical equations.

—Is it theirs, Romey? You sayin' it's theirs?

I nod. I feel the claws of excitement scratching inside my chest. Complex variables, imaginary numbers, the binder must be my father's, but I search and search and can't find his name.

—You see any music? Violet says.

—Damn, Violet, it's my father's notebook. Frequency variations in molecules. No doubt about it. Notes on composite waves, Jesus!

Mr. Blakely shoves another box to us. It has the same aged look with split sides and rotten bottom and this time with the name Bishop written beside the 3B. I want to rip it apart and dig inside, but I carefully drag it to an open spot and open the top. I take things out, one by one, and hand them to Violet who places them into a row along the basement floor. A pot and two skillets, a dust pan, four novels, an alarm clock, five plates with unmatched patterns, silverware, salt and pepper shaker, and local newspaper turned inside out with a story of the rumors about Justin Bishop and the University's pushing for the Nobel.

My grin is infectious, and even Mr. Blakely's cigarette-stained lips turn up in a smile. We carefully lay the items into long rows. These are hallowed possessions that touched my parents' hands, and now they're touching mine. Violet can no longer contain herself, so she digs further into the box and pulls out a crumbling book.

—A phone list, she says and fans it from A to Z. The pages are dark and the pencil notations faded. She has trouble making out the names, as she begins reading: Jonathan Ivy, Morris Fletcher, Grace Bethlehem. Hey, Romey, Vira Pierce, Music Department.

I snatch the book. There's a phone number beside the Pierce entry. We rummage in the boxes until we're satisfied that the phone list is the only thing that will give us more clues as to where the music might be found. Mr. Blakely is getting nervous, as if suddenly he's not as comfortable with letting us rummage through other people's possessions, no matter if their owners are long gone and never coming back. He grumbles another oath about the new super and walks to the door and jingles the keys. I pack most of the things into the boxes. I tuck the notebook under my arm and shuffle the phone list pages into their original order.

—Don't show me, he says. I didn't let you in. I didn't see you take a thing. You keep getting me into trouble, you know.

We thank Mr. Blakely and Violet kisses him on the cheek. He locks the left-behind room and we watch him disappear inside his sad basement home, then we race up the steps and out the front door to the street. We flag a cab and in a few minutes we're back to the hotel and calling Vira Pierce.

—I'm very sorry to bother you, I say and hang up the phone.

—No luck? Violet hugs on my arm.

—Vira Pierce died in ninety-eight.

—Try this one, she says and points to another name. Don't give up, Romey. Grace Bethlehem, the name sounds like a professor. Never know until you call.

She reads me the number and I try it, but the phone has been disconnected. We try several others, Jonathan Ivy and Benjamin Knewley. Then we come to the middle of the book and a quick notation: Leon Harrad, Royal Holloway. It has no address and no number. I pick up the London area phone book and look for the number of the college.

—Can I help you?

—Leon Harrad, please?

—Harrad? the voice repeats and pauses. Sorry, it's not on my list.

—Could you transfer me to the physics department.

There's another pause and a new receptionist answers. I ask her about Harrad and she says the same thing. He's not on her list.

—It's urgent that I get in touch with Leon Harrad. He must have worked there, but it could be twenty years ago.

She covers the phone with her palm and begins speaking to someone else. Then she comes back on the line.

—Dr. Leon Harrad was the Dean of the College of Physics about ten years ago. I wish I could help you. I don't have his number.

—Someone must have his number. I really need to get through to him. Is he still alive? Could you tell me that?

—We think so, she says after another consultation. I'll take your name and number and get it to him. That's all we can do.

—I appreciate it.

I tell her my name and that I'm the son of Justin Bishop. I give her the hotel name. I return the phone to the cradle and feel a steady flow of adrenaline as if I'm standing in water and there's a leak of electricity. If anyone would remember my father, it would surely be the Dean of Royal Holloway College.

THIRTY-FIVE

—Justin Bishop was a boy of great intelligence.

—Then you do remember him? I say.

Dr. Leon Harrad can barely keep his eyes open, not from lack of sleep, but from the sheer energy it takes to lift his massive lids. The way he bellows orders at the nurse, he must have been a tangle in his day, but now the Dean Emeritus is over eighty. His nurse pulls a shawl around his neck.

—Of course I remember him, he says. Why wouldn't I remember? You think I'm dotty, young man?

I nod my head sideways, but I can't think of an answer more convincing, so Violet jabs my arm with hers.

—Don't worry about Romey, she says. He's just nervous, learning about his father and all. If you got something, Leon, we would be real glad to hear it.

—I did know Justin Bishop, he says. A fine student, but he had little regard for rules, I remember. We need rules. We need the method. Scientists would be lost without it, I fear, but some of us get lost in it. That's the way Justin got lost.

—Because of the plane crash? Violet says.

—I can't turn back the clock, he says and shakes his head.

Nothing to be done, but there should be a way, you see, to do just that. Time was my specialty, the focus of my research. When I think of how I could have made a difference with just a little more effort, it makes me angry, that's the worst thing. Justin Bishop could have been a great physicist, but they got hold of him too early.

—Who got hold of him? Violet says.

He curls his shoulders forward in a sigh. The nurse hovers over him as if he could go downhill any second.

—The great debate of this new century, he says after clearing his throat, will not be cloning or creating new life, but how we use science. Do we stay within the framework of mathematics and the scientific method? Do we let our obsessive search for cause put blinders on our research? We put such high faith in the markets to deliver innovations from obscurity, that we've ended up making science a product farm, nothing more.

—I don't understand, I say. What has this to do with my father?

—It has everything to do with Justin Bishop, he says. If we are to progress at all, we've got to come to grips with the untestable, the unobservable. Everything is not causal. That is the great truth of quantum mechanics. All things cannot be framed within the trajectory of time. Indeed, the creative urge must remain free of trajectory. The scientific method has its place, but it must adapt to the quantum uncertainty. We must respect creativity, see science as an art form, merge science and faith into one. Only then will we prevent such a waste as Justin Bishop.

—My father's life was a waste?

—His ideas could not be tested, the old man says with a sigh. Your father was speculating on a world that is beyond our machines of measurement. How can you measure a vibration? The elementary wave would be way over a billion times smaller than a proton. Too tiny for any of our tools and, even then, to measure it would be to lose it. Uncertainty reigns supreme. Justin was a thinker, indeed, one of those ahead of his time. He was too young. He needed grants, which we gave him, but we withheld what he desired most.

Harrad's body shakes in a spasm and the nurse pulls the shawl tighter around him. It takes a few minutes for him to regain composure. Violet sits beside him and puts her hand on his, and the protective nurse comes around closer.

—You withheld something? I say.

—Approval, he says, the freedom to explore the uncertainty. Your father needed validation. It's what all of us mortals want, and it's what men of power use to control men of ideas.

—You think his ideas were right?

Suddenly, Leon Harrad opens wide his eyes and stares as if he's never seen me before. Then a wave of recognition comes over him and his lids fall back down.

—His son, you say? I didn't know Justin Bishop was married, or that he had a son.

—He wasn't married, Violet says. He and Romey's mother lived together, just like me and Romey. Her name was Maria.

—She had dark hair, he says. Very lovely, like you, my dear.

—I'm not really blond, Violet says. Maria was a cellist and I don't play anything. Maybe someday, though.

—Do you remember my mother's music? I say.

—I was a scientist, not a musician, he says, though Justin would have us think there is no difference. He would have us combine every discipline into one universal field, I suppose. Your mother was very quiet, almost delicate. I always thought she could have been broken with a harsh word.

Violet rubs the old man's hand and the nurse cranes her neck so she can see what Violet is doing. Violet whispers something into the old man's ear, and he smiles as if she has just propositioned him, and maybe she did.

—Dr. Harrad is very tired, the nurse says. He must rest, now.

—He's fine, Violet says and leans on the wheelchair so she's in front of his face. We're looking for some music, Leon. Romey's mother wrote it just before she died, and we would like to get hold of it. You know anything about that music?

—I played a little piano, he says, here and there, mostly when I was very young, a child really. Now, I couldn't play a note. If this young man's mother wrote some music, maybe they preserved it. Physicists are very good about preserving their work. Musicians, as well. All is built on what has come before. Nothing is lost.

—Preserved how? she says.

—In archives, libraries, now it's the Internet, I suppose. At Royal Holloway during my time, it was standard for all works of possible scientific importance to be catalogued in Royal Holloway's library.

—My father's work?

—I ordered it myself, he says. They keep everything, notes, drafts, newspaper clippings, anything that might be of historical importance.

—That's it, Romey! Violet says and kisses the old man's cheek. I'll bet they have a whole room for your work, Leon. A whole room.

—Indeed, he says. You're very kind, dear. What is your name?

—Stephanie, she says, but you can call me Violet.

To the irritation of the nurse, she kisses the old man again. I shake his wrinkled hand as hard as I can without hurting him. The nurse says good day and before the Dean can complain, she turns him away. We watch the wheelchair disappear down the hall, then Violet and I find a pay phone. She calls ahead to Royal Holloway and finds out the library stays open until eleven o'clock. Violet screams the news to me so loudly that the nurse follows us with accusing eyes until we leave.

We flag a cab and it gets us to the college before six. I'm so revved up, I can feel the valves of my heart open and close, swish-boom, swish-boom, like brushes on a snare drum. We fill out the forms and get permission from the head librarian. There's a catalog, but the notations mean nothing to us, so we request the entire archive. We sit at a conference table in front of two large boxes with numbers printed on labels attached to the sides. I open the first and rummage through. Most are typewritten papers, but a few are handwritten, drawings, diagrams, mathematical formulas and my father's personal notes on the beam experiments at Fermilab.

The second box has more personal effects, cards, receipts and schedules. Near the bottom of the box, Violet finds something entirely different from the other items.

—It's a bunch of letters to somebody named Alberto, she says.

—My uncle?

—Jesus, Romey, they're from your mother. Right there in the return address, it says Maria Argasti.

I snap the bundle from Violet's hands. It's a packet of letters in discolored envelopes, tied together with hemp string. I see the same elegant script that was on the envelope to my grandmother. I untie the butterfly bow.

—The envelopes are sealed, I say. They were never opened.

I look to see if the librarian is looking, then tuck the first one under the table and tear it open. Some words are in Italian, but most are in English.

—Alberto told me there were letters, but how did they get in my father's archive.

—And why didn't he open them? Violet says. Maybe she didn't send them, Romey, and they got mixed up in your father's things.

—The seminary must have sent them back. My grandfather kept them from Alberto. Must be thirty or more.

Violet scoots closer to me so she can read the letter. I scan a few lines but nothing sinks in, so I skip to the end of the letter, then put it aside. I drop the envelopes on the floor and get them out of order.

I open another envelope and read the letter start to finish. The dots begin to connect: the apartment, the physics, a rift in the family.

I open a third letter and my skin feels like nettles. I read of a night when a man came to my mother. I read how this man threatened her, terrified her. Hit her. My heart rips open. Silvie was right. I bleed on the floor. The atoms in my hands and legs shudder and thud. If only I hadn't dropped the envelopes. They're out of order. There must be context, an error of some kind. My mother must have been writing about someone else, not the Whirl, no matter how much he drank and thought the whole world was his to control.

—What is it, Romey? Violet says.

I tuck the stack of letters beneath my shirt so it looks as if I've got a huge gut. Violet closes the two boxes and returns them to the desk. Two male students monitor the checkout counter, but I know there is no possible way they're going to look at me instead of Violet. We make our way past them without questions and lunge through the turnstile. The letters don't set off the alarm, thank God, so I keep walking without looking back. It's dark as we emerge from the library. I sit on the steps under a pole lamp that casts an umbrella of light around us. Violet leans against me and puts her head on my shoulder.

—Is it bad? she says.

My head spins like a pulsar. Tree limbs lash wildly from a wind that roars as though a hurricane is about to hit.

—This is why he couldn't tell me, I say.

—You're not making sense, Romey. You gotta talk to me.

I scoop the letters into a pile, stuff them into my shirt and run to the road. Violet yells after me. I stop to let her catch up, then we walk fast in front of the brownstone houses that go on to infinity. I can't speak about the letters. Violet just holds my hand and suffers with me without knowing what for, only that she knows more about suffering than most.

THIRTY-SIX

Violet stands behind me and rubs my shoulders. I lean in front of the bathroom mirror with one hand on the sink and the other grasping a crinkled letter. I scan back and forth so quickly I can barely distinguish one word from another. One thing for certain. My mother was deeply in love with Justin Bishop, but even such intensity couldn't keep her from the pain.

—It started with my grandfather, I say to Violet.

I crush this new letter into my fist. I stare at my face in the mirror and see the curve of Sergio's chin and the horizontal of his eyes.

—No shame on you, Romey, she says. It's not you who's in those letters.

She squeezes my shoulders so hard it hurts, but it keeps me from going too deep into imagining Sergio's stolid face being bloodied by my fist. My mother's words could never be used in a court of law, but she was witness to many crimes, and it fuels my rage.

—I should have know when I was in Mariano. Nobody keeps beating themselves with the past unless there's shame.

—Whatever the bastard did, Violet says, he'll burn in hell, Romey. All the bastards will burn in their own hell, all together, the bastards, that's what the Bible says.

She pulls me away from the mirror to the bedroom with its made-up bed and hotel Bible that Violet took from the top drawer. It's open to a page that neither of us have read.

—She thought Justin was going to save her, I say. She trusted him, took care of him.

Some of the envelopes are spilled on the floor. I take one and use my index finger to slit the seal. I read slowly to Violet because she's hanging on me and won't let go. The letter tells how Maria and Justin became lovers, how she felt about him, his skin, the fragrance of his hair. Contradictions of sin and delight split every sentence. At first, the young lovers were happy in their isolated world, two souls living in the present without pressure from the future or burdens from the past.

Trouble only came when outsiders intervened, offering rewards for changes, boons for contrition. If Justin and Maria wanted the womb of family, the safety of wealth or the pride of recognition, they would have to choose a path designed by others. That path would become a trajectory that inevitably split their love.

In rushes and stops, I read how Maria fought Justin's depressions and took them on as her own. I read of their first encounter with a much younger Frank Whirlpool with all the anger and none of the wisdom. The Whirl had told me how he had learned, too late, about the good in life from my mother. If she hated him as much as she says in these letters, how could she have let him become my guardian?

My head feels too heavy for my neck. I take another letter from the stack on the floor. I begin to see an order, past to present. I skip ahead to where my mother's world changed forever. Now my world changes, too. She was pregnant. When Frank Whirlpool attacked her, he left her with more than shame. He had raped her.

I drop the letter. Violet snatches it from the floor. She reads in a monotone. The words build walls that rise up and crash down. If physics is a fundamental truth, how can the physicist be such a lie?

—I don't think we should read anymore, Violet says and crushes the letter in her lap.

—Read! I scream. The bastard took everything, Violet, even my mother.

Violet mumbles words, but I can't listen. I lie back on the bed and put a pillow over my face and pull tighter and tighter until I think it might stop the air.

—That's not what it means, Violet says. She doesn't say rape, Romey.

I spring from the bed. I pace the small bedroom with the pillow crunched in my arms.

—It was rape, I say. All those years when the Whirl told me nothing about my mother, he was just hiding his crime.

Violet puts the letter aside and pulls me to the bed. She wraps her body around me like a blanket, but I push her away and demand that she read on. She shakes her head, but finally starts, this time the words spitting from her mouth like bitter food. My mother's solitude, the seed of Sergio's violence sprouting anew, the struggle to keep her music as the one place she could rest and still believe in God.

—I'm not reading anymore, Romey, Violet says and smashes the letter face down on the bed. It's no good dragging all this up. Even if it's true, we can't do anything about it. They're dead, Romey, all of them.

I slide off the bed to the floor. I take the letter from Violet's hands and smooth the pages. I search for the place where Violet stopped reading.

—If Justin is not my father, I say, then Hope is not my aunt. She wanted to be my aunt.

—She's family, Romey. You're freaking me out. You shouldn't do this. You don't have the right to bring up the past. None of us do.

I pick up some more envelopes. I crawl on knees and hands to the bathroom. I sit like a wounded animal beside the sink and tear another envelope open.

—She tricked Justin into thinking I was his son, I say to myself, just like the Whirl tricked me.

In the other room, Violet slams drawers and kicks clothing across the floor, but I start reading aloud. The final days of my mother's life come in a few short letters, but I can barely concentrate, the thought of rape and birth banging inside my head like a piston.

—I know where it is, I say.

—What is?

—The music.

—Don't tell me that, Violet says and comes into the bathroom, not if you don't mean it.

She sits down with me. With all the spite I can muster, I read the paragraph where my mother tells Alberto how she sent a copy of her composition to the Whirl, not to make him feel her pain, but because she wanted him to understand the depth of her sorrow.

I fold the letter. My heart beats to the rhythm of the piston that continues to fire in my head. Violet takes my hand and pulls me from the floor. I sprinkle water on my face and tell her I'm going to the payphone in the lobby to tell Oscar I know about the music.

—If you know, Romey, she says, you can't tell him. You can't trust him.

I nod and allow her to plot and scheme and make sure my blind obsession for my mother's music doesn't hurt us in the end. Violet hands me the receiver and dials the number I give her for Boyer, Fine and Roberts. The receptionist answers and gives me Oscar's voice mail.

—Music found, I say simply and slam down the receiver.

—Let's walk, Violet says. I need air, Romey. You need a little air?

Step-by-step, I do my best to match Violet's feet. She puts her arm around my waist and holds me, and this is the first time in a long time I really see her for who she is, a lover, a friend, a womb.

We come to Winton Avenue, pass the library and walk on to Bloomsbury Square. We sit on a cold bench where my mother and her lover must have sat, and I remember the two letters I stuffed in my pocket. I open one and read aloud to Violet. In places the ink is smeared, but it's too dry to mix with any moisture of my own. I try to imagine my mother with Justin Bishop and Frank Whirlpool, and how they loved in opposite ways to produce the same result, the suffering of my mother. I think of the true shame in it all, that I will never really know her pain, and she will never know mine.

The setting sun breaks through the hulking oaks of Bloomsbury Square. It illuminates for a moment the steeple of the church on Chester Avenue. I pull the last letter from my pocket. In disjointed English, Maria writes to her twin brother about Justin's ideas. She does her best to describe the waveform theory, how matter and even human beings can be understood more clearly as energy waves. A circle of creation, she calls it. Energy transforms into matter, like her music that vibrates from strings to air. Human beings are energy in the form of composite waves traveling to create their own space and time.

This is what the Whirl in his shame had taught me, but I was too young and impatient to understand. There are two types of waveforms, causal and spontaneous. Causal waveforms depend on what has been. They are trapped energy, particles that interact in a trajectory of past, present and future.

It is the spontaneous waveforms, Justin Bishop had imagined and my mother believed, that provide the opportunity of physics. Virtual particles, quantum tunneling, free energy: the spontaneous movement of energy is a natural state of the universe.

In the simple words of her letter, Maria completes the circle.

Free energy is free will, she says. Free will is love. Love is the *logos* that created all things, which is what she and Alberto as children saw as God. Then the waves that move in circles go back to the beginning. God creates humans. Humans are vibrations. Vibrations create space and time, on and on.

They lived such short lives together, Maria and Justin, intersecting waveforms, a composite wave of love corrupted by fear. Trapped energy. It was a waveform in conflict and, unfortunately, it formed a causal trajectory toward their own destruction.

"Life is propagated on a wave," Maria had scribbled in her light script, "and it can be changed, Alberto, even prolonged by the constructive or destructive interference of waves, but it takes courage on the part of all."

For my mother, the musician, all was harmony and dissonance. She understood creativity as an artist. Spontaneous creation is beyond measure, beyond interference. Human life is differentiated by the ability to create new waveforms, new music, new ideas, even string quartets that get lost in the shuffle of life.

Humans get lost that way, too, but even death has a different frame of reference in Justin Bishop's language of energy. Death is the destructive interference of waves. Energy is ultimately conserved.

I put the letter into my pocket with the other one. I'm wide-awake, bursting with a new desire to know everything. I can feel my mother's life and music running through me. I take Violet's hand and we run back to the hotel and reach the lobby just as the sun's last light disappears. I check at the front desk to see if Oscar has called, but the wide-eyed clerk shakes his head and doesn't speak, which is strange because every other time we see him he always asks about our business.

We climb the stairs to our room. As I open the door, I smell perfume and so does Violet. She says maybe the maid has been in the room, but it smells familiar. I try to think of where I've smelled this fragrance before, lemon and roses. I close the door and toss the two letters on the bed with the others, then I realize the envelopes are not in the same place. They are all on the bed and the room is too quiet. The air is dense with presence.

—Romey! Violet screams.

She lunges across the bed. Tuf is stretched in the corner. His tongue is out and patches of his fur go opposite ways. Violet pulls him from a pool of dark liquid and she presses him to her chest. The smell of death mixes with the scent of lemon and roses, and I suddenly remember where I've smelled that combination before, in the bedroom of the manor, mixed with the scent of the Whirl dying.

I grab Violet and try to run, but the tainted air closes in. I see a handkerchief reach around Violet's face, then another one covers mine. As if we're praying on bending knees, the three of us drop to the floor. The smell of chloroform overwhelms the scents of death and perfume, and Violet clutches Tuf in a life grip to no avail.

THIRTY-SEVEN

I squint at the light of the lamp on the bed stand. My head pulses with a dull pain. A spot on my right cheek stabs at the center of a lattice of pain that crosshairs from my temple to my chin. The Whirl taught me about pain. Emotionally and physically. It's causal, one electron to another. In the hypothalamus of the brain, the neurons explode into action; extra blood is rerouted to the muscles; adrenaline is increased to the heart and liver; a blast of quantum particles superimposes from cell to cell in an energy transfer that has evolved from the beginning of humankind. In the infrared spectrum, the healthy human body emits about 200 watts of radiation, but I've expended so much energy all I can hope for is mercy, as if my pain has a mind of its own.

—Ahhh, Silvie says. It's about time you came to.

I see her slight form in a chair not far from where I lie on the bed. She's wearing plastic gloves. Her silver hair and aquiline nose meet at the hawk eyes that spy on me as if I'm a specimen.

—I must have used too much chloroform, she says. You've been out for hours.

Violet is curled into a ball on the chair by the window. Her hands are bound with rope. Her mouth is covered with tape. Tuf is beside her in a dark mass on the floor. I try to go to them, but my arms are lashed to the bed.

—Your little whore will be fine, Silvie says. Just worry about yourself, Romeo, though you do seem to bounce back well. When I hit you with that tire iron in Frank's office, it left quite a gash. Now it's barely noticeable.

—You, I say, not Philip?

—Not Philip, she says and laughs. Poor Philip has no stomach for such things. That's why we have politics, for weak men who think they're strong. But you, my boy, have a more dangerous flaw. You seem to think you can change the order of things.

—You poisoned Frank, I say and a spasm in my gut launches vomit to the base of my throat. I can almost see her tipping powder into the Whirl's drink, or hiding it in his food.

—May God rest his ungrateful soul.

A drip of saliva rolls from Violet's mouth down her cheek and onto the chair. I'm dripping, too, but it's blood from the cut on my cheek.

—Are you going to kill us like you killed my…like you killed Frank?

—We'll see, Silvie says, won't we? I am a little tired of this game you've been playing. As the years go on, I have far less patience. Frank wasted a great deal of my time, you know, and he was about to waste more.

With her gloves and a tissue, she wipes the blood on my cheek before it hits the sheet. She reaches into a bag on the bed and pulls out more of the rope, which she fashions into a hangman's noose and settles around my neck.

—You need to understand the seriousness of your situation, Romeo. If you do everything you can to cooperate, I won't hurt your precious whore, though she is a thief. I found the ruby in her baggage. I knew it would be too tempting for her. I planted it in the limousine in case Oscar became troublesome, but it just goes to show you how things turn out to be different from the plan. Can you imagine that ridiculous waif heiress to the Whirlpool fortune? What were you thinking, dear boy?

—Just tell me what you want, Silvie, and let her go.

—A little patience, Romeo. Did you think I would ever let Frank give you the money, make this huge mistake? I worked twenty years to build the Foundation, while Frank did nothing but drink with his political friends. Twenty years of toil and he decides to take over the Board and push me out.

—He was always pushing you, I say, and you were always pushing him.

She leans forward and pulls the noose tighter. The lamp on the bedstand is sparing of light, but Silvie's pupils are like an animal's in the dark.

—I said nothing when he took you in, she says, a bastard, nothing more than a mistake from a fling. But we had an understanding, Frank and me. He would have his life and I would have mine, but nothing was said about a child. Never trust a spurned lover with your medicine. It was Frank who caused this when he took you in after your mother died.

I taste blood where I bit my tongue. Silvie pulls from her purse a short-barreled gun with a long silencer. She slithers across the room to where Violet is curled. I pull the ropes and try to roll, but the knot just tightens more. I open my mouth to yell, but Silvie lunges to me and presses the gun against my temple.

—One mistake, she says. First you, then her. Do you understand?

I nod. The cold barrel scrapes across my skin. She glares at me. Her face is frozen in a mask of hate. The gun travels down my cheek to my chin and her finger tenses on the trigger, then releases slowly as if she's considering every motion. Her huge pupils drift up to mine, but she looks through me to somewhere deep inside her mind.

—You could have been our child, she says as her mask melts for a moment, then she shakes the thought away and lifts the gun level with my cheek. She slinks away and back to the chair in the corner.

—So pretty, Silvie says and smooths Violet's hair with the tip of the gun barrel. Too bad beauty fades, she says, but we're working on that. Frank thought the idea was silly. He knew so little about women. Skin care matched to the frequency of a woman's derma cells would be a gift of the gods. Smooth skin like your little Jezebel's here may soon be available to every woman, and it's more than vanity. It's science, frequency injections, electron infusion, photon phase modulation, we're even working on a method to replace chemotherapy, but there's a shortage of capital. Frank died just in time. His fortune will do the trick. Now he can do in death what he was too obstinate to do in life.

Silvie reaches for one of my mother's letters and tears open the envelope. Silently, she reads and the more she reads the more her face loses her determined expression. Her eyes grow cold and distant, and the gun slowly drops until Violet moves and Silvie shakes herself back to the present.

—This must have been her last letter, she says, poor soul. I was with Frank when you were born, you know. It doesn't say that in any of these letters, I suppose, how you came between us. It's not the fact of a child, really, it was more what we had promised. What we had hoped for. When Frank had your whore of a mother, it ruined us. Everything I had worked for came to nothing, and your mother was the start of it, Romeo. This one, she says and presses the gun harder on Violet's cheek, reminds me of her. The same appearance of frailty when inside there's nothing but nerve.

—Let her go, Silvie, I say and pull harder on the ropes.

—I would advise you not to struggle, she says. The more damage that shows, the more I'll have to consider killing you. A bullet in your head, your girlfriend's prints on the gun, problem solved.

Violet flinches from the cold barrel. Her eyebrows stretch and her mouth puckers, but she doesn't wake. With the tip of the gun, Silvie pushes a tuft of blond hair away from Violet's forehead.

—Let her go! I scream and Silvie's eyes widen. She drops the letter and leaps to me before I can yell again. The barrel lodges between my lips and clicks on my teeth. I taste the oil and gunpowder. I imagine the silencer puffing and the cold bullet blasting out the back of my head, but all I hear is a mix of nervous breathing, different tempo, different beat, Silvie and me.

—You can survive this, Romeo, she says, if only for some misplaced regret for what I did to Frank. Your whore can go free and so will you, but you've got to concentrate on what I'm saying.

She draws the gun from my mouth and reaches for a paper on the table. She lays it on the bed beside me. I remember when the Whirl would take me to Silvie's house on Fifth Avenue. Every wall and open space were the spoils of her gruesome hobby. Mounted like the musical instruments in the Whirl's collection, dead animals were poised: stags in flight, boars at charge, lions leaping on imaginary prey.

—Sign the paper, she says, and your whore will survive.

Violet squirms and stretches her body against the tape. Silvie scrambles on all fours and puts the silencer to Violet's face, and I think the gun goes off, Puff! Yet the room is silent.

—I'll sign, I say. Just don't hurt Violet.

She smiles and drops the gun from Violet's cheek. She leaps to the bed, unties one of my hands from the bedpost and puts a pen between my fingers. As she slides the document beneath the pen, I scribble my name.

—Good boy, she says and tucks the document and my mother's last letter into her bag by the door. I feel a bit cheated, she says. I feel most alive when I'm stalking prey. Frank was not my first, you see.

There was a lover in Norway, but that was when I was much younger. One shot was all it took. When people realize they're about to die, they have such lovely faces, as if they know something we could not possibly understand.

Silvie's eyes are so wide they no longer show white. She points the gun at Violet and squeezes slightly on the trigger, so with my free hand I swing, but she's too fast. The gun slams against my temple and I shudder on the bed.

—More blood on the linens, she says. Such a fool.

She grabs a towel from the bathroom and wets it. My head wound has split open. She daubs my scalp and tries to wipe the sheet.

—I really should kill you, she says as she unties my other hand. Leaving loose ends was Frank's weakness. Now it's mine, I suppose. Frank's last favor. I don't want to see you again, Romeo. Take your whore and run as far and as fast as you can away from here, away from me.

THIRTY-EIGHT

December 23, 1986

My baby is born, Alberto. The air is filled with the scent of soft blankets and salty skin. As I write this letter, he sleeps in his cradle, but I am as close to this baby as if he were still in my womb. His eyes are deep green, almost black like an Argasti. A swirl of dark hair barely covers his skin, and his nose, you should see, could only be that of his Uncle Alberto. So proud is he of his beauty!

We named him after Mamma's papà. Justin and I have never married, so the baby keeps *il mio cognome*, and though I fought against it, we have given this poor baby the middle name of a particle. Imagine, Alberto, your nephew facing the schoolyard with the name Romeo Quark Argasti!

He is *perfetto*, brother. Whether he becomes a great physicist as Justin believes, or a great musician as I do, Romeo is an amazing creature. When I hold him to my breast, his tiny mouth sucks away my breath. He will be the first of a new generation of Argastis. Once Papà sees Romeo, surely he will realize no child is a bastard. For that, I hold faith above hope.

On the day when Romeo was born, Justin was with me. We talked and imagined how this child's life will go, but as soon as the baby was home, Justin was gone. He stays long hours at the laboratory, and with all there is for me to do and learn about a new baby, it has been difficult. If it isn't Romeo needing to be fed or changed, it is someone at the door hoping to find Justin at home. He has become a celebrity. Dean Harrad called two days ago, not to congratulate Justin on the birth of his baby, but to tell him Royal Holloway is approaching the Nobel committee.

Justin belittles it. He says it is just a publicity stunt, more politics than science. He deserves recognition, I tell him. His ideas have helped me. They give me courage to bring a baby into this world, but it is Romeo who teaches me, now. He helps me understand what Justin has always believed, that we are stardust and separated only by the blindness of birth. Babies are created, Justin says, as all things are created, by these elemental waves that combine and recombine from the most ancient forms. New life is old life continued, and I believe that now more than ever. To hold Romeo in my arms is to feel myself breathing. He is connected through me to the past, and I am connected through him to the future.

This baby is a Godsend, Alberto. Little Romeo shows me nothing on this earth can be evil, even those who would hurt us. We are only particles colliding, pure notes in an infinite measure, set upon this trajectory from the beginning of time. Yet even as I begin to understand Justin's physics, the physicist seems to forget. He finds little time to be with us. Like most scientists I meet, he is blind to the beauty of his ideas. He can barely contain his excitement about the nomination, though he contends it is nothing. I see great hope in his eyes. It is the same look he gives the baby.

As if I should be impressed with the great people that shake his hand, Justin called tonight from the college. He told me who was with him, a friend from America, a scientist from Spain, another from Denmark. He said Frank Whirlpool asked about my health. I asked Justin if Silvie had been so thoughtful, but he did not answer.

He and Frank must tremble for what Silvie knows. She is their lover, and lovers are always confessors, and Silvie is not a woman to hold secrets without gain. These two men make a grave mistake. She will ask a payment that neither will be able to give.

I try not to think too much of it. I play my cello softly until Romeo goes to sleep in his cradle. I am nearly finished with the string quartet I have been working on for so long. A few notes linger and refuse to go on paper. I sit and squeak the bow lightly across the strings, but awake or asleep, Romeo absorbs the sounds as if it were sustenance. I play him parts of the quartet and the air fills with the sounds of nature, whales crooning, gulls screeching and waves crashing on the sand.

When the sun goes down, I hum a mother's lullaby. This is how I find peace, Alberto. I do not want parties or dinners where Justin speaks from his head and seeks fortune. I do not share his need to escape the long shadow of his father's time. For me, I prefer the stillness of motherhood. It is a shame that being a wife and mother is not one and the same. The happiness that should be ours, the bond between man, woman and child, has been corrupted. Justin speaks of the baby and his nomination as if they were the same. He turns physics to ambition instead of love.

This is my life, brother. I will live with my shame until someone tells me, maybe God, that truth can be told in full. Justin wants me to go with him to Stockholm, though I have told him to go alone. I test him, as I test myself. I can use the time, I told him, to finish my music. How can I explain to him that I find more peace in work than in being with my lover?

It is not Justin's fault. We are all weak in our ignorance. Surely, he must suspect. When he looks into my eyes, I turn away or pretend something has distracted me. I do not play for him anymore. I play only for Romeo. He and Frank Whirlpool are the only ones who have heard a bit of my final composition. Justin is too busy and my professors at University have not called since they heard news of the baby. I have only to see Romeo opening wide his beautiful eyes to know my music will live on. He will understand what lovers understand, that when each note leaves the page and flows freely, it is created anew.

What more could a woman want, Alberto? I have a beautiful baby boy, a scholarship at the Royal Academy, a lover who says he loves me. I hear Romeo talking to me with the rumbling song he sang for so long in my belly. I live with the fear of all mothers, that when I wake my baby will not be beside me, but in more deserving arms.

I must give him everything I have to give, the love of a mother, the truth. As I look at Romeo's sweet mouth and sleepy eyes, he gives me strength to carry on in this ocean of lies. I must tell him all. He should know his father from his birth father, though of how I am still unsure. You must promise me, brother, if something happens to me, you will tell your nephew what I have told you. He will need to face the truth, or the lies will keep him from peace.

THIRTY-NINE

Violet is potential energy, a boulder held high, the force of gravity warping spacetime until it draws its victim near. It's only my plan that keeps her from launching a vigilante hunt for Silvie Nels. Violet knows I know where the music is. It's a continent away, but it's ours if we stay focused. From the moment we buried poor Tuf in a corner of Bloomsbury Park, I saw in Violet's stolid eyes a determination as clear as the deadly warning of the murderess.

We land at Kennedy International in the early afternoon. Violet is back to dressing in a midriff and shorts, so the sky caps fall all over themselves to help. We find our luggage and make our way to the curb for ground transportation, but the cabbies are not so obliging. One of them in a Sikh turban walks around our tattooed bodies and grabs the bags of three businessmen in cheap suits. The next driver in line doesn't think so quickly, so we have him.

—New Jersey? he says. That's a long way. I need the fare upfront. If you've got it, get in. If not, move outta the way.

Violet throws her bag into the trunk and stares at him as if to say the world is screwed by people like you, and the more you distrust me, the more I can't be trusted. She's looked at me a hundred times that way, but she softens because she knows I'm not going to fight

her. I want the music as much as she does, if not for the same reason.
I'd do anything to hear the song of my mother.

—What's going on here? I say to the guard as the cab pulls beside
the guard shack at the driveway of the Whirlpool estate.

I get out of the cab and take a short puff on the cigarette I bummed
from Violet. I give the driver another fifty and ask him to wait. A
New Jersey State Trooper steps from a cruiser that's parked in front of
the guard shack. Two more police cars are lined along the drive and
three more are at the house. The trooper asks for identification, and
I give him my passport and ask him why the driveway to the manor
house is barricaded.

—This property is under police orders, he says as he scans his
clipboard. Unless your name is on this list, you can't go in.

—I live here.

—Your name's not on this list. You've got to turn that cab around
and clear the lane.

—Did you hear him! Violet screeches from the window of the
cab. He lives here, dammit. It's his fucking mansion.

—Watch your mouth, young lady.

Then before I can stop her, Violet opens the door of the cab and
lunges toward the officer. I step between just in time.

—My mouth's none of your damn business, she says and tries to
push around me, but I hold her. Check your records, she says. Call
his lawyer. That's it, call his lawyer. Tell him, Romey.

—Get back in the cab, the officer says. If your name's not on the
list, I can't let you in. Now get this car out of the driveway.

He shoves my passport back into my hand. The cab driver starts
to back out of the drive, but Violet's door is still open and it stops
him from leaving. I pull Violet back to the car and give the driver
another fifty. I change my strategy and tell the trooper my orphan
story and he seems to weaken a little. I spell my name again, but he
shakes his head and tells me the prosecutor's office is reviewing the

records of the estate.

—There's a lockdown, he says. People are suing. It's a mess. Yesterday, it was all over the papers. Where you been?

The officer goes to his cruiser and picks up his radio. I climb into the cab next to Violet and shut the door. I tell the driver there's no problem, but he's bucking to leave because he's already been paid. Violet sits with her arms tight around her. The trooper comes back and bends at my window.

—I checked again, he says. There's no Argasti on the station's database. I talked to the detective in charge, but he doesn't know anything about you. You'll have to go.

Violet punches the door with her elbow. The trooper shakes his head and goes back to his cruiser. The cab driver makes a three-point turn and a left out of the driveway. We're about a mile from the estate when I tell the driver to pull to the side. It takes some time for him to realize I'm serious, but eventually he stops. I hop out and Violet starts screaming but hops out after me. The driver sees the opportunity to escape, so he jumps out and opens the trunk. With one motion he heaves our bags to the culvert. Violet and I stand next to the road and watch the cab disappear.

—Why the hell did you do that? she says. He left us in the middle of nowhere.

—There's a way in, I say.

—Yeah, she says, we go back there and tell the bastard you're the damn owner. We make it his problem. That's what we do. You can't let them ignore you like this. It ain't right, Romey.

—Give me a cigarette.

—I'm out, thanks to you.

—Now we wait. It's still a little too light out. Trust me.

She holds her hands high, and she's about to scream again, but the trust part works its magic. We find a place in a grove of trees on the opposite side of the road. We wait until the sun works its way below the trees and leaves a trail of darkness. I dash to the opposite side of the road and to the fence I remember. It runs along a manicured lawn for a few miles, then through a tangle of woods for another five. When I was young, the Whirl took me on long walks around the estate as an excuse to teach me physics or tell me stories about how he grew up poor in Brooklyn. Now the memory of those walks has a different feel. It's confusing, the hate and love, but if time could only go backward, father and son.

—I played on these grounds my whole life, I say to Violet. I know the woods. I made some holes in these fences so I could get through without climbing. There's a path beyond these trees and a ditch where the dogs always got loose.

—And when they shoot us? she says. What good is a sheet of music when you're dead?

—You don't have to come.

—Yeah, well, who's going to watch your back. Tell me that, Romey?

—You are, I say and her eyebrows furrow.

We hide our bags in some bushes by the culvert. She holds my hand and follows me along the fence until we find a hole large enough to slip under and into a bramble of berry vines. We hunch down and run along a narrow path that's less dark than the woods. We come to a clearing at the back of the manor. Security lights pulsate like bright stars. We have no choice but to risk the expanse of mowed grass that's narrowest on the south. The prosecutor's lockdown has effectively cut the back of house off from the front lane. Six troopers are posted at the side entrance, but to control the open land around the Whirlpool estate would take a small army.

—It's in the den, I whisper.

—The music?

—It must be.

—You said you knew. You told me you knew exactly where

it was, Romey. These guys got guns, and now you don't know for sure?

—I know how the Whirl thought.

—I guess you would, she says, the bastard.

We run low to a bank of windows and wait for a few minutes to see if there's any movement in the Whirl's old office. I see tiny lights from the security alarms on the windows and doors, all but one particular window, third from the left. I remember once after returning from a walk, the Whirl realized he had forgotten his keys. It was about the hundredth time, so he decided to fix the problem. He pulled the window's wires and close-looped the circuit for good.

I look behind a bush and find the short screwdriver we always used nearly buried in the dirt. I insert the rusty blade where the window meets the sill. I push slowly, then jam it hard and the window springs open.

—Damn, Romey, Violet says, that's very cool.

—My father taught me how to do that, I say and, for a moment, I feel butterflies flutter in my chest.

Violet lifts the window, and we wait for a sound, but nothing happens. I toss the screwdriver behind the bush, then quietly slip over the window sill and wait for Violet to do the same. The den is dark except for a night light by the door. A faint glow shows the outlines of a pile of instruments in the corner.

—So where is it? Violet says.

—Emilio Dentrante, I say.

—Emilio what?

—The Whirl's instrument repairman. Once a month, he made a stop with his tool chest. The Whirl kept all the instruments that needed repaired in here. One instrument Emilio never seemed to take back to his shop. It just sat there in its case. I always figured it was too far gone.

I close the window and reset the latch. I decide not to risk a light, so I ask Violet to use her cigarette lighter and we follow its glow to where the moon has made an outline of the forgotten instrument in its tall black case. I lay it on its back and carefully open the latches. With both hands, I lift the wooden mass and carefully lay it on the rug.

Violet touches the long, wooden neck and by accident strums a string. We freeze while an open C note vibrates across the room and dissipates. We wait a minute or two, but there's no sound of anyone in the hall.

—It's a cello, I say.

—I know it's a cello, Romey.

I shake the instrument to see if anything has been stuffed inside the curling sound holes that flank the strings, but there's no rustling. I check the main compartments in the case, but I find only bow resin and a wiping cloth. I feel along the sides of the velvet liner and find the edges where it meets the leather. In the middle of the case, where the instrument has matted the velvet, I feel a square edge. I follow the raised line across, then down and across again. I put my finger into one of the frayed spots at the edge and tear the cloth like a zipper.

—You find it? Violet says. Is that the music?

I pull the square through the torn velvet. I raise Violet's hand with the lighter so the glow covers the entire case.

—Is that it? Violet says. Tell me, Romey.

The papers are lined in staff notation with scribbled notes above and below. My hand is shaking, so the sheets rustle like autumn leaves. In the light from Violet's lighter, I see several pages in handwritten notation showing which notes are stopped and their durations.

—My mother's hand, I say.

—Jesus, Romey, it's the same writing as the letters. I know it.

My heart pounds a monster beat because I see the signature: Maria Elana Argasti, 1987. I lay the music carefully on the floor. I ask Violet to hold the lighter higher so I can see both the cello strings and the sheet of music. Still sitting on the floor, I position the cello between my legs and lift the bow, but I can't manage because the frets are too high.

—What the hell are you doing? Violet says.

I nod as if it's an answer. Violet can't keep the lighter lit so I stand and switch on the small light that illuminates the fake Vermeer. I pull a chair over and sit upright with the cello. All those lessons the Whirl made me take were for something. They taught me how to tuck the huge curved body between my legs and hold my arms lightly above the strings. What else did the Whirl do and know?

—It's for a string quartet, I say.

—You're not gonna play it. Not here.

The first note is loud and out of tune. I pluck a string and turn a tuner on the dusty instrument. Violet tries to shush me, but I ignore her. It feels too right, holding my mother's cello and reading these mottled notes inked by her precious hand. I pluck another string, then run the bow along for one full measure. The sound is too loud to stay in the room, but I can't stop myself. I read the notations. I try to decipher her notes and find the rhythmic structure, the quavers and semiquavers, the beams and slurs.

I try more notes, measure upon measure, following the staff across the discolored pages. At first the notes build in what is clearly a chamber music score, sad and sallow, but as I find my way through the rhythm, it breaks down to something less than what I imagined. I'm not sure if it's the music or my poor ability to play, but my heartbeat skips a nervous beat. There's something missing. More notes are needed to fill in the gaps.

—That's horrible, Violet says.

—It needs two violins and a viola. Dammit, I need more light, Violet.

She clicks the lighter harder and holds it close to the music, but it doesn't help. I can barely make out the faded notations and handwritten notes. I flip through the sheets. I imagine the other instruments in my head, one folding across the other as layers of a whole. Finally I sense a melody, but it's too complex for someone of my talent to do justice.

—That stinks, Violet says. Maybe your mother, you know, not meaning any disrespect, but maybe she wasn't very good.

I flash Violet the angriest stare I can muster. I feel woozy. I shift to the next sheet. I draw the bow across the strings and play a few more measures. In my head I begin to add a few notes from one violin to create a melody, *vibrato* upon *vibrato*. My hand shakes with the bow. Ripples of tension move up my arm and through my shoulder. The notes become louder and louder. The cello wails as if it's still not in tune, but I swear it's the way she's written the music. I keep playing, shaking and grating across the cello's body until the end of the score, one last note, a lone A that fills the room with a bold sound as if all the dissonance and resonance comes down to one frequency, clear and long.

Then it hits me. As the A-note ricochets back and forth across the room, I realize it has left me weeping. Tears hit the mottled wood of the cello and I look at Violet to see if she sees me, but she has her eyes closed.

—You hear that, I say. Tension and release, Violet, like she had us, then let us go.

—I heard it, she says, then she suddenly jumps up. So did they, Romey. You played too loud, now they're at the door!

—Doesn't matter.

—The hell it doesn't, she whispers. Grab the music, Romey.

She shuffles the sheets into a pile, but I grab them before she can take them. There's a few papers that are not like the others, no lines or measures. I stare at them as a pounding begins at the door.

—Let's go, Romey! We can make it.

I lay the cello on the floor. I turn on the overhead light so I can see the typed papers more clearly. The pounding is getting louder, but I'm beyond caring who finds us, who finds me. It's a scientific paper, just like the one Bill had in the box in his closet.

—Open up! comes a yell at the door.

—It's Justin's paper, I say to Violet who waits at the window. And there's a letter, I say.

—Who cares, Romey. We've got to get out of here.

—Jesus, Violet, it's to the Nobel committee.

She forces the window back open with her fingers. There's the sound of keys in the lock at the door. I hold the letter in the light. It's an apology, I realize. His experiments, it says, failed to verify his conclusions, just like Bill said. Justin asks them to withdraw any record of his nomination by Royal Holloway. It accuses Frank Whirlpool and Silvie Nels of changing his paper. It accuses them of fraud.

—That's why, I say, she tried to murder Bill, but Violet doesn't hear because she's already out the window. Bill's paper must have been the only evidence, I realize. Until now.

The key in the lock jingles and the doorknob turns. Two troopers plunge into the room with guns drawn. I hold up my hands and see Violet at the window. She tries to run, but one officer bolts to the window and raises his gun.

—Don't! I scream. She doesn't have anything to do with this.

I see Violet stop. She turns and comes back to the window. She puts her hand on the sill and climbs back inside.

—The hell I don't, she says. I do have something to do with this. It's me and you, that right, Romey?

I nod and put my arm around her waist. The trooper holds his gun steady. He sees we don't have any weapons, so he eventually points his down. I hand the papers to the one who seems to be in charge, and I tell him it's evidence and not to let anyone, for any reason, take them away until he gives them to the prosecutor.

The truth is beginning to come clear. The data the Whirl used to make his fortune was falsified from the beginning. He and Silvie used Justin's nomination to justify their claims of frequency modification. The Foundation's line of frequency drugs, after all, was based on a scam.

While Bill's copy gathered dust in the shoebox, there was no threat to Silvie or the Whirl. When Violet and I showed up at Bill's door, the murderess was watching.

In the end, the Whirl has done the same to Silvie as she did to him. Destruction comes in many forms. One wave crashing on another, energy trapped in a field of avarice and ambition.

The officer reads us our rights. He handcuffs us more for procedure than because he thinks we're any danger. Several more officers come and, as if they might uncover a conspiracy, they go to search for others. What they don't know is there *has* been conspiracy. Two conspiracies that started twenty years ago: one to keep a son from his mother, the other to keep their fraud from ever being known.

FORTY

The last letter from Maria to Alberto was used as evidence in a New York court of law, though it was not written as a means to judgement. The letter was intended by Maria as a search for forgiveness, and if it had not been taken from the hotel that night by Silvie, my future might have been much different. If I had read the letter, my mother's depth of forgiveness might have seeped into my soul and been enough to sustain me. Her music might still remain hidden, the Whirl's request for redemption from the grave denied. Yet that would be in a perfect world where the suffering of others is embraced as the suffering of self. And this is not a perfect or imperfect world, rather one where beauty is obscured in a quantum uncertainty that will only make sense when we embrace forgiveness.

February 12, 1987

I write this letter without knowing whether you will receive it or it will go unread. Perhaps it is better that my life goes unmeasured by eyes that see only God on High. I live in the world God began, the one where nature is not so intended or destined that we can conform it to our desires.

I am leaving in two short hours with Justin for his presentation in Stockholm and what should be the start of our brightest future. It should be Justin's moment, an acknowledgment of his achievement, but now it is fixed by a lie.

This morning as if his enemies had gathered, Justin stood in the kitchen with his back against the wall. In his hand, he held some crumpled papers that were shaking just as he was shaking. As if he had gone mad, his eyes were wide and he ranted that everything he had worked for, his ideas, the nomination, all had been ruined by these papers.

Then before I could stop him, Justin lit the burner on the stove and touched the paper to a flame. *Calmarte!* I screamed, but smoke clogged the room and the fire alarm screeched and the baby began to cry.

On Justin's face was a vacant look. Then I realized, Alberto, no matter what he said, the nomination meant everything to him. I grabbed the flaming papers and doused them in the sink, but the building manager had heard the alarm. He began to pound on the door, but I was too stunned to answer.

He did not wait. He used his key and rushed in to open a window and fan the smoke. What is wrong with you! he screamed at us, but he saw our faces and he knew that more was ruined than those papers. If you can't think of yourselves, he said, think of others. Think of your baby! The whole building could have gone up in flames.

He reset the alarm and left Justin and I in the kitchen staring at the charred papers in the sink. The author's name could still be read on one of the blackened pages. He does not think I know what happened, what caused this, but I know more than he imagines. This trouble is only part of the shame we share with those who will go to any length to destroy themselves and those they hate and love.

Justin saw his name and ripped the rest of the papers into pieces. They altered my words, he said. They sent these lies to the committee. The nomination means nothing. All my work for nothing.

In my apron pocket, I curled my fingers around the plane tickets. Romeo was still crying, but I did not go to him as usual. I hung my head to keep Justin from seeing the shame on my face. Against my heart, I had resolved to go with him, to stand by his side as he answered the committee's questions. Anything to have a little time alone with Justin, if only to see if things can ever be right.

This morning, he said, Frank admitted at least one of his lies. Frank said it was Silvie who changed the accelerator report, but he and Silvie are both to blame.

Justin vowed to put an end to it, expose their fraud, his fraud. I helped him to the couch. I put my head on his shoulder. I could feel his heart beating in unison with mine. Now, betrayal is something we have in common. He knows what it is to be violated, raped of honor, so I rocked him until he could turn his anger into a pain I could share.

This will do more damage than they imagine, he said. Facts based on a lie are no more than beliefs. That is the way these things work, Maria. Once the belief begins, it is perpetuated on a wave of ignorance. Unless the committee realizes this fraud, the lie becomes a force on its own. Then the belief becomes me, Maria, and I become the lie.

I held him as if letting go would risk me losing him forever. I whispered into his ear that I loved him and that the rest of the world should be ignored. Others mean nothing if the two of us are together, I said. The three of us, I meant. It is not so bad, I said, a minor nomination, a mention to be lost in books.

I ruined my father's name, he said angrily and stood from the couch. My son is lucky he has a different last name.

Then as if his thought had mixed with my own, I saw fear grow in his eyes like a storm. He saw my doubt. He could feel my shame as if the whole evil story had escaped my lips.

If he is my son, Justin said with barely a breath, then he looked from me to the room where Romeo was crying.

I have not seen such a look of utter defeat, Alberto. Before he could think or say anymore, I left him and ran to the bedroom where the baby was tangled in blankets. I picked up Romeo and rocked him on my knees. I asked Justin to come and look at our baby, but it was as if the genius of physics had been struck dumb, so I dressed poor Romeo in his little blue sweater and rolled him in the scarlet blanket.

The baby will go with the sitter, I said to Justin. Our son will be fine, Justin. Everything is arranged. We are tired. The baby is colic. I have not been sleeping. I am no good to him. I need time away. Remember, it is not only you who has been betrayed.

I put the tickets on the table. While I rocked the baby, Justin gathered the scorched pages of his paper into a pile. The minutes went by, one by one, as I waited for him to determine our future.

My father would have fought them, he said as he took the tickets from the table. Our son needs a father who knows how to fight against a lie.

Then he kissed me on the cheek, a simple kiss that surprised him as much as it did me. That kiss held a measure of forgiveness, and I did not wait for him to explain or change his mind. I took the tickets from Justin and put them in my purse. I finished packing our suitcases. I kissed our sweet baby over and over and rocked him to sleep, then I took our Romeo to Mrs. Donnely, our neighbor on the second floor who will keep him safe for the few days we are gone.

Now Justin sits in silence at the kitchen table and writes his courageous letter. He will tell the committee to reject the papers that were submitted without his approval. His ideas are not to be measured so easily, he will tell them, but they are important just the same.

I have also written a letter against a lie. In some ways it took as much courage as Justin's letter. Mine was addressed to Frank

Whirlpool. It tells him what he already knows and what Justin may have guessed, that poor Romeo is the beautiful and innocent result of a violent seed.

The window is now streaming with a chilling rain. Soon, Justin and I will leave for the airport. I know my sins have helped these devils play with our lives, but sin is fear and fear, as I have learned, is only a vibration. For all its frightful character, fear is the ambivalent motion of nature, nothing more. I learned this in a hard way, by failing to understand how Silvie's fear of this baby would be so deep she would exact a lasting price on Justin. Ambivalence in love is desperation. Does she love Frank too little, or too much?

Soon there will be time to think more about the present than the past. Justin and I will be together in Sweden. He will stand shoulder-to-shoulder with the great men and women of our time. When he gives his letter to the committee, I will hold his hand as a lover and friend. I will stand by him as he tries to stop the motion of a lie.

If only I can show such courage. When I tell Justin the whole truth, without omission, it may heal us or destroy us, only God can know. If Justin can expect forgiveness from such a grand committee, I shall expect nothing less from him. The truth will build on what he begins in Sweden. It will not stop until it collides with what we have started in error at home. Justin's action will testify to the soundness of his ideas, that despite his weakness and mine, he has found something that makes sense of the world, even the lies.

FORTY-ONE

The wave function in quantum physics is a mathematical tool based on the equations of Austrian physicist Erwin Schrödinger. The wave function is related to the probability that a particle will be in a particular place at a particular time. It takes into consideration all the possible routes of the particle, which are infinite, and gives a picture of what might happen next. Most importantly, the wave function collapses when all possible paths cancel each other out, but one. The remaining path is what we call reality.

The canceling of these infinite possibilities is in some ways as important as the final wave. The Whirl understood this process all too well when he created the waveform Violet and I had just collapsed.

—Danny busted us, Chalice says. You must be psychic, Romey. We need a drummer. Only trouble is Danny stole everything but the platform, even the sandbag for the bass.

—That's okay, I say. Just say the word and I'll buy a whole new set.

—Go ahead, Chalice says, like you got that kind of cash.

I shrug my shoulders and Violet pinches my arm, and we yuck like two fools over the uncertainty of it all. Not only do we have more than enough cash, but enough to buy a thousand drum sets, and Bonner's, and the whole damn city block. So Violet and I leave Chalice in a state of confusion and hoof it to a nearby pawnshop. We pay cash for a new set of drums and have it delivered by show time. It's a beautiful composite, a percussion hybrid of traditional pads and cymbals, rattles and shakes, two congas and a small Chinese gong.

—*Seven rollers on a play*, sings Chalice as he shakes his shaggy mane at the crowd that's come to hear us, *Seven players on a roll...*

Bonner's is full of street bikers and weekend junkies, but the beat hangs in the background of Chalice's lyrical circles and the band is tight, so the crowd stops hustling for awhile and pays attention. I still can't say I'm one with the drumsticks, but I'm slowly getting the hang of it again. It's good to see Chalice so into his music and hear Violet laughing out loud. It's good to be playing drums like old times in New York City. The future comes in tiny segments, rapid-fire riffs, twists and turns of a phrase, spontaneous energy in and out. Each present moment is a new universe so unlike the old it could be a new dimension, but I think it must be the same one despite the infinities.

Just a hunch, I suppose. Einstein said God doesn't play dice, and I believe it. Nothing so probable as a simple toss of the dice and I'm all for loading them way up front. In the end you've got to let the dice go, so I hit the floor tom hard as if I'm trying to pop its skin, but it jumps back and tempts me to bring on even more. A double crash on the piggyback cymbals ends the set, and Chalice bows and steps down from his platform to shake my hand, fist-to-fist.

—Whew, lover, Violet says as she sweeps up to the drum platform and leans over the snare to kiss me. You're on fire, baby. It makes me hot, it does.

I grin with embarrassment because two drunks have overheard, though they nod with us and it seems as if nothing can go wrong. I hesitate before I stash the sticks in the hollow of the bass drum. If Danny comes and steals them, I'll just buy more. I'll buy him a whole new setup, no hard feelings. I walk on the balls of my feet with Violet hanging on my shoulder. We go to the bar and order two beers.

—Oscar's outside, she says. He won't come in. Does he have any clothes besides that double-breasted piece?

We finish our beers in big swallows and work our way through the crowd with lots of "how-you-doings" and a blast of smoke as we bust through the door to the street. Oscar is pacing across the street in front of an old, brick building that's splashed with ten repetitive billboards of another revival of the Grateful Dead, minus the dead.

—Good, you're here, he says and shakes my hand. Why haven't you called me, Romey? We've needed to talk.

I light a cigarette for Violet and she lets loose a circle of smoke that Oscar tries to brush away before it reaches his suit. I sniff the night air of Water Street and it stinks, which is normal. Without a doubt, it's home and I feel a certain thrill in the background of sirens and the clicking of spike heels and boots. It's more than edgy, or hip, or down. It's the physics of humanity. It's probability waves to infinity, the universal wave function in micro and macro, the uncertainty of position and momentum at its best.

—I knew you'd never agree to it, I say. I don't need you to come all the way from Thirty-Seventh Street to yell at me, Oscar. It's done.

—It's insane! he roars. That's what it is, Romey. Silvie's in jail, Philip's in the Caymans, and Frank's nieces are preparing a legal challenge that, undoubtedly, will take decades to fight. All for what, I ask you? Take a few bucks and give the rest to science? What the hell is that, Romey? Only the dying give their money away.

—What's he talking about? Violet says. She takes a puff and looks at me with her face askew.

—Didn't tell her, did you? Oscar says. I knew you wouldn't tell her. This lunatic is giving away the money, Stephanie. He's gone insane.

—What's he saying? she says to me.

—We don't need the money, Violet.

—Like hell we don't.

—It's done, I say. I was going to tell you later.

Violet puffs on her cigarette as if it's the last one she'll ever smoke, which is what she keeps telling me, but it's never the one.

—You're a shitass, she says. All we've been through and you give the damn money away?

—Except for pocket change, Oscar says, not billions, not even millions for Christ's sake, but thousands, a few hundred thousand.

—We won't starve, I say. Look, I still feel a little dirty. My father lied to a lot of people, Violet. He and Silvie took a good thing and made it bad, so I put a stop to it.

Violet holds my eyes ransom. She shakes her head back and forth.

—After all we went through, she says, half way across the world.

She stares at me and I stare at her until we both break into a smile, then a laugh.

—You shitass, she says and flips the cigarette butt on the ground and grinds it with her shoe. Okay, we're poor, she says. No shame, is there, Oscar? No shame to be poor, big boy? You'll loan us your car, won't you?

Oscar pinches his lips, but it's less at Violet's jab than because he knows she was his last chance to change my mind. He shakes his troll head and sniffs the night air.

—Jesus, he says, how can you stand the smell of this place? It's disgusting. I don't know why I stay in New York. Maybe Miami.

He turns to leave, but I stop him and ask him the latest. He tells me Silvie's getting her just reward. They tested the Whirl's last bottle of his morning freq pills from the Foundation and detected the residue of poison. They traced the bottle to the manufacturing plant in Denmark on a night when the spurned lover was working a little late and Frank Whirlpool's prescription was on the line. A little strychnine into the Whirl's morning dose, one waveform so caustic it could collapse another. The whole universe is changed forever.

—As far as they know, Oscar says, it was just Silvie. Your uncle wasn't involved, though he still comes out a loser. Philip spent a couple million of estate funds on his campaign, and that's something the prosecutors won't forget, let alone the Methodists. I hear the new sanctuary at the Riverport Church will be dedicated to a congressperson from Newark.

I shake my head and smile. It all makes sense in the *logos*, like my father said, but I know it wouldn't be right to say it aloud. It's too personal. Too spontaneous. To understand how things were from the beginning of time takes a good reading of Maria's letters, and a visit to the time-warped village of Mariano, and an infinite view of a universe where solid ground vibrates and the sky quivers like the strings of a cello.

—You sure about the money? Oscar asks as we walk to where his Lincoln is parked. One billion dollars for particle research, he says. That's insane.

—You're just worried about losing a client.

—The appeals will cost millions, he says. It's never going to end.

—That's why I named Fermilab and CERN the trustees. Their lawyers can handle the lawsuits. I've had money all my life, Oscar. I saw where it got Frank. What comes around goes around, they say. Eye of the needle, and that's not so far from the truth.

—I knew you'd get religious, he says. Just keep enough cash to stay out of jail, Romey. With the way you live, that's not going to be easy.

I nod my head and shake his hand. Violet gives him a kiss on the cheek, which makes him fall humpty-dumpty into the back seat of the Lincoln. Violet finishes one more of her *final* cigarettes while I use the drumsticks to get the buzz of lawsuits and ambition out of my head. Like Violet, ever since I decided, the world has been a little easier to handle. No ambivalence. No vibrations out of fear. Now and again, the negative waves still do their thing, but I know it's just nature doing its thing.

When you speak the language, you realize it's how you handle it that makes the difference. There's no such thing as perpetual motion. Destructive waves collapse into energy. Constructive waves expand to infinity. Violence begets violence, peace begets peace, and the quantum fact of it all is that the universe taught us the way over fourteen billion years ago. Antimatter lost to matter, and the truth is no more amazing than what the Whirl told me before he rejoined the cosmos. It's more what you do with the field and less what the field does with you.

A few days later, Violet and I meet Oscar one last time. He set up a private concert at Lincoln Center. It's the Philharmonic's day off, so two violins, a viola and a cello are in the arms of four musicians in jeans and sweaters. On their music stands are copies of my mother's composition. The musicians seem confused, not just because the audience is just three people, but the notes on the pages don't match their sense of what a string quartet should be.

The first violinist tells me he's got a theory. He says my mother may have studied the *structures sonores* of the Baschet brothers, unconventional musicians who composed music in the 1950's. Their work had to do with the idea that vibrations build exponentially. The resonant energy that results from two sympathetic vibrations lasts a lot longer and gets a lot louder than the individual notes. Multiplied by hundreds or thousands, you have a tidal wave of sound.

—Sound sculptures, he says, like the Greek Aeolian harps that played as the wind blew, or partially filled glasses that vibrate when you run wet fingers around the tops. It's the intersecting of waves that creates something larger than what individual notes can do on their own.

He raises his bow and announces *Logos Sonores*, a string quartet in A minor by Maria Elana Argasti. The three other musicians raise their bows and the cellist starts rocking her fingers on stopped strings for a warm, fluctuating pitch. In unison, the two violinists rub their bows across the f-shaped sound holes and emit a shower of piercing C's. For a long while the tiny viola stays quiet in the background, then it surges forth and climbs the octaves to a quivering peak.

With what the Whirl taught me of physics, I understand the mechanics of music a little more than Violet or Oscar. The melody focuses on a series of A notes at 440 cycles per second, which conflicts with a succession of cross-rhythm D's at a completely different frequency. *Vibrato* and *tremolo*, the vibrations hang in the air above our humble diversiforms, the lawyer, the drummer and the whore. At first, we sit like absentee generals reviewing our unfamiliar troops, then the melody takes over and we become like old beatniks on the corner of Ninety-Sixth and Coronado when jazz throbbed in the street. Tap, tap, tap; bam, bam, bam, the beat captivates our hands and feet.

You would think with all the fine shivers and shakes, the quavers and rolls, that the music would build to a monstrous finish, but on the last measure it squeals, then quiets and stays high in the rafters. It's as if that simple harmonic A has exploded into oxygen, and now it forms the air we ingest without thinking. The music lingers in an echo that curves along the parabola of the ceiling and hangs out with the photons from the light fixtures, and the matter-waves of our seats and the cacophony of crickets a thousand miles away in a field that takes little notice. It blends with the distant turbulence of history.

Finally as my mother's long-lost musical wave begins to subside, the musicians begin clapping, and we clap, too. Yet the music keeps flowing like a quiet wind behind a storm, or the expansion of the universe, or a breath of God that blows away all fear.

The four players pack their instruments and Oscar gives them an envelope with a contribution. We say goodbye to our lawyer-friend, then Violet and I take a cab to the Bowery. As we climb the stairs, the risers don't shift and we don't feel as if we're risking our lives. The Hovel is new and not even close to the dregs. The stairway is painted to match the doors, but the carved windowsills tell of the factory days when blue-collar workers still pounded the streets of downtown Manhattan.

—You in? Gabby says as she passes us a box of pizza with cheese stuck to the cardboard.

I know they're playing strip poker, because Brownie sits in his underwear and a grin. Things at the Hovel are not by any stretch of the imagination like the old days. The warehouse glows with painted pipes and track lights. There's no dirt or broken glass. Even the Bowery moves on.

—Not me, Violet says. I just wanted to see Brownie in his skin. See if Gabby's been telling me the truth about him having a body of steel. Go, baby, go!

Gabby gushes with laughter and Brownie raises his shoulders as if he's bragging. I lean on Violet and we walk around the far side of the loft to where we've been sleeping on a real bed behind a drape.

—Romey! she screeches and scoops up a white and orange kitten, which settles in her arms and purrs.

—It's not Tuf, I say. It's a girl, but it reminds me of Tuf, something in the eyes.

—She's gorgeous, Romey. Isn't she gorgeous?

We hike our legs through an open window and sit facing the cool breeze on the steel platform that holds the emergency stairs. Violet rubs the kitten with her chin. The neon of the night is gorgeous, all red and orange, yellow and green. The buildings are indigo and violet as if someone went wild with phosphorescent crayons.

It's good to have my color back. I'm taking shots of vitamin A. The doctor said it was probably the shock of seeing someone die that caused me to lose my colors. A rare form of macular degeneration, he said, a temporary blocking of the blood vessels in the eye. The physics tells the story. The cones in my retina failed to fire the color pigments that signal the visual cortex, but I know it was the Whirl all along. He was reaching out from the grave to his prodigal son and teaching me his final lessons.

There's no such thing as redemption, only healing, and God is more awesome than we could ever measure. It's infinite possibility in a universe where all energy is intimately connected. Uncertainty is the process. It makes all things possible; waveforms that have been rolling along since the very first vibration. The next moment is our choice. We can act spontaneously or causally. Spontaneous actions are free energy. Causal actions are trapped in the field. Both are natural states of the universe, and the creative juices come only from letting nature take its course without collapsing the wave out of fear.

It all makes sense in the language of energy. Yet for each of us lost in our own wave, every single one of those thoughts must be an insight, a personal epiphany of extraordinary depth.

—You remember what I told you, Violet says as she holds the new kitten like a baby. I've got to go, Romey. He's a sad bastard, but he's got cancer and I'm his daughter. I can't let him die without people.

I nod because I feel what she feels, fear what she fears. We let each other go before by mistake, but I can't argue with her logic. The simultaneity of events is not just Einstein's dream. It's the decisions we make and the mundane actions of life that make relativity and quantum physics so relevant in our lives. It's the electrons we make jump through the gaps in our neurons, synapse to synapse. It's the color and speed of objects and the joy and tragedy of the human condition. It depends on how we look at things, where we are in this life, the acceleration of our mind. Mostly, it's our inertial frame of reference when the other guy swears he sees the same event in a different way. You've got to give them freedom. It's just waveforms collapsing, time after time.

 —Promise you'll come back?

 —You keep the kitten, she says. I wouldn't leave the kitten for good, Romey. I decided, you know, and that should be enough.

 She hugs me as if she's holding on for life. The neon signs on the corner blur with Violet's tears that mix with my own and jostle with the vibrations of the kitten purring.

 I tell her I'm thinking about starting school. New York University, in physics, no surprise. And the news doesn't seem to faze her anymore than me. She knows it's more than fate. It's the wiring, past and present. It's the choices others made before me, and the ones I've made, too. I've got work to do, oscillations to jiggle, wavelengths to extend, amplitudes to increase. Justin Bishop may not have been my father, but his unmeasurable ideas are a part of me as sure as the DNA of the Whirl. It doesn't matter that Justin's hypothesis about time was right or wrong. Theories in physics will constantly evolve. Yet he changed the language for me, and that's a start. Life is no longer so solid and still.

 It's like music, or building a house, or making good with your lover. You can vibrate simultaneously in the past, the present and the future without worrying about whether the interference of waves is constructive or destructive. Both are part of the eternal conservation of energy. It's the negative energy that hurts so badly, the people that suck energy out of others only to spit back hate. Frank Whirlpool plotted for redemption after death, and he found it not so much because Violet and I found the paper and exposed the fraud. He was redeemed through Maria, and the forgiving hearts of history, and the physics of love.

—You be good, Violet says as she packs her things. Are you sure you can take care of Tuf? she says. I named her Tuf. Is that okay?

I tell her it's okay. She doesn't need to worry. She's an orphan trying to find family, just like me. These last few nights, as I held Violet in my arms, I understood when our lips touched and the particles coalesced that I was finding what my mother found with Justin, and with Frank, and with everyone she ever met and hated or loved. Electrons collide and energy flows, and the breath of God flows freely between us. The universe has been and will always be a singularity, an infinitely small space where all are redeemed without trying, without dying, and without the need for fear.

ABOUT THE AUTHOR

J. Frederick Arment winters in the Florida Keys on the sailboat *Serenata* and summers with his family in Yellow Springs, Ohio. After an early career in secondary school teaching, he went on to lecture for Wilberforce College and in the MBA program at Wright State University. As a technical writer, he has penned numerous publications for Fortune 500 companies as well as non-profit and governmental organizations. He holds a bachelor's degree in history education as well as a master of humanities degree with a focus on the eighteenth-century American and French Enlightenment. His post-graduate study has focused on the integrated disciplines of philosophy, theology and physics.

ACKNOWLEDGMENTS

I would like to thank the many individuals who contributed to the publication of this book, including Timothy Waterman, Ed Davis, Irma Wright, Edgardo Alvarado-Vazquez, Vick Mickunas, Viki Church, Judy DaPolito, Naomi Ewald-Orme and Kate Meinke. My appreciation also goes to Shirley Strohm Mullins for her musical expertise and the use of her beautiful cello, created in 1855 by Jean Baptiste Vuillame.

Any similarity between this novel's waveform or dimensional time literary devices to past or current physical theories is purely unintentional. My gratitude and respect goes to the many scientists, philosophers and theologians who have experimented, speculated and created the hypotheses, theses and insights of quantum physics that are just beginning to have a profound effect on our language and lives.